Escaping His Grace

KRISTIN VAYDEN

LYRICAL PRESS
Kensington Publishing Corp.
www.kensingtonbooks.com

LYRICAL BOOKS are published by

Kensington Publishing Corp.
119 West 40th Street
New York, NY 10018

All Kensington titles, imprints, and distributed lines are available at special quantity discounts for bulk purchases for sales promotion, premiums, fund-raising, educational, or institutional use.

Special book excerpts or customized printings can also be created to fit specific needs. For details, write or phone the office of the Kensington Sales Manager: Attn.: Sales Department. Kensington Publishing Corp, 119 West 40th Street, New York, NY 10018. Phone: 1-800-221-2647.

Lyrical and the Lyrical logo Reg. U.S. Pat. & TM Off.

First Printing: February 2019
ISBN-13: 978-1-5161-0570-0
ISBN-10: 1-5161-0570-2

ISBN-13: 978-1-5161-0571-7 (ebook)
ISBN-10: 1-5161-0571-0 (ebook)

10 9 8 7 6 5 4 3 2 1

Printed in the United States of America

To Grandma Lainhart (or Grandma Hart, as the great-grand kids call her). Going to Scotland with you and all the girls was one of the most amazing—and hilarious—adventures I've ever experienced! Thank you for your love, insight, delight, and humor in all areas of life. Your legacy is incomparable, and if I become half the lady you are, I'll be grateful. I love you so very much! #bridgmanbabesabroad

Acknowledgments

Thank you, Jesus, for expanding my time so this book could get written! We caught the epic flu of 2018, all in succession. It was a winter for the record books.

Thank you, Yessi Smith, for all your feedback, insight, and words of wisdom on this manuscript! I absolutely adore you! And thank you, Kensington Publishing, for all your faith in me, and this series! Rachel, I will ever be thanking you, acknowledging you, and mentioning you because of all the insight, wisdom, and questions you patiently and lovingly answer! You're the best sister ever! And, of course, my husband, Harry. He's my mountain man, my hero, and the source of most of my humor. I'd be so boring without you. Thank you for your love, your support, and your willingness to make dinner.

Prologue

The Honorable Heathcliff Marston, eldest son of the Viscount Kilpatrick, had quite a perfect childhood. With parents who held a true affection for each other, he was born into a life that was the product of a real love match. It was rare as hen's teeth in society, but being young, he didn't have the experience to realize what a boon it was to have parents who actually loved each other, not just tolerated each other's company. He had the luck to be the son of an Englishman, and the misfortune, as some would say, to have a Scottish mother. It was because of his mother's estate near Edinburgh that his father elected to keep his family in Scotland, and travel to London for the Season.

Even as a lad, Heathcliff adored the wilds of Scotland and abhorred the visits to the city of London. When he turned of age and took his education at Eton, he carried a reasonably large resentment toward his father for the first few weeks until he met Lucas Mayfield, the heir to the earldom of Heightfield.

It was friendship at first fight.

And a fight it was.

Lucas had always had a biting way with words, and Heathcliff had the temper of his Scottish mother, so the combination was volatile, and often troublesome for those around.

Ramsey Scott, the Marquess of Sterling, eventually joined their circle of friends, adding a bit of gravity to their otherwise unruly bunch. He was often the voice of reason, the restrainer of fists, and the only one without a bloodied nose or knuckle. In short, he was the buffer between the two.

It was those friends who stood by him at his mother's funeral, silently offering their support when words wouldn't suffice.

And damn, he wished he would have listened to them and stayed in London rather than travel home the summer of 1809. He had endeavored to be home to be a comfort to his heartbroken father. It was a worthy cause, but it had become abruptly sidetracked when he reacquainted himself with the daughter of a local squire, Margot Reynoldford.

He remembered her from his childhood, but she was a child no longer. Flowing chestnut hair, hazel eyes, and an easy smile, Heathcliff had fallen hard and quick for her charms.

He'd spent most of his summer in pursuit of her affection, which she gave readily. Expectation was thick in the air as whispers surrounded their courtship. It was nearly the end of July when Heathcliff notified his father of his impending engagement to Margot.

Never once had he expected anything but an acceptance of his offer, never once expecting his father to do anything but congratulate him on finding his own love match. He was shocked when his father advised against the match.

Heathcliff tried to convince his father it was a love match. Heathcliff adored her, worshiping her every smile as if it were the sunrise and sunset of his life. Surely his father could understand! He had enjoyed his own affectionate relationship with his wife; surely he would want one for his only son? When his father explained his hesitancy, Heathcliff ended the argument abruptly by stating that his father was simply heartbroken, not wanting anyone to experience joy because he no longer could. It had been a low blow, one that would echo in later fights with his father on the same subject.

Heathcliff stormed from the study, chose his own path and proposed that evening to Margot.

They were married as soon as the banns could be read, neglecting even to invite his closest friends, pride and folly whispering that they might not approve of the match. Even when he knew it was his own misgivings that had begun to surface.

Eager to please his bride, Heathcliff had thrown his whole heart into the marriage, deferring to her wants and wishes, however outlandish they seemed. He simply delighted in her smile, feeling as though it were the rising sun in his life.

Only to find out she had her own rising sun.

It wasn't even six months into the marriage when his world shattered. He'd come back from Edinburgh earlier than arranged, expecting to surprise his wife with a beautiful music box from Italy, a gift he had ordered months before.

He'd sprinted up the stairs, only to find his wife astride another man, in his bed. The music box met a swift end when he hurled it across the room, alerting the lovers of his presence. The sound of it smashing against the wall echoed in his thoughts.

She didn't even have the good grace to pretend shame.

He'd stormed off, knowing if he stayed there would be blood on his hands. A divorce was the only option. He wouldn't share his wife with another, nor would he be fool enough to pretend it could work to look the other way.

That was when she confessed to being with child.

If betrayal were a coffin, that revelation was the last nail in his heart.

Because she wasn't sure who was the father.

Which only meant it may, or may not, be his child.

Did he dare risk abandoning his own son or daughter? He couldn't, wouldn't risk it—regardless of the mother's sins, the child was innocent of them.

So, he sent Margot away to his estate in the Scottish Highlands, and waited.

Heartbroken and bitter, his father was the only voice of reason to reinforce his decision not to put away his wife in divorce. As a reminder of the heartbreak, he ordered a replica of the music box he had bought for Margot.

May he never forget.

The child was stillborn, and Margot followed shortly after.

If that weren't enough heartbreak for one man, there wasn't an end in sight.

The next day, Heathcliff strode into his father's study and found him slumped over in his chair. The doctor said it was his heart.

And in one week, Heathcliff had lost everyone.

Including himself.

He returned to London, finding that Lucas's life had suffered a similar upheaval.

Ramsey was the last man standing.

But he too would fall.

It was only after they all survived the betrayal of others that they turned their efforts toward alienating the society that had made light of their pain.

When Lucas came up with the idea for the gambling hell, both Heathcliff and Ramsey were quick to throw their hats in on the idea. Titled, dedicated bachelors, it was time for them to enjoy life, instead of dwelling on the pain dealt so cruelly by the fates. Lucas's idea had a name—a bloody insightful one.

Different than all the other gaming hells about London, this one would thrive on anonymity. No names. No faces. Masks and the uttermost exclusivity no other hell could boast. No strings attached, where your privacy was also your security, your pleasure.

Temptation.

Short, sweet, and directly to the point.

Because when you live in the moment of temptation, you're too consumed to dwell on the past—and the ghosts that haunt it.

London, 1815

"I'm so very disappointed you will not be able to make the acquaintance of your new employer, Miss Miranda." Lady Barrot's clear blue eyes conveyed sympathy. She reached over and placed a gloved hand upon Miranda's as they took their afternoon tea in the Barrots' parlor.

Miranda—she practiced the name in her mind, wrapping her head around the new identity, and the necessity of taking it—nodded once. "I understand, Lady Barrot. It's unfortunate, but it's clear there are other implications one must consider." *Implications* was a simple way to state it. In the past twenty-four hours, her life had changed significantly.

Viscount Kilpatrick was not only her new employer but the best friend of her sister's new husband, Lord Heightfield. It was under that close connection she had secured a way to elude her tyrannical father, the Duke of Chatterworth, by taking on temporary employment under the protection of the viscount.

In hiding till the carriage to Edinburgh, Scotland, could convey her to safety, she was now in residence at the home of Lord and Lady Barrot, trusted friends and benefactors of her new brother-in-law's clandestine business. She wasn't quite sure of the details of said business venture, but she knew it was of the scandalous variety. So, she found herself in the sumptuous London parlor, awaiting the time when she could escape fully. In the interim, she was expected to meet the viscount, though they had just received a missive from his estate.

Several private investigators had questioned him earlier concerning the whereabouts of the duke's missing daughters. It was paramount that he allay any suspicions they had. To be sure, Miss Miranda was surprised her father hadn't alerted the local magistrate at the sudden disappearance of his two daughters, but as she considered it, he likely didn't want to raise awareness of their absence. To not be in complete control was a cardinal sin.

So, rather than meet the viscount, the man behind so

many of her sister's stories, she simply accepted Lady Barrot's word, and awaited the time when she could leave behind everything she'd ever known and seek the adventure she never had wanted to take.

But freedom was always the first choice of captives, and while her cage was gilded, it was still a cage. And for the first time, she was about to test her wings. Hoping that somehow, she would instinctively know how to fly.

And the place she was to test her wings was Scotland.

Chapter One

Edinburgh, Scotland
Two days later

Miranda took a deep, calming breath through her nose before releasing it slowly and forcing a calm demeanor. The footman extended his hand, offering his assistance from the carriage, and with a resolute step forward, she accepted.

Her eyes were drawn to the large manor before her. Gray stone rose high above the courtyard, with beautifully trimmed boxwoods that made her immediately homesick for London. Stepping from the carriage, her foot crunched along the gravel. She released the footman's hand, and met the curious gaze of the elderly woman beside the door. Her back arched in a perfect posture that bespoke some English training. Miranda was drawn to her inviting smile, which was decidedly Scottish, not distant like most proper English servants.

"A pleasure, Miss Miranda." The woman nodded

kindly and stepped forward. "I'm the housekeeper, Mrs. Keyes. We're quite delighted to have you on staff here at Kilmarin; you'll be a blessin' for sure." A slight brogue leaked through the crisp accent.

Miranda nodded kindly, her mind whirling as to how to act like a governess when she had been raised the daughter of a duke. She gave a slight curtsey. "It's a pleasure to be of assistance. Is the young lady I'm to educate in residence or still en route?"

Mrs. Keyes gave another smile, and a measure of Miranda's tension melted. "She's is most certainly in residence, Miss Miranda."

Miranda wasn't sure how her words were intended, but a shiver of foreboding trailed up her spine. Perhaps this wouldn't be as easy as her sister, Liliah, had led her to believe.

Even as she thought of Liliah, her heart pinched with sorrow. How she missed her, and it hadn't even been a fortnight! She quickly reminded herself that she would soon see her once again. As a newlywed, her sister surely deserved a measure of privacy.

A blush heated her face at the thought, but she pressed it to the back of her mind and focused on the task at hand

Blending in.

Being someone she was not—but that shouldn't be too much of a problem. Hadn't she done that most of her life?

"If you'll follow me, Miss Miranda, I'll show you to your room and give you some time to freshen up before dinner." Mrs. Keyes signaled a footman with an efficient twist of her wrist, and Miranda followed the woman as she ambled up the marble stairs.

Mrs. Keyes nodded to the butler at the door. "Sothers,

this is Miss Miranda. She is to be Miss Iris's governess."

The butler nodded his salt-and-pepper head and murmured a soft welcome.

Miranda curtseyed to him as well.

Her gaze lingered on the foyer. The flagstone tiles were a rich green color, one she would have associated with Ireland rather than Scotland, yet the color somehow fit. A coat of arms decorated a wall, along with an ancient-looking suit of armor. She eyed the sword dubiously, hoping it was anchored well to its position.

"Yes, Lord Kilpatrick keeps that old decrepit thing in the foyer. We've all done our best to encourage him to move it elsewhere, but it belonged to his grandfather, then his father, both of whom kept it in that very spot. A tragedy, if you ask me. So many other things would be far more welcomin' for guests. Not tha' we get them so often." She shrugged and moved on.

Miranda bit her cheek to keep from grinning. Scotland was quite different from England; either that or servants spoke to other servants vastly differently from their betters. She had a suspicion it was the latter.

Even though it was acutely awkward to bypass the private quarters and follow Mrs. Keyes into the section of the house dedicated to the nursery, she reminded herself that this place was *safe*.

It was strange how such a small word would mean so much.

As Mrs. Keyes opened the door, sunshine beamed through wide windows. Several tables were strategically positioned on the wooden floor, with several shelves of books lining the walls in between the windows. Miranda stepped into the room, her gaze taking in the vast view of the gardens that appeared to be behind Kilmarin. Green hills rolled in the distance, creating a picturesque scene before her. Hedgerows lined the gardens and stone archways led away from the middle courtyard into smaller ones, a fountain in the middle of it all.

"It's majestic, is it not? Of course, I'm partial to the manor because I've been here since the master was in leading strings. But if I do say so myself, it's stately enough." Mrs. Keyes chimed in as she stood beside Miranda.

"It's lovely," Miranda agreed. "And the sky." She blinked at the azure blue that seemed to be so much brighter than in London.

"Ach, that's right. You're from London. It's a bit brighter here. Not always; we get our share of the rain, bein' so close to the sea. But at least you're not downtown Edinburgh. It's more of the smoke you're accustomed to. Though we're only a mile out, it's a bit fresher—yet you can still taste the sea." She gave a carefree shrug of her shoulders.

Miranda inhaled through her parted lips, smiling as the tang of the sea teased her tongue, reminding her of the times when the wind blew from the sea into the City. "I do love the sea."

"I'm sure Miss Iris will love an excursion or two." Mrs. Keyes remarked, then stepped back away from the window. "Speaking of Miss Iris, you'll be meeting her at dinner, and because none of the family are in residence, I've taken the liberty of setting the family table for just the two of you. I'm not certain how you'd prefer to take your supper, but being just the two of you, I figured you'd not want to eat alone."

"Thank you, I'm sure that is preferable," Miranda added, glancing to a nearby bookshelf.

"And do look over the volumes we have, then let me know if there's anything you're missing. Lord Kilpatrick wishes Miss Iris to have the best education possible, I'm sure you understand."

Miranda agreed. "I'm sure what you have here will suffice for a while, till I can . . ." Miranda paused, thinking over how to actually teach what needed to be taught . . . "Ascertain where the pupil stands in several subjects," she finished, feeling quite relieved at how she had handled the question. Tonight she would need to look over all the books, and make notes on what she remembered from her own governess. It couldn't be *that* difficult, could it?

"Then I'll leave you to find a few moments of rest." Mrs. Keyes nodded and turned, but Miranda could have sworn she whispered, "You'll certainly need it."

Before Miranda could question her, she gestured to an open door. "If you'll follow me, I'll show you to your room."

Miranda paused, but didn't remark on the housekeeper's words. She followed the woman's mobcap into the next room.

"Again, if there's anything you're needing, please notify me at once." Mrs. Keyes gestured to the room.

A small writing desk was beside a tall, stately window that overlooked another aspect of the gardens. A pitcher with water rested upon the large dresser, and a dressing table boasted a small mirror. By governess standards, it was quite impressive.

By a lady's standards, it was underwhelming.

A small bed rested in the middle of the room, and immediately, Miranda missed her feather bed, and the warming pan that would heat the sheets before she snuggled in deep, listening to the crackling fire.

She glanced to the opposite end of the room, and re-laxed slightly at the sight of the larger hearth. At least she wouldn't be cold—even if it was still summer.

She had heard about Scottish winters, and she hadn't a clue how long she'd be in residence.

A delicate shiver ran up her spine.

Belatedly, she realized Mrs. Keyes was awaiting some sort of response to the room.

"Thank you, I'm sure it's more than adequate," Miranda replied, keeping close to the truth so she wouldn't have to remember a lie.

"Lovely." Mrs. Keyes beamed. "I'll send Maye up to fetch you when dinner's ready. We keep country hours, even if we are close to town." And with a warm nod, Mrs. Keyes quit the room, leaving Miranda to her thoughts.

At the housekeeper's departure, Miranda sighed in the most unladylike fashion, quite reminding her of her sister's antics on multiple occasions. And once again, a pang of homesickness waved through her.

But she wouldn't dwell on what she had left behind.

She glanced to the door, seeing the footman had de-posited her belongings on the floor.

As she studied the parcels and bags, she noted she had never once unpacked her own things.

A maid always assisted—with everything.

But now, she was the help. She glanced at her two hands, which had only seen delicate needlepoint and piano study, and wondered if they were capable of more.

If perhaps *she* were capable of more.

She wanted to be.

Which was a good thing, because she was going to have plenty of opportunity to test her strength, inside and out.

And maybe, just maybe—she'd discover she was stronger than she thought.

That maybe, just maybe—she was more like her sister than not.

She certainly hoped so.

Chapter Two

"For the last time, I've never met this Samantha before, nor am I associated with the Duke of Chatterworth!" Heathcliff Marston, Viscount Kilpatrick, was about to lose the last of his patience as he studied the men before him, drinking his brandy and lounging about in his study.

"We have reason to believe—"

"And I have appointments and other responsibilities!" he all but shouted. He took a small sip of brandy, using it as a buffer between his anger and the men provoking it.

They exchanged a glance, the kind that said *we're going in circles here*, and then the older one rose from his chair.

Heathcliff almost wept in relief but kept his gaze hardened and trained on the interlopers.

"You'll be in contact if you hear anything." The man set his calling card on Heathcliff's desk. He noted the question wasn't exactly that; it was a demand.

Heathcliff wanted to take the card and toss it into the fire, then pour brandy over the flames just to make the point more spectacular, but working with Lucas and Ramsey had taught him to temper his, well . . . temper, and he suppressed his somewhat barbaric reactions.

Most of the time.

And this was, regrettably, one of the times he suppressed his baser reactions.

"Of course," he lied smoothly, watching as the younger gentleman, probably in training, followed the older man to the study door.

"We can see ourselves out."

Heathcliff withheld a grin at the sudden appearance of Wilkes, his longtime butler, at the door. "If I may, gentleman?" he offered.

Damn butler was worth his weight in brandy. French brandy.

Heathcliff gave an approving nod to Wilkes as he led the men from the study to the front door.

Good riddance. Bloody blooming hell. That was the third time in the past fortnight the investigators had come knocking at his door. The first time had caused him to miss the introduction to the governess for his newly acquired ward.

Though that particular instance wasn't exactly a hardship. He wasn't looking forward to meeting a sour woman who educated other high-maintenance women for a living. Regardless of how highly recommended she came, he had no desire to meet her. He simply wanted her to do her job well.

Lord willing, if she was as good as Lucas, the eighth Earl of Heightfield, his best friend and business partner had suggested, soon he'd be marrying off his bloody ward to the first man who showed the slightest bit of interest in her. Then he could be finished with the whole bloody lot of them, and go back to his bachelor ways.

Not that he had any intention of quitting his bachelor ways in the interim, but he did have to be moderately careful—wouldn't want his reputation to sully his ward's. Then he'd never be rid of her!

The fire crackled and sparked, bringing his attention back to the moment. He bloody had to stay in residence for at least another week to allay suspicion. Damn, Lucas owed him.

Not only was he covering for his friend's hasty marriage, but he was also dodging the duke's private investigators. Heathcliff couldn't suppress a grin at the memory of the last few weeks' events. In fact, he felt a smug satisfaction in knowing his friend's future before his friend did. It didn't take a scholar to know that Lucas was utterly undone by Lady Liliah Durary. Of course, his friend wasn't willing to admit the truth till it had been almost too late. But all was right in the world now, minus the fact that the duke had never approved of Lucas's secretive marriage to his daughter. This was truly a case of knowing the right people and having the right leverage.

There weren't many who would risk the ire of a duke, but when you had the right dirt on the right people, the reward far outweighed the risk. And in their line of business, secrets were their currency.

And they were wealthy in that specific currency, wealthy indeed.

Heathcliff's thoughts drifted to their business, and he set down his glass and shifted the papers across his desk till he found the one he needed. He, Ramsey Scott, the Marquess of Sterling, and Lucas Mayfield, the eighth Earl of Heightfield, operated the most secretive, selective, and seductive club in all of London. Temptations was the brilliant idea of Lucas, but as Lucas was currently on his honeymoon, the operation of the club fell to him and Ramsey. It was almost the end of the Season, and the final masquerade loomed on the horizon. It was a large, heavily attended event by most, if not all, of the exclusive members and their . . . invitees. Heathcliff smirked. Courtesans, mistresses, strumpets would be better terminology, but he wasn't one to judge. Rather, he was only concerned with their ability to pay for membership and gamble at the tables. With whom they spent their time was none of his concern. The masquerades seemed to bring out more of the demimonde than the regular events, which seemed to spawn a heightened flair to the parties. He was certain this last event would be no different.

He made a note to check whether the Duke of Chatterworth—Lucas's unwilling father-in-law—planned to attend. That could be problematic, but Heathcliff didn't suspect he'd show his face in his new son-in-law's den of iniquity, even if his son-in-law was astoundingly monklike before his marriage.

The irony was thick amongst them all.

"My lord?" Wilkes bowed as he entered the study.

Heathcliff nodded once.

"Lord Sterling is here to see you." Wilkes waited expectantly.

Heathcliff waved his hand. "Show him in, of course."

"About bloody time." Ramsey strode in, giving an annoyed glance to Wilkes, who ignored the slight, bowed, and left the gentlemen alone.

As the door closed, Ramsey turned to Heathcliff. "I

suppose you've been interrogated as well? What was he thinking? Does he know the depths of the scandal involved here? A duke's daughter!" Ramsey tugged on his cravat, then took a seat opposite Heathcliff.

"It will all blow over soon enough," Heathcliff remarked calmly, quite accustomed to Ramsey's aversion to scandal of any sort.

"Twice! Bloody investigators have been in to see me twice."

"I only just excused them, yet again. I've lost track. This was either three or four times," Heathcliff remarked, then stood from his desk, lifted his glass, and raised an eyebrow of inquiry to Ramsey.

"Thank you." Ramsey accepted the invitation.

Heathcliff poured a generous portion into a clean glass for his friend and refreshed his own brandy. As he handed the amber liquid to Ramsey, he took a seat on the edge of his desk. "It could be worse." He took a sip.

"Enlighten me," Ramsey remarked dryly and sipped as well.

Heathcliff shrugged. "They only have suspicions. And I'd wager they already know Lady Liliah Durary is now the Countess of Heightfield and are only looking for more information. What's done is done."

"True, but what of the other daughter?" Ramsey asked stiffly. "She is still in question."

"I know nothing of her. So I'm not helpful in the least."

Ramsey nodded. "I heard something about America, but who's to say? Still, it makes me nervous. A little too close for comfort. I always knew Lucas would create a scandal."

Heathcliff chuckled. "Ramsey, we *are* scandal. The

three of us! Think upon our reputations! Not even the current ones, but the rumors that surrounded our descent into hell," he remarked, standing up. "What redemption is left for us? None."

Ramsey twisted his lips, then adjusted his spectacles. "Indeed. Regardless of what truly occurred, our reputations do precede us."

"And we've used it to the best advantage possible."

"Very well, you've made your point."

"Thank you." Heathcliff lifted his glass to salute his friend.

Ramsey stood. "Are you still planning on staying till this dies down? Heightfield said you might return to Scotland for the off-Season."

Heathcliff shrugged. "I was intending to leave earlier, but I'll wait till the situation rights itself."

"Thank you." Ramsey nodded, then headed to the door. "And for heaven's sake, talk to that butler of yours. He's worse than a watchdog. You'd think I've never come in without announcement." Ramsey shook his head, then quit the room.

Heathcliff chuckled. He could easily have asked Wilkes to admit Ramsey without hesitation, but it was utterly entertaining to watch his friend become irritated.

Yet, as he turned toward the fire, his thoughts wandered.

It was a truth that never left his mind but was also not always at the forefront.

Reputation.

It was a heartless bitch.

Unfair, unkind, and many times a liar of the worst sort.

Yet, he, Ramsey, and Lucas had turned their misfortunes into another sort of fortune, and the secrecy it created into a sort of armor.

But watching Lucas's heart open to another had reminded Heathcliff of the betrayal of his past.

And while he was thankful for his friend's second chance at love, he didn't think he'd ever be willing to risk the same.

Because how could you ever trust love when all it had handed you was betrayal?

And nothing was so deceptive as betrayal at the hands of a beautiful woman.

Nothing.

Chapter Three

Miranda took the stairs carefully as she made her way to the dining hall. The air was crisp, and a shiver trailed down her back. Again, she was reminded of the coming Scottish winter, and she wondered how she'd purchase appropriate clothing. She'd never had to think about money before, and now it seemed so important and quite evasive.

So many questions.

Not enough answers.

After a fortifying breath, she followed the footman down another hall and inhaled deeply of the rich scent of pheasant and some sort of broth. Her stomach rumbled quietly in appreciation. The hall opened into a grand dining room with gold and red accents. A majestic table was the focal point of the room, lined with velvet-covered chairs. Her gaze shifted to the two place settings at the very end of the table, one beside the other. Apparently, she was first to arrive for dinner.

"Good evening!" Mrs. Keyes bustled into the room. "I wanted to make sure this was to your liking before we summoned your pupil."

Miranda blinked, then turned to the table, then back to the housekeeper. "I'm afraid I don't understand," she replied, hoping she wasn't giving away her inexperience.

"Oh, forgive me. You see, we've not had any experience in training up a young lady. We'll be relyin' on you for the proper way of doing things, Miss Miranda."

Miranda swallowed.

But after a quick moment, she was quite thankful that clearly there were no expectations for her. She could set them herself, which was an acute relief.

"Of course," Miranda answered, then turned back to the table with a fresh perspective. "The table is splendid, and I agree with the way you've placed the settings together. Later on, we may practice what it would be like to have a larger party, but for now, everything is as it should be."

"Good." Mrs. Keyes beamed. "I'll go and have Miss Iris fetched for dinner, then." With a soft smile, the woman disappeared into the hall.

Miranda exhaled in relief and walked to the table. It was odd, to be looking at things from such a different perspective. Yet, at the same time, she could see the way her upbringing and training had given her more than adequate experience for the job at hand.

Perhaps she would not only know enough but also excel at something. It was a revelatory thought, one that boosted her spirits in a way she hadn't felt for some time.

The sound of footsteps alerted her to the approach of her pupil, and she turned, straightened her shoulders, and waited.

At first glance, Miss Iris Grace was pretty enough, though her red hair was almost vulgar in its bright color. Miranda watched her walk, noting the confident stride that was almost masculine in its approach. Shoulders back, her posture was perfect, but her air was casual. Miranda made mental notes as she watched her enter the room.

"Miss Iris, allow me to introduce Miss Miranda, your governess." Mrs. Keyes gestured to Miranda.

Belatedly, Miranda curtseyed. It was odd to curtsey to her pupil, but she remembered her governess always curtseying to her because of her higher rank.

A smile curved her lips as she considered this twist of fate.

"A pleasure," Miranda spoke demurely as she rose.

Miss Iris watched her, a tiny frown forming between her green eyes, before she curtseyed as well, albeit it a little awkwardly. That was certainly something they'd have to remedy quickly.

"A pleasure, Miss Miranda." Iris spoke with a slight accent to her English tones.

Rather than remark or inquire, Miranda gestured to the table and watched as her pupil walked around the table to her place setting.

Mrs. Keyes glanced from Miranda to Iris, then back. "Please let us know if you need anything else." She bowed her head graciously, then left.

Two footmen stood beside the place settings and withdrew the chairs. Miranda watched as Iris took her seat, then followed suit.

"So, Miss Iris, can you tell me about yourself, maybe starting with your age, interests, education?" Miranda asked, starting the conversation.

A rich broth was brought out as Iris began to answer. "Old enough to wonder why my guardian thought I'd need a governess, quite honestly." Iris's tone wasn't unkind, just forthright.

Miranda suppressed a smile. "Perhaps he wanted you to have companionship as well?"

"Perhaps. I'd find that easier to believe if he'd taken the time to even make my acquaintance." Iris spoke dryly as she took a sip of the soup before them.

"I see," Miranda remarked, then took a sip as well. It was rich and flavorful, reminding her of the beef and barley soup at home.

A pang of homesickness waved over her, but she pushed it away. She had a task to complete, and complete it she would. "Why don't you tell me of your interests? Surely there is something that sparks your curiosity?"

Iris met her gaze, measuring her with her green eyes, as if trying to determine Miranda's character. "I enjoy traveling. My parents, before they passed, were avid explorers, and I went everywhere with them."

"That sounds like quite the adventurous life. Where are some of the places you traveled?" Miranda asked.

"Egypt, India, the West Indies . . . to name a few." Iris shrugged, as if traveling half the world wasn't of any consequence.

Miranda took another sip of her broth, hiding her reaction. Exposure to the world didn't necessarily mean an understanding of it. Yet she suspected in Iris's case, it did. And if so, her pupil was of a vastly different caliber than she'd expected.

"Have you traveled?" Iris asked, pulling Miranda from her thoughts.

"Some," Miranda answered, not wanting to give away the fact that the only other country she'd visited was the one in which she was currently in residence.

"I already miss it. Meeting new people, studying different cultures. It's quite fascinating, you know," Iris said.

"Indeed. Please tell me of your education. What subjects have you studied?" Miranda asked.

Iris watched as a footman removed her almost-empty soup bowl. "Arithmetic, I've read most of Shakespeare, and I can speak a few languages. My father taught me to read and write Greek, which isn't my favorite, but I can do tolerably well. Botany is something I do truly enjoy, but I don't think I'll find much to study around here; it seems pretty common to most of the continent. It was a better subject of study in India. I've studied Egyptian history, and my father made sure I understood how to navigate by sea as well—it was quite fun to work with the captain when we sailed to the Indies."

Miranda schooled her expression, trying to keep from showing either shock or a feeling of inadequacy. "You've quite the education, Iris."

"Thank you. So, you can see why I'm curious as to your necessity. But as you said, it would be nice to have companionship." She lifted a fork to taste the pheasant just placed before them.

Miranda swallowed back the feeling that her assistance was indeed utterly unnecessary. Yet, as she thought over Iris's words, she noted a few missing elements.

"Iris, you spoke beautifully of your father. What of your mother's contribution to your education? I'm sure you're just as accomplished in other areas as well, perhaps things your mother taught you?" Miranda asked, taking a small bite of pheasant. The gentle flavor filled her with delight.

"Well, I mentioned my father, but he and my mother did most things in tandem. So everything I learned from my father should give credit to my mother as well. It was my misspeaking that didn't include her. For that I apologize. My mother thought it important that I be able to do all that a man could do, so she gave a far greater weight to my father's education of me, versus the more ladylike aspects."

Miranda nodded, inwardly affirming her suspicions. To confirm, she continued to ask several questions. "Have you studied the pianoforte?"

Iris glanced to the side. "No, and before you ask, I can't embroider and have no desire to learn either."

Miranda nodded. "Both are worthy venues of education, but if you're not interested, have you learned how to dance? Surely you have some delightful experience in other cultures' expressions of dance?"

Iris toyed with her pheasant. "No. My mother wasn't much of a dancer and my father had no rhythm."

Miranda's feelings of inadequacy fled like the darkness at daybreak. Not only was she more than adequately educated, she was utterly necessary if Iris were to appear on the marriage mart next year.

"Have you any social experience? Have you been to parties, a ball or two?" She highly doubted it. Iris hadn't had a come-out, but she asked regardless.

"In India we attended a wedding," Iris replied, her tone hopeful.

"I'm sure that was delightful," Miranda replied, noting that the first area of her education needed to be of the social variety. And that was going to be a challenge in Scotland, especially because she didn't know the area well. Certainly Mrs. Keyes would be willing to provide the necessary information.

"Iris, I'm going to be quite frank, because you seem to appreciate forthright conversation." Miranda set down her fork and regarded her pupil. Iris nodded, though suspicion was evident in her gaze.

"Your education has been exceptional, and you do not need my assistance in furthering the basics of reading, writing, or arithmetic, as I'm sure you are aware." Miranda paused, watching as Iris nodded once.

"But you do need my assistance in the more feminine pursuits. For example, if we were at a dinner party, who would be sitting in your place?"

Iris blinked, then studied the table, then turned back to Miranda. "A countess," she answered confidently.

Miranda called her bluff. "That's indeed true, if . . ."

Iris confident façade fractured a little. "If a duke was sitting over there?" She pointed to a chair.

Triumph washed over Miranda. "No, and there aren't a great many dukes who attend dinner parties." She would know; her father was a duke after all, she added to herself. "At a dinner party, the host will sit at the head of the table, then from there you'll have assigned seating to benefit the flow of conversation. The highest-ranking men and women will usually be seated toward the head of the table by the host, but in some circumstances, they will not. We will learn all this, and much more."

"Why?" Iris asked, her light brows arching.

"Because if not, you'll appear the fool should you be invited to a party, and no one wishes to feel that way, Iris," Miranda answered, using the response that would hit the weak chink in Iris's armor, her confidence.

"Oh." Iris bit her lip. "But what about embroidery? I can't see any benefit in learning it." Her confidence returned in full force.

Miranda lifted a delicate shoulder as the footman took away their plates. "Perhaps, but that's simply one area of study, and probably not the most important."

"What would you suggest is the most important?" Iris asked, a slightly impudent tone to her voice.

Miranda smiled, not even trying to hold her response in check. "Dancing."

Iris's brows pinched, her confidence faded, and she took a deep breath, as if steeling herself.

"You might even enjoy it."

"Entirely doubtful."

Miranda chuckled softly. "It's actually delightful, and as bright as you are, you'll catch on quickly, I'm sure."

"You've just met me. You'll be taking back those words once you see me try."

"So, you have danced?" Miranda caught her.

"No. I said I've tried. There's a difference," Iris remarked, folding her napkin and setting it to the side.

"Well, there is no time like the present." Miranda gestured for a footman, and he quickly pulled back her chair. As she stood, she realized Iris had scooted her chair back on her own.

"We wait for assistance." Miranda gestured for Iris

to sit back down, and she reluctantly obeyed. "When you're finished at the table, signal for the footman and he will help you withdraw your chair.

Iris signaled for a footman with a quick and impatient gesture.

"No. A lady is always patient," Miranda remarked, mimicking the tone and words of her governess when coaching her older sister Liliah. In a way, Iris reminded her of her sister: headstrong, stubborn, capable, and confident.

Iris resignaled the footman, and Miranda noted the slight twitch of his lips, as if he were amused. She wondered just how many times her own footman at home had suppressed grins at her and her sister's antics.

"Much improved," Miranda encouraged as Iris rose from the table properly.

Turning to the footman, she requested the presence of Mrs. Keyes.

In a moment, the woman entered the dining room, a smile on her kind face. "How can I be of assistance, Miss Miranda?"

"Mrs. Keyes, Iris and I are going to have a short dancing lesson. Where would you suggest we attempt such an activity?"

Mrs. Keyes thought a moment. "I do believe the red parlor will suffice. There's a pianoforte and ample room for the two of you. If you'll follow me?"

At Miranda's nod, Mrs. Keyes led them down the hall.

It was a lovely thing, to be needed. And Miranda wondered if somehow she'd been missing that sensation all her life. To be more than just obedient but to contribute.

Maybe she had something more to offer the world than just a pretty face.

Who would have thought?

Chapter Four

Heathcliff signed another document on his desk as he waited for his carriage to be ready. It had been a hell of a week, and he was more than thrilled to escape London and once again feel the Scottish country air. In part, the events of the week were his own fault.

After another visit from the investigators, he took it upon himself to leak the information to the *Times* about the marriage of the Earl of Heightfield to the Duke of Chatterworth's daughter, Lady Liliah Durary. The ton had buzzed with the sensationalism of it all, which only put the bloody duke in the forefront of the fanfare. It was a scandal of biblical proportions, with many voicing their opinions at the recent party at Temptations. Of course, that there had been a large betting pool placed in favor of the duke's daughter marrying the son of the Earl of Greywick only added fuel to the blazing fire. But with Greywick now admitting to his empty coffers, it was a delightful ending for Heathcliff to witness.

He couldn't stand either of the men. And this was more than their due.

He mused over the story the duke had created to explain the absence of his youngest daughter, and Heathcliff hoped that wherever she was, it was far from his clutches.

The party had been heavily attended, as was their silver ball. Every member, with the exception of a select few, one of those being the Duke of Chatterworth, had come to the event. The brandy had poured forth like the Thames in spring, and the gambling tables were overflowing with willing gamers. Ramsey left the safety of his office to attend Heathcliff in the ballroom, policing the event. The news of Heightfield and Lady Liliah was the prime subject of the evening. Heathcliff couldn't walk two steps without having some lord inquire about Lucas's quick work in marrying the duke's daughter. Lord Greywick didn't dare show his face in the gambling hell, not with the debt he owed. Before Lucas had spirited Lady Liliah away to wife, the Duke of Chatterworth and Lord Greywick had had an understanding for their son and daughter to be betrothed. It was a miserable arrangement for both but satisfied the fathers' needs; the duke needed Greywick's silence about his scandal and Greywick needed the dowry to fill his empty coffers.

It was a horrible mess, but one that seemed to have some silver lining, at least for Greywick's son. It would seem that Lord and Lady Grace had finally approved of the match between their daughter and Meyer, heir to the Earl of Greywick. It was a love match that had been whispered about for months. And while Lord Greywick was no longer plump in the pockets, Lord and Lady Grace had more than the necessary to redeem the title. It wasn't Heathcliff's usual mode of operation to follow gossip, but in this case, he was certainly glad for the news. Happy endings rarely happened these days.

He would know.

But now that Lucas had settled in Scotland for the time being, or so he assumed, based on his friend's earlier plans, Heathcliff decided it was time to head back home as well. As much as his title was of the English variety, he never felt as if London were home. No, that name was reserved for Edinburgh. So it was with great anticipation that he awaited the few days' travel to his beloved estate. The only thorn in the situation was the bloody ward waiting for him at his residence. With any luck, she'd been trained enough that the governess could shine her up a bit and send her off to be married next season.

A man could hope, could he not?

Wilkes bowed as he entered the study. "My lord? Your carriage is ready."

"Brilliant," Heathcliff remarked. "Please make sure Ramsey receives this, and if there are any questions, he knows how to reach me." He handed several documents to his butler.

"Of course, my lord." Wilkes replied. "Have a good journey."

"Thank you, I'm sure I will." Heathcliff tugged on his great coat and strode toward the foyer. Already he could feel the freedom of the countryside calling his name. He took the stairs to the courtyard quickly, and soon he was traveling away from the smoke, the ton, and the expectations.

He only hoped that what awaited him was tamer than all he was leaving behind.

But if history had taught him one thing, women were almost never tame.

Chapter Five

"**Y**es, like that. Hold your frame," Miranda coached Iris as she held her in a position of a waltz. A pang of sadness ached in her heart as memories of doing the same sort of practice with her sister filtered through her mind. They had practiced dancing for hours in the parlor of their home, perfecting each step. It was abundantly clear that none such practice had happened at Iris's house. It would seem that dancing was the poor girl's Achilles's heel. Even after two weeks of coaching, Iris still failed to use the correct footing.

All because she insisted on leading, not following.

Miranda rather thought it was a thread that ran through her life.

Lead, don't follow; it was Iris's unspoken motto. It would be commendable if it weren't so painful when she stepped on Miranda's toes because of her insistence on leading.

"I'll just dance the cotillion." Iris spoke through clenched teeth. Her brows were so light, one could hardly see them, but her frown highlighted their position.

"Afraid of a dance—is that what you wish to be, Iris?" Miranda asked, keeping her smile in check as she neatly dodged one of Iris's feet as they turned. It hadn't taken long for Miranda to note that logic wasn't the best way to change Iris's mind, but give her a challenge? She couldn't turn it down.

"You've said that before," Iris grumbled, biting her lip as she clumsily took the next few steps.

"And it remains true, unless you've decided to give up?" Miranda asked sweetly.

"I know what you're doing." Iris glared, misstepped, and landed on Miranda's toe . . . again.

Miranda sucked in a breath as she winced in pain. Her toes were ever so sore, but just as Iris couldn't back down from a challenge, nor could she. "I'm attempting to teach you to be a lady of quality."

"I *am* a lady of quality," Iris enunciated.

"Then waltz like one," Miranda replied, holding out her hand once more and counting. "One, two, three . . ."

Iris sighed, stepped into the frame of the waltz. "One day—"

"You'll meet a gentleman you wish to dance with, and you'll thank me. Because my toes will have taken the punishment in his place, saving your pride," Miranda finished, turning cautiously. "And for heaven's sake let me lead!"

"I don't follow well," Iris grumbled.

"You don't follow at all," Miranda replied, but even as she said it, Iris relaxed slightly and performed the steps with adequate grace.

"See, it's possible." Miranda released her and stepped back, smiling with encouragement.

"Just not probable," Iris retorted.

"And a quick tongue is not something you should exercise on the dance floor. Ladies think before speaking."

Iris's expression turned mutinous, but she didn't say anything. Wonders never ceased.

"Now that's been accomplished, why don't we turn our attention to the pianoforte?" Miranda had learned she had her work cut out for her regarding the ladylike pursuits in Iris's education.

"That's almost worse than waltzing." Iris sighed but turned toward the grand instrument in the corner. "I can't see why it's so bloo—"

"Iris," Miranda cut off the vulgar word.

"Important," Iris finished as she sat on the bench, her hands hovering over the keys.

"At least you have some experience."

"Not of any merit. You *have* been listening, have you not?"

Miranda nodded. Listening to Iris play was as much punishment for her ears as waltzing was for her toes.

As Iris began to play the simple song before her, Miranda decided governesses were grossly underpaid if the torture she was enduring was any indication.

She winced as Iris hit the wrong key, then another, before finding the correct one. "That's better. Already an improvement." She gave a cheerful response.

Their old governess should be sainted just for enduring her and Liliah's education.

Right now, Miranda thought she should be on her way to being sainted as well.

"Must I continue?" Iris asked.

Miranda was about to reply when there was a knock on the door. Turning, Miranda nodded to Mrs. Keyes, who entered.

"Good afternoon, ladies. I've just received word that Lord Kilpatrick will be in residence this week! I thought you'd wish to know. I'm sure he will be thrilled with your progress, Miss Iris. And I'm certain he will be impressed with your tutoring, Miss Miranda," Mrs. Keyes said encouragingly.

Miranda thought it was an overly optimistic opinion, but she didn't offer any correction.

"I find that highly suspect," Iris remarked to the housekeeper. Apparently, *she* had no hesitation to voice her opinion.

Not that Miranda found that surprising. Iris's opinions were rarely thought, simply spoken.

It was another area they were working on . . . amongst many.

"Iris . . ." Miranda coached, offering a stern glare.

The young lady sighed. "And *when* may I voice my opinion?"

"After you've thought about your words and their implications. And then I'd still wait a few moments," Miranda explained, not for the first time.

"By then the time for saying something—"

"Will likely pass, and you'll have saved yourself the trouble," Miranda finished.

It was becoming a common theme, Iris voicing her opinion and Miranda intercepting and correcting it.

Mrs. Keyes chuckled. "I don't know what we all did for entertainment before you two! It's just wonderful to have two young ladies in the house. Heaven knows it's been a long while." Mrs. Keyes's joyful expression sobered, and Miranda took note of her change in demeanor.

"Oh, and I almost forgot." Mrs. Keyes's expression buoyed. "You've a missive, Miss Miranda. I wasn't aware you had connections in Edinburgh," The housekeeper remarked. "I placed it in your chamber."

"Thank you," Miranda replied, her heart pounding as she anticipated finally hearing from her sister. It had been longer than she had thought, and a thread of anxiety had woven its way through her heart as the days passed without any correspondence.

"Can we have a short break, Miss Miranda?" Iris asked.

Miranda nodded, thankful for the excuse to read her missive.

"We'll meet again in a half hour to review conversational topics acceptable for mixed company," she replied.

"How thrilling," Iris replied dryly.

Mrs. Keyes pressed her lips together as if suppressing a laugh.

Miranda gave her a wink, then excused herself. Each step down the hall toward her room was tempered with impatience. Finally, when she had reached her chamber and bolted the door, she lifted the note from her small desk and ripped it open with the old wooden letter knife.

Dearest Sister,
Please accept my earnest apologies for this
letter's late arrival. There were many obstacles
to its being written, many of which were in direct
relation to our father. However, I'm pleased to
say that there is a rumor circulating in London

*that states that you are visiting a distant aunt in
America, Boston more specifically. It seems our
father has admitted a defeat of sorts. In this I
rejoice, because it means you are, at least for the
moment, safe from his reach. Dear Sister, I cannot express to you how much I miss you, but
please know that I'm supremely happy as the
Countess of Heightfield, and though your
acquaintance with your new brother-in-law was
brief, I'm utterly convinced you will come to adore
him. He has taken every effort to protect your
whereabouts from all, all in an effort to preserve
your safety. This alone endears him further to my
heart, but that is simply a small token of his affection for me, and, as such, for you, his sister-in-law.
But I must also make known the fact that Lucas
did not confide your identity to the Viscount
Kilpatrick. He is not aware of your connection
with me or his friend. We are traveling to Edinburgh now, and I expect we shall arrive a day
after you receive this missive. Lucas has reason to
believe the viscount will not be far behind us.*

*Rest assured that we will notify the viscount
of your connection once we are all safely
ensconced in Edinburgh, but till then, may I encourage you to keep all secrecy until Lucas can
make everything known?*

*I sincerely hope you are finding your wings as
you experience freedom, dear Sister. You are so
much stronger than you ever thought, and I wait
in great expectation to see you soon, but not
nearly soon enough!*

*With all my heart,
Liliah*

Miranda read, then reread the letter, committing her sister's words to memory as she lovingly caressed the paper. Her heart rejoiced in knowing she would soon see her, yet she wondered how such an arrangement could be made before her true identity was made known. Wouldn't it seem suspicious to the staff if the countess visited her sister, the governess? Miranda gave her head a slight shake. If Liliah and her husband had been so cautious thus far, they certainly knew how to address further matters as well.

A smile tipped her lips as she considered the truth that Liliah was happy in her marriage to the Earl of Heightfield. She hadn't expected any less, but to hear it from her own hand was a blessing. Liliah was a rare spirit, and Miranda was thankful she had found her love match in the earl. It would be a great boon to be able to further her acquaintance with her brother-in-law. She hoped his intentional neglect in divulging information to the viscount wouldn't affect his friendship, but as she thought it, a wary notion flickered through her mind.

Not only had she never met the Viscount Kilpatrick, but he hadn't any clue of her identity. Would he be kind? While she didn't think her sister would approve of her taking the position in his house if he was suspect of a violent nature, she still felt a shiver of trepidation run the length of her spine. She set the missive down on the small table, then glanced back at it. Dare she keep it?

Reluctantly, she stood and carried the missive to the low-burning fire.

No chances.

With a flick of her wrist, she sent the missive to the

coals, watching the fire lick at the words and consume them.

It was symbolic.

No chances, no looking back.

Move forward.

And pray the past didn't somehow catch up to her.

For certainly, if it did, she would burn as well.

Chapter Six

Heathcliff watched the horizon, anticipating the next curve in the road that would lend the first view of Kilmarin. As the bays rounded the bend, a smile broke across his face at the bloody wonderful sight.

Settled against the rolling hills, the Kilmarin estate grew larger with each step of the horses. It was a bitter yet sweet sight.

One that reminded him that freedom was never free.

But it was worth every penny.

Already, he could hear Mrs. Keyes's gentle scolding, and taste the haggis and biscuits made by his cook, Mrs. Mertle. His mouth watered. The only damper on his peace of mind was the expectation that he'd need to meet and engage in conversation with his unwanted ward.

And the bloody governess.

There was no way but through it, so he was determined to accomplish the unsavory task as quickly as possible and then avoid them both like the black plague.

He took a deep breath of Scottish country air and watched as the horses took the turn into the Kilmarin courtyard. The large stone building had been in his family for generations. Of all the places he had ever been, it was the only place he called home.

The carriage halted before the front entrance, and Heathcliff tugged his gloves into place and waited for the footman to open the carriage door. His boots crunched on the gravel as a wide smile spread across his face as he met the warm welcome of Mrs. Keyes.

"Milord! It's a pleasure to have you home at last!" The grandmotherly woman's green eyes twinkled with delight as she gave a slight curtsey.

"None o' that, Mrs. Keyes. You dinna lower yourself when I was a wee one, you needn't do it now." Heathcliff grinned at the warm reception, his body relaxing.

"We've ladies, Lord Kilpatrick. I'm setting a good example, that I am," she answered with a sassy tone.

Heathcliff grinned in spite of the reminder of the two ladies in residence. "Ach, and what do you think of the lasses?" he asked in a teasing tone, though he was honestly curious. Mrs. Keyes would be kind, but she wouldn't not mince words. He paused before the older woman.

"I think you'll be pleasantly surprised. No doubt you're expecting a harridan." She arched a gray brow even as her lips quirked into a grin.

"Possibly," Heathcliff answered, glancing into the distance, then turning back to her.

"The only harridan you'll find here is the one you'll see in the mirror," Mrs. Keyes sassed, a familiar Scottish lilt to her words and a welcoming smile teasing her wrinkled face.

Heathcliff chuckled. "I knew the pretense of your good manners wouldn't last long."

"Ach, they are in the house. They can't hear my words, just see my actions," she replied, dropping her words to a whisper.

"You always were a sly one."

"It's why you couldn't get away with anything." Mrs. Keyes batted the air with her hand as she started toward the entrance to the house.

Heathcliff followed her up the stairs, a smile tipping his lips at the familiarity that washed over him with each step. "You always knew what shenanigans I was attempting."

"You weren't as sly as you thought," she said in a huff.

He paused as he nodded to his longtime butler, then glanced around.

Home.

\It was bloody lovely to be home. As he followed Mrs. Keyes down the hall, he smirked as she glared at the suit of armor, then cast an irritated glance at him before continuing on her way. "I'm assumin' you're a wee bit hungry."

"You'd be assuming correctly," Heathcliff replied.

"Figured as much. Cook has been in a dither, trying to anticipate when you'd return. She baked treacle tart on a whim you'd be here today."

"God bless her." Heathcliff could almost taste the hint of lemon in the tart, surrounded by the shortbread crust that was amazing. Scotland and shortbread: it was a match made in heaven.

And it was only a few short steps away.

If he closed his eyes, he could smell the sweet dessert's precious aroma. The sound of a door being wrenched open interrupted his revelry.

"Ach, Miss Iris!"

Mrs. Keyes's voice had Heathcliff opening his eyes from his reverent appreciation and regarding the reason for the interruption in his sensory delight.

Heathcliff looked at the woman pausing in the doorway of the green parlor, gripping the doorframe as if supporting herself from tumbling into the hall. Her green eyes flashed with mutiny, even as she straightened her shoulders and lifted her nose just slightly. "Forgive me, Mrs. Keyes," she replied with a clipped tone, as if trying to be polite but finding it difficult.

"Well, now is as good a time as any." Mrs. Keyes shrugged and turned to Heathcliff, pulling his attention from the young lady in the doorway. "My lord, may I introduce you to your ward, Miss Iris Grace Morgan."

Heathcliff bowed smartly, confirming a few of his preconceived notions regarding his ward. The young lady's fair skin paled further, and she dipped into a slightly awkward curtsey. "A pleasure, my lord," she replied, her tone soft.

"Dancing again, Miss Iris?" Mrs. Keyes asked, a smile in her tone.

Heathcliff turned to the housekeeper, noting the familiar expression of amusement. How many times had he seen that same expression when inquiring about his activities as a lad?

His heart softened a bit toward Iris as he awaited her response.

Iris's lips twitched as she cast a furtive glance to Heathcliff, then back to Mrs. Keyes. "Yes, ma'am."

"You'll catch on soon enough," Mrs. Keyes encouraged. "But let's take a short break for the moment. I'm assuming Miss Miranda is just behind you."

Iris sighed and stepped from the doorway and glanced behind her. "No doubt awaiting to torture me further."

"With dancing instructions?" Heathcliff couldn't resist asking. Never before had he considered a lady might loathe dancing. Reasonably, he associated the two closely. It was intriguing.

"Indeed," Iris replied simply, yet he sensed a simmering frustration below the surface. His attention was stolen by a movement just behind Miss Iris, and only years of self-discipline enabled him to hold his reaction in check.

In a word, the young woman was angelic. Beautiful in every sense, she was a feast for his gaze. Long, thick dark hair framed a delicate, heart-shaped face with wide, expressive brown eyes that seemed to radiate kindness. After performing a curtsey that would be welcome in Prinny's court, she straightened and offered a reserved smile.

Mrs. Keyes coughed.

Heathcliff then realized he was expected to say something. He cast a quick glance to Mrs. Keyes, who was hiding a knowing grin. Bloody cheeky thing.

"Miss Miranda, I presume?" he inquired, offering a grin that surely bordered on the wolfish.

A leopard can't change his spots; neither can a wolf tame his instincts.

"Yes, my lord," she replied. "A pleasure to make your acquaintance. Forgive our interruption." She gave an amused glance to Iris, then met his gaze once more. "Surely you just arrived?"

"Indeed. I've only just walked through the door."

"You are certainly in need of refreshment, then. We apologize for detaining you."

"Yes, pardon me," Iris echoed.

Heathcliff noted the way she was quick to respond to her governess. It gave him hope that the impish streak could be tamed.

"It's of no consequence," he replied. "It was a pleasure to meet you both." He bowed once again, and as he regarded Miss Miranda again, a vague familiarity teased the back of his mind.

He almost asked her if they had met before.

But he gave a quick shake of his head and started toward the kitchens once more.

Certainly he'd remember meeting an angel like Miss Miranda.

After all, darkness was always attracted to light.

And if one thing was certain, he was of the darker variety.

Which made Miss Miranda all too tempting.

Chapter Seven

Miranda waited until the viscount turned the corner, then released the breath she'd been holding. Dear lord.

His voice made her insides melt like butter on hot toast, and his eyes—that caramel shade warmed her from the inside out. For the first time, she had an inkling of what her sister felt for Lord Heightfield.

"That was close." Iris turned around, her gaze wide.

Miranda smoothed her skirt in an effort to collect her wayward reaction to her new employer. "Well, I think we made an impression."

"Not exactly the kind I was hoping for." Iris scrunched up her nose.

"Nor I," Miranda responded. "But what is done is done. Shall we continue?" Miranda bit her lip to keep from smiling as she gestured to the dance floor.

"I'd rather . . . not," Iris replied tersely.

Oddly enough, Miranda smiled. That was progress!

A polite decline was a milepost in Iris's education. A week ago, she wouldn't have been as kind.

That should have given Miranda hope. Instead, it simply reminded her just how far they had to go.

Yet, it brought up a question that had plagued Miranda from the beginning: How does one teach without extinguishing the spirit? It would be easy to require Iris to suppress her fire and energy, but in the end, was that what was best for her?

She thought about Liliah, and how any pressure to conform only made her more rebellious. It was a miracle she kept to the social rules as well as she did. Each day, Iris reminded Miranda more and more of her sister, only the roles were reversed. Where Liliah tried to set a good example for her, Miranda was trying to set the good example for Iris. It was opposite, yet not.

And still utterly confusing.

"Miss Miranda?" Iris inquired.

Miranda shook her head to dispel her thoughts. "Yes, we can take a break. I'll ring for tea." She smiled to Iris, then went to ring for the tea service. As she came from the bell, she took a seat across from Iris on the sofa. Rather than engage in conversation, Miranda watched.

And in observation, she noted the way Iris's shoulders curved in on themselves. Iris picked at a frayed edge of the upholstery and sighed. A thought flickered through Miranda's mind.

"Iris, did you know that my mother died when I was around twelve years old?" Miranda was taking a risk. Never had her governesses spoken to her about their family or private life. They had only worried after her education and performance of said education when called upon.

She and Liliah had made it through life because of each other.

Iris had no one.

And maybe, just maybe, Miranda could be that someone for her.

So she took a shot in the dark, wondering if it would hit a mark or not.

Iris's hand stilled, and she lifted her gaze to Miranda. "Truly?"

Miranda released her pent-up breath. "Yes. I know the pain of missing a loved one."

Iris nodded slowly, then bit her lip. "How, rather, when does it get easier? To not miss them?"

Miranda glanced away to the ground, gathering her thoughts and the unexpected onslaught of emotion. When she felt mostly in control of herself, she glanced back to Iris. "It never stops hurting, it simply gets easier to adjust to life without them."

Iris gave a slow nod. "I see. Is it horrible of me to say I miss my father even more than my mother?"

Miranda shook her head. "No. I missed my mother significantly more than I miss—missed my father," Miranda amended belatedly.

Iris twisted her lips. "When did you lose your father?"

Miranda took a deep breath, wondering how to answer that question, when a knock sounded at the door. A parlormaid came in with the tea.

Miranda gave a silent sigh of relief at the appearance of a distraction. Perhaps Iris would forget the question.

Miranda thanked the maid and said they would serve themselves. "How do you wish your tea this afternoon, Iris?" Miranda asked. Early, she had learned

Iris didn't simply take her tea the same way each time, but tended to cater it to her mood.

"Cream and sugar today, please," Iris answered.

Miranda poured the amber tea into the china cups, watching as the steam swirled above it. The aroma was bitter and sweet all at once, so much like life. The cream lightened the tea and halted the swirling steam as soon as it was added to the cup. After dropping one sugar cube, Miranda carefully stirred the liquid and set the spoon to the side before handing it to Iris.

"You make serving tea look lovely. How do you do that? Everything you do is graceful," Iris added just before taking a sip of tea.

"Thank you," Miranda answered. Though she wasn't sure how serving tea could appear graceful in the least, it was still a kind word from Iris. "I'm simply doing what everyone else does when pouring tea."

"Yes, but . . . I'm not sure, you make it look effortless. It's the same as when you dance. I'm not sure I'll ever be able to learn it, which is daunting."

"I have a few more years' experience," Miranda answered, pouring her own tea and adding a small splash of cream. The steam swirled above her white china cup and she inhaled the sweet scent before taking a sip.

"I'm sure a hundred years' more experience for me still wouldn't make it stick," Iris replied wryly. "But I digress. Tell me, when did you lose your father?"

Drat. Miranda didn't wish to lie; she hated it. After all, hadn't her father lied enough for them both? Why add to it? She took a fortifying breath. "I never really knew my father." She answered honestly, hoping it wouldn't invite more questions.

"I see," Iris replied. "Well, it is a tragedy to be without one's parents. But I will say it is . . . soothing to know I'm not alone in my grief."

"You are certainly not alone. And I'm thankful that we have each other. I realize that I can be exacting, but in the end, I only wish the best for you, Iris. Please know that."

Iris's eyes turned glassy and she looked away. "Thank you. Forgive me for my stubborn nature. My frustration isn't aimed at you but closer. I aim it at myself."

"And such an action will only serve to defeat you as well. You are a very strong young lady, and in that you will be either celebrated or shunned if you don't manage that strength properly. But you will. It just takes time."

"And dancing lessons," Iris replied, gaining some of her cheeky behavior back.

"Many, many dancing lessons," Miranda said, chuckling softly.

"Speaking of dancing, I've never seen a gentleman quite so . . . broad as Lord Kilpatrick." Iris leaned forward. "Tell me, are all the gentlemen in London like that?"

A shiver of appreciation traveled down her spine at the memory of the viscount. Never had an introduction to a gentleman had such an effect on her, and she'd been introduced to quite a few. "No, most are far less . . . imposing."

"Good heavens, all I could think of was that I can't even dance with you and you're of my height, how will I ever master dancing with a man that tall!" Iris giggled, setting down her empty teacup.

Miranda grinned. "It isn't as difficult as you make it sound. You'll see."

"Do you think he'd be willing to let us practice with him?" Iris asked, tilting her head thoughtfully.

Miranda almost choked on the sip of tea she'd taken. The thought of dancing with the viscount was both thrilling and terrifying. "I'm not sure. We can . . . ask," she answered, albeit reluctantly.

"Perhaps." Iris twisted her lips. "But not anytime soon. I need to master the steps first. Wouldn't want to hurt his toes."

"Simply mine," Miranda replied dryly.

"You're accustomed to my abuse," Iris said teasingly.

"Sadly, yes," Miranda replied, shaking her head. "Iris, why don't we take the afternoon off? You've worked hard all day, and I'm certain tonight we'll be dining with the viscount. You'll want to wear something appropriate, and it will be a good opportunity to practice table conversation and manners."

Iris sighed. "I was quite thrilled till you mentioned dinner. I suppose there's nothing to be done to change it?"

"I'd think not."

"Then I suppose I'll be happy with my freedom this afternoon, however short lived."

"Unless you've changed your mind—"

"No, not at all. Thank you." Iris stood from her place on the sofa. "In fact, I shall take advantage of this time while it's still being offered. Excuse me." Iris curtseyed, grinned, and headed to the door.

With a quick glance behind her, she darted out into the hall, leaving Miranda quite alone with her tea and her thoughts. She lifted the cup to her lips once more, remembering the introduction to the viscount. There was a flash of something in his gaze. Recognition? Did he see the resemblance between Liliah and herself? It was unlikely. It did beg the question, however, how would he take the information concerning her close connection with the new lady of Heightfield? Would he resent his friend's dishonesty regarding her identity? Would he perhaps understand the necessity of it?

Would he resent her?

The questions continued to flicker through her mind, and as she gazed into her almost-empty teacup, the now-cold tea gave no answers.

She supposed only time would tell.

And she was growing tired of waiting.

It seemed so much of her life had been consumed by it.

Wait till you master the waltz.

Wait till your French is flawless.

Wait till you come out.

Wait till you meet the man I've chosen for your husband.

Wait, wait, wait.

Even in her escape from her father, she was in a perpetual state of waiting.

Waiting for her sister.

Waiting for the viscount.

Waiting for the truth about her identity to be revealed.

When would she finally move past the purgatory of her life?

She set down her teacup and smoothed her skirt out of habit.

Because it was what ladies did when they waited.

She was bloody tired of waiting!

A blush heated her face at the thought of the vulgar word, but it was also honest.

What would it be like for the world to wait at her

leisure? To have that kind of power, that control? To determine her own course, to be brave enough to try? She wanted to have that kind of courage, but the truth about courage was that you never knew you had it till you used it.

Or failed.

Well, she had gotten this far, hadn't she? There must be some courage buried deep within her. Impossibly, her father hadn't extinguished its flame. Resolved, she decided to fan the tender fire. Who knew? Maybe it would grow.

It had to, because the opposite was unacceptable.

She simply had to await the opportunity to feed the flame.

Bloody, blasted waiting.

Chapter Eight

Heathcliff licked his fork clean, then glanced at his plate, which held only the crumbs remaining from the treacle tart. Never in his dreams had he tasted anything so delightful, and he had tasted a great many things—delightful, pleasurable . . . things. The wicked thought brought a grin to his lips and he set the fork to the side of the plate, then rose from the table. It was blessedly quiet, and he paused to absorb the peaceful atmosphere of the room. Certainly it would be far more crowded during the evening meal.

Three constituted a crowd in his opinion—especially when the facility was his home.

His normally reclusive and very private home.

Bloody women.

But even as he thought back to the ladies in question, he couldn't help but allow himself to linger on the governess. There was something about her that seemed . . . more. It was a simple word, with a complex meaning. Belatedly, he wished he had asked more questions regarding her background and references, but at the time, he was simply happy Lucas had solved his problem.

The nagging sensation remained, and in his gut, he knew something was amiss with the governess. And in his profession, one always trusted their gut instinct.

People lied.

They cheated.

And would risk everything to keep from being caught in either trap.

He wasn't sure which category the beautiful woman fell into, but he was certain it wouldn't take long to discover.

In fact, it would be a diverting little game he'd engage in, flirt with, and enjoy.

"Ach, did you taste it at all?" Mrs. Keyes rounded the corner and placed her hands on her ample hips.

Heathcliff chuckled. "Near enough."

"Well, 'twill be more at dinner tonight. I'm taking the liberty of inviting the girls to dine with you," Mrs. Keyes informed him.

"I see you're still not asking my opinion on matters and such." Heathcliff gave her a wry grin.

"I ask ye on the matters I want your opinion. On the others, I'm inclined to give you the option that's best for ye," she sassed with a grin. "Are you opposed to dining with the ladies?" she asked, growing more serious.

Heathcliff shook his head; no need to make her question her decision. After all, it was the one he'd have made as well, even if he hadn't felt like it. "'Tis all well and good."

"Good," Mrs. Keyes replied. "I'm assuming you're heading to your rooms to freshen up a bit. I had Emily tidy up the room this week, and I just sent up the footman to ensure the fire's warm for you."

"Mothering me still," Heathcliff teased, bowing to the woman.

"Ach, you still need it," she replied, hitching a shoulder. With that, she bustled past him in the hall, leaving him to the promised refuge of his rooms. He strode down the hall, the ground slightly creaking under his weight. A pained smile pulled at his lips. The house was alive with memories; even the sound of footsteps told a thousand tales.

Of when his father would stride down the hall, so powerful, immovable, strong.

Till he wasn't.

And the stride became a shuffle.

And then nothing at all.

But it was an honor to the great man's legacy to remember the years of health, of strength. It was also a painful reminder of how short Heathcliff had fallen when trying to measure up to the standard his father set.

He shook his head to dispel the memories and took the stairs that wound up to the second floor. Sunlight spilled into the room from the grand windows that stood guard over the hall, the air warm. He glanced out to the hills beyond the windows, mentally making plans to take his leisure in hunting the grouse that wandered there. It would be a welcome change of pace from the bustle of London.

London had its other charms.

But he didn't miss those at the moment. He would eventually, but now . . . now he was simply happy to keep to himself, to have no expectations placed on his character, his reputation, or living up to either.

The metal of the handle was cool against his hand as he opened the door into the first of his suite of rooms.

Sure enough, his room was comfortably warm from the fire crackling in the hearth. Even though the end of summer, Edinburgh's air was still damp enough to carry a chill. The scent of sunshine and lye soap filled the room, and he inhaled deeply. The fresh smell of laundry was vastly different here than his home in London. Never did the sheets fully become fresh from the clean air as they did here, and he breathed greatly, anticipating the delightful sensation of his bed that evening. Tugging on his cravat, he loosened the offensive garment and shrugged out of his coat. Twisting his neck, he tugged on his shirtsleeves and loosened his top button. Far more relaxed, he took the few steps to the window that overlooked the back of his property. Just as when he was a lad, he traced the correct path of the maze with his gaze, but as he reached the end, he paused.

Someone was in the maze.

He took a step closer to the window to inspect. Sure enough, a young lady—the governess, he suspected— wove through the path with expert ease, taking each turn correctly till she emerged on the other side of the puzzle. She walked toward the hills then, abandoning the maze and disappearing behind a hedgerow. His gaze darted ahead to where she'd emerge in the break between the hedges. It took only a few seconds and he saw her once again. The slight breeze was teasing her bonnet ribbons, and he saw her reach up to their drifting ends before disappearing behind the row once more.

He glanced to the next separation and grinned when

he noted the absence of her bonnet. Perhaps the governess wasn't quite as prim as she pretended.

He found he liked that idea.

Dismissing it, he was about to turn away when he saw her disappear once again. Out of habit, he glanced ahead to the next row, but after several seconds, she didn't appear.

Curious, he waited a few moments longer.

Nothing.

Now confused, he placed his hands on his hips and studied the courtyard. She hadn't turned back either.

Odd.

He waited a few moments more, and when she still didn't appear, he disregarded the wayward woman and turned his back to the window.

But he wasn't able to dispel his curiosity.

It was both his greatest asset and his greatest fault.

He changed his shirt, then turned to the window.

He washed his face, then turned to the window again.

He looked to the door, then to the window.

"Blast it all," he muttered before opening his door and all but stalking out.

He moved down the hall and then opened the door to the servant's stairway; it would be the quickest way to the back of the estate. He took the stone steps two at a time, then paused on the landing below. The wooden door creaked loudly as he opened it, spilling sunshine in over the gray stone. The call of a dove was the only sound above the gentle stirring of the wind. He took the path that led away from the house and toward the maze, then took a smaller fork in the path to where the hedgerow started its division of the property. Rather than follow the path the governess had taken, he opted for a more relaxed route, deciding to at least appear as if it were happenstance.

No need for the lady to think he was watching her.

He was simply curious.

It was innocent enough, yet how long had it been since anything he'd done could be considered innocent?

He glanced to the hills as he walked along the outside of the hedgerow, his hand tracing the lower hedge beside it, brushing the bright green leaves with his fingertips. When he reached the place he assumed the lady to be pausing, he gentled his steps and listened.

Nothing.

As he made it to the next break in the hedgerow, he turned, expecting to startle the young lady.

But the there was no young lady.

Unaccustomed to being surprised, Heathcliff frowned, then glanced around, scanning the property. It was entirely likely she had moved while he was traveling between his room and the staircase, but wouldn't he have seen her then?

And why in the bloody hell did it even matter? He didn't need to chase a skirt; hell, skirts chased him.

In droves.

But it was something of a thrill, however small, to solve the mystery. He didn't have any pressing plans for the afternoon.

And surely it wouldn't take long.

Decision made, he glanced about once more, looking for clues as to where she might have endeavored to disappear. He noted a hill cresting perpendicular to the hedgerow. If she had crested the hill, he wouldn't have seen her digress in her path, nor would he see her now.

It was a possibility.

He followed the deer path up to the hill and, as he crested it, paused to absorb the sight.

Nestled amid a copse of birch trees sat a forest nymph. She reclined lazily upon a rock, her stockings removed as she kicked a toe in the small pond just beyond. Her hair was pinned up properly, which was the only detail out of place. Didn't nymphs, fairies, and the like have unbound hair? All the pictures he'd ever seen in the more salacious books he'd read had used the unbound hair to cover the more . . . delicate areas of the beauty, only to keep the reader fully engaged in imagining what was hidden.

It was a pity the fairy was utterly and properly clothed.

He'd like to remedy that.

She moved her foot about playfully in the water, and her chest rose and fell with a contented sigh. The movement highlighted the delicate curves and valleys of her feminine form, a heated and feverish fantasy in daylight.

The rational part of him knew it was simply the governess he'd hired for his ward—he was uncertain if he was bloody brilliant, stupidly lucky, or headed for destruction because of that decision—but the less rational and more amorous part of him was finding great satisfaction in the fantasy.

It was ironic.

He owned and worked at the most exclusive gambling hell in London. Courtesans and the like were in constant company—yet none of them had utterly stolen his attention, for however long.

She reached up and swiped a stray hair from her face. The motion so smooth, so graceful, it was art simply to watch.

He had to put an end to this madness, preferably before he did something stupid.

"Good afternoon." He released the words into the silence, and watched as her body froze, then her head turned just enough to see who had spoken.

Her eyes widened, and she slowly rose from her reclining position and moved to stand.

His gaze flickered to her foot in the water, watching as she placed her other foot down on a nearby rock.

It wobbled.

She shifted, gasped—then, as if time had slowed down, she fell backward into the pond.

Chapter Nine

*C*old.

The first thought that went through Miranda's mind wasn't the need for air, or the inclination to swim. It was the idea that her body was going to freeze into a block of ice, like the Serpentine in winter. At least she'd had the good sense to take a deep breath and close her mouth as she fell.

Good Lord. He'd scared the wits out of her!

Her hands found the bottom of the rocky pond, and she pushed herself up into a sitting position, taking a lungful of air. Thankfully, the pond was only a few feet deep, just enough to give her a proper soaking. Immediately her teeth started chattering while she wiped the water from her eyes.

"Good God, are you all right?" a deep baritone asked with a rich brogue.

Miranda glanced up to see the man who had ignited her fright, the man who was also her employer, reaching out a hand toward her.

Reaching up, she was all but flung from the water and onto the shore by his powerful grip. Warm hands grasped her shoulders, and she wanted to melt into their comfort. Quickly, too quickly, the touch was removed as she gained her balance. "Thank you," she spoke between teeth chatters.

Even though she really didn't feel thankful in the slightest. She turned to him then, waiting for an apology.

She blinked.

He tilted his head.

Was the man daft? Didn't people apologize? Wasn't she owed one?

"We should get you indoors." He nodded once, as if his idea were brilliant rather than simple common sense.

While she, on the other hand, still waited for an apology.

She wasn't sure why it mattered so much; it just did.

Maybe it was because her father never apologized for anything.

Maybe because she wanted to be treated well.

Regardless, as she waited one moment more, something inside her snapped.

She. Was. Done. With. Waiting.

"Aren't you going to apologize?" she bit out, trying to make her tone serious even while her teeth chattered.

The irritating man tilted his head, as if the thought had never occurred to him.

Perfect. From one arse of a man—her father—to another.

Well, this time she refused to stand by and allow it to happen.

Not when she knew Liliah would arrive soon.

Not when she *knew* her rank, her worth—regardless whether anyone else knew.

She. Did.

"Do you need coaching? I'll help. 'I'm sorry I snuck up on you and—'"

"I know how to frame a proper apology," he interrupted, his caramel eyes dancing with . . . amusement?

What part of this was amusing? Miranda began to seethe.

"You simply are miserly in handing them out, even when they are grossly necessary?" she asked, her tone clipped. This time the chattering of her teeth added emphasis.

He opened his mouth, fought a grin, and glanced to the ground. "A thousand apologies, miss."

Lady, she corrected in her mind but held her tongue. "Thank you," she replied in more of a retort, and started to march up the hill toward the manor house.

"Isn't it customary to accept an apology when one is given?" His tone was challenging.

She paused halfway up the hill and turned to regard him. "When the lady is so inclined, yes," she answered, then turned, a smirk on her lips at her own smart remark.

"And you don't include yourself amongst the ranks of ladies?" he asked, his voice sounding much closer.

I'm more of one than you think. "When it suits me," she replied instead.

A deep chuckle radiated from him, giving her body a rush of warmth even with the biting chill of her wet skirts. "I'm thankful you amuse yourself, my lord." She stomped up the rest of the hill and started down the other side, her skirts sticking to her legs with each step.

"Wait," he called out to her.

"I'd rather not. I'm not comfortable just now," she remarked over her shoulder without breaking her stride. She made it to the gravel path beyond the hedgerows and noted the way her skirts dripped water upon the stones, leaving a trail. Drat; she wouldn't be able to make it up to her room without making a mess. She stopped and glanced to the house, debating which entrance would be best to take.

A warm hand rested on her shoulder. She should have shrugged it off, but the warmth was irresistible. Settling for a glare, she turned to the owner of the hand.

"Come with me. It's the least I can do," he remarked, amusement still thick in his tone and apparent in his expressive eyes.

She shouldn't notice.

But she was realizing that he was impossible to ignore.

She gave a small nod, and lamented the loss of heat when he removed his hand and started for a small entrance not far from where she stood. With his back to her, she took the liberty of studying the infuriating man before her.

The man whose benevolence she still needed.

For the moment.

Drat.

Yet her irritation melted into appreciation as she studied the broad length of his shoulders, the tapering of his waist down to a powerful stride.

Belatedly, she noted he didn't wear a coat, just his shirtsleeves.

It wasn't proper.

But she wasn't exactly proper at the moment either.

The improper attire did afford her a much clearer view of the gentleman's form, and it was . . . intriguing. Angular yet rounded. She fleetingly wondered if he was as granite solid as he appeared.

"Here." He opened the door, pulling her fairly scandalous thoughts from the forefront of her mind. If she hadn't been so terribly cold, she was sure a blush would have given away her private musings.

She was no sooner through the door when she was shocked once more by the absurd gentleman. One moment she was walking on her shivering legs, the next she was holding the man's neck to keep her balance while he carried her up the stairs.

"This, no." She shook her head.

"Ach, wee-shet," he muttered, grinning wolfishly. "Mrs. Keyes would tan my hide if I let you traipse about the house dripping all over."

"I highly doubt that your housekeeper—"

"You don't know her as I do. Trust me, I'm saving my hide here. And maybe yours too." He gave her a wink.

While he carried her.

In his arms.

She'd never been carried before.

Warmth seeped through her as she pressed against the fabric of his shirt. The initial shock of her cold skirts pressed tightly against her was now being replaced with warmth from his arms.

If she weren't so frustrated, she might actually enjoy it.

"I see you're not giving any argument," he said.

"I can't see how my arguing would change anything," she replied.

He chuckled, the sound vibrating deep in his chest, resounding against her limbs. "You're right in that."

She was about to say something but noticed he was walking out into the second floor. "My roo-chambers are not here my lord, but . . . below." She spoke, the idea of it reminding her of her humble position.

He paused, turning a confused glance to her. "You mean Mrs. Keyes gave you the nursery quarters? When we've at least thirty rooms available?"

Miranda frowned, not seeing the problem. "Of course. Why would I be anywhere else?"

Something flickered in his gaze, an understanding of sorts before he gave a small nod. "I see."

"I'm afraid I do not. And I'm soaking you as well." She glanced to the almost transparent white shirt pressed against her skirts. Belatedly, she realized she was able to answer her own question.

Yes. His body was as solid as granite.

Her fingers, pressed against the back of his neck for support, registered a thousand sensations all at once, as if absorbing as much information as possible, as quickly as possible. Soft, warm, smooth, tight, it was an over-load of her senses, and she scrambled to identify each one.

"Let's count it as my penance for a late apology." He smiled kindly, then continued down the hall.

She opened her mouth to say something in reply, then closed it when no intelligent remark came to mind. She was growing far too . . . aware of him. His arms were placed just beneath her bottom, and his hands gripped her upper thighs as he walked. His other arm wound around her back, making his hand scan-dalously close to her—

"What in heaven's name!" Mrs. Keyes all but shouted, drawing Miranda's attention.

"Ach, I scared the wee lass and she tumbled into the pond," he answered with a hint of remorse.

She was shocked it held any at all.

"She's drippin' wet!"

"I said she fell in the pond, Mrs. Keyes. Did you think she miraculously didn't get wet?" he answered with a chuckle as he turned toward a room with a double door.

"There's nothing to be done for it now, I suppose. I'll fetch some clothes for the poor lass."

"Thank you, Mrs. Keyes. And I'm dreadfully sorry I'm dripping on the floor," Miranda added.

"Isn't your fault. It's his." She jabbed a thumb at the viscount, cackled, then rushed off to collect the items.

He opened the door and took a few steps inside, then, with a gentleness she wouldn't have suspected, he tenderly set her down on her feet.

"Th-thank you," she murmured, missing the heat of his body immediately.

"You're welcome." He ran his hand through his sandy hair, stretching the fabric of his transparent shirt over the skin of his chest.

Miranda's face heated with a blush even as her heart beat faster at the imagery it created. "I'm sure Mrs. Keyes can assist me from here," she added, wanting to be rid of him. Her senses and emotions could only take so much.

He'd wreaked havoc on both.

He nodded once, his gaze meeting her eyes, then lowered, traveling the length of her body till she was sure he was studying her slippers. His gaze was like a touch, caressing every inch of her body, making her breathless. With a low curse, he turned and left.

It was a few moments later, after she'd recovered, when she glanced down at herself.

Just as his shirt had become transparent from the water, so had her dress.

Chapter Ten

Heathcliff Marston, Viscount Kilpatrick, was not a stranger to beautiful women. Nor was he a novice when it came to the naked female form.

Rather, he was considered an expert.

Lord knew he'd had more than enough experience.

Yet he still felt the lingering intensity that threatened to make him combust.

He tried to remember the trek to the house. Surely he would have noticed the transparency of the fabric before? Yet it was also reasonably sound to consider that the water continued to soak through the layers of clothing till . . .

He slid a hand down his pants to ease the ache between his legs.

And there was something else.

Employees did not demand apologies from employers.

He'd seen it in her eyes the moment they flashed at him in irritation.

She had expected one, and when the expectation wasn't met, she had demanded it be satisfied.

It was rather erotic. The forest- turned water-nymph had a bit of a temper.

He liked it, but it was an untried emotion. One she didn't use often.

Apparently, he had the knack for bringing it out.

That could be intriguing.

The nagging curiosity ate at him yet. Who was she? He'd often heard of ladies of good breeding falling on hard times and turning into bluestockings. Hell, they'd employed a few ladies who'd turned into ladies of the night because of financial destruction. It wasn't often, and they came to Temptations because they'd at least be treated and paid well, but it made him wonder what trauma had befallen the nymph now next door.

That was another problem. Of course Mrs. Keyes would put the governess in the nursery rooms, but when she said it, it seemed wrong, like petting a hound against the grain of his fur. But that didn't bloody well give him license to deposit her in the room across from his.

As if she didn't present enough of a temptation.

Damn it all, she was the help!

Nothing could come of it.

Except pleasure.

Only that was one particular pleasure that wasn't to be had, or so he tried to remind himself. In an irritated motion, he unfastened the wet shirt that clung to his skin, gritting his teeth against the memory of how *her* clothing had done the same. Tossing the offensive reminder to the floor, he all but stalked to the adjoining closet and selected another. He should call his valet, but he wasn't the kind who required constant assistance from others. No, he preferred to accomplish tasks with his own two hands. His fingers fumbled slightly with the buttons, but soon he was tugging the sleeve of his shirt into place while he finished dressing.

The generational clock sounded in the hall, and Heathcliff counted the chimes, *four.* They kept country hours here, and he expected dinner to be served at around six, which left him two hours. Much could happen in two hours, but there was only one thing that was a necessity.

He had to calm the hell down.

It wasn't an impossible feat, but it was a feat nonetheless. Governesses weren't to be trifled or flirted with. That was simply the end of it. Yet, as he shrugged on his coat, his mind drifted back to the perfect outline of her waist swelling to perfectly rounded hips. His memory traveled the length of her waist, higher . . . he shook his head. In truth, the fact that he was attracted to her should be the first sign to be wary.

His judgment in women had never been good. Rather, it was a universal truth amongst his friends that if he found a woman interesting, she was trouble.

It would behoove him to remember that, and apply it to this situation. Miss Miranda may be beautiful, with the form of a goddess, but fine figures often hid black hearts.

After all, a beautifully wrapped poison was still lethal, no matter how lovely the paper and bow.

He headed to the door and strode out into the hall. It had been months since he'd been in residence; he needed to address the small mountain of correspondence and documents requiring his attention that had taken habitation on the mammoth desk in his study. As he took the stairs down to the lower floor, he caught a glimpse of Mrs. Keyes leaving one of the parlors and entering the foyer.

"I see you're all cleaned up as well," she said, her brow arching.

Heathcliff narrowed his eyes. "Indeed."

She shook her head. "Scaring the wits out of the poor thing. You should know better," she scolded without any heat.

"You should know better than to expect much from me." He shrugged and started toward the study again, then paused. "Mrs. Keyes?" He turned.

The woman folded her hands and inclined her head. "Yes?"

"Can I speak to you in private?" He gestured to his study, just ahead.

"Of course." She followed him in, then took a seat when he indicated she should.

The fire crackled softly in the otherwise quiet room, and Heathcliff set a stack of papers to the side of the desk before he sat down, facing Mrs. Keyes. "What do you know of Miss Miranda?"

Theoretically, finding out about her history and other information would reinforce the necessity to keep away. He only hoped Mrs. Keyes had some details.

"I'm afraid I don't know much about her, my lord."
Blast.

Mrs. Keyes twisted her lips, then continued. "She's very prompt, exceedingly polite, and I'm certain she was a lady of quality at some point in her young life. She carries herself with more grace than any lady I've ever seen, though you'd be a better judge than I, with all your experience in London."

"Indeed." He waited.

"She's kind to a fault, never cross as far as I can tell, and has the patience of a saint to deal with Miss Iris. Who, I might add, is a delightful girl as well, simply inclined to more of a stubborn nature, you understand."

"I quite gathered that." Heathcliff arched a brow. "So you know nothing of her life before her employment here?"

Mrs. Keyes shook her head. "No. I thought you had that information, my lord."

Heathcliff leaned back in his chair. The mystery continued. "Thank you, Mrs. Keyes. I appreciate your insight."

"Not sure how much insight I have, but you're welcome. If you're interested, why no' ask the lady herself?" Mrs. Keyes asked, her brow furrowing.

Heathcliff gave a disinterested grin, the kind he gave to gamblers who tried to convince him of the worth of the collateral they used to place bets at Temptations.

Mrs. Keyes arched a brow, as if awaiting his response, not believing his bravado.

Damn, it was bloody well irritating to have someone read your expressions. He almost had sympathy for the gamblers.

Almost.

"I don't wish to bring up memories that could be painful," he lied smoothly.

"You and your tender heart," Mrs. Keyes remarked, smirking. "Will there be anything else?" she asked in a kinder tone.

Heathcliff shook his head. "You're dismissed."

"Thank you." She stood slowly, then bustled out of the room, shutting the door with a soft click.

Heathcliff folded his hands on his desk, staring at the swirling wood grain but not seeing it. It would be a terrible lapse in judgment to ask Miss Miranda questions. Who was to say she would tell the truth? And while he prided himself in reading others' body language, women were of a different sort, and his confidence was lacking in that area.

It had been ever since the godforsaken disaster that was his marriage to Margot. Even thinking her name made bile rise in his throat.

It was one thing to marry for convenience; the expectation for affection was low, and if it grew, it was a boon to both.

But his marriage to Margot was of love, at least from his side of things.

The memories flooded back, unwelcome and unwilling to leave till they'd spun their stories. He leaned back in his chair, giving himself over to the torture, to the ghosts that haunted him.

Hadn't he fought with his father in this very room?

Everyone seemed aware, or at least suspicious of her duplicity—everyone but him.

Love was not simply blind, it was hazardous.

Many a man had stared wars over the love of a woman, and he was not immune to the inclination. It was only the wisdom of his father that had ended the argument before it came to blows.

Even now, Heathcliff could see the expression in his father's gray eyes when he spoke. "I love you, and if this is your choice, so be it. And when your world crumbles, because crumble it will, we will still be here. Just promise me one thing . . ."

Oh, he had hated his father in that moment, but his

honor wouldn't let him refuse the challenge in his father's words, so he had fisted his hands and listened.

His hands flexed instinctively at the memory.

His father had made him promise not to run away, but to run home.

He'd been doing it ever since, in one way or another.

His father's words had been prophetic.

How Heathcliff wished he had listened, and if he had, perhaps, perhaps it would be different today.

The betrayal of Margot was swift in its reckoning.

In hindsight, he could see her behavior was overly flirtatious, but his inexperience had whispered the lies to his heart that gave him the freedom to believe them. Certainly a well-bred lady wouldn't become a strumpet once married.

After all, she loved him, didn't she?

He was quick to propose, and she swift to accept. Certain of her affection for him, he had battled his father's wisdom against their quick engagement. It was the spark that ignited the fight between him and his father, only to result in an agreement where there would be no winner.

He took a deep breath, banishing the ghosts and memories from his mind. He focused on the fire, the sound of the sparks kindling, and the shuffle of papers as he lifted them from his desk.

He was a shell of a man when Lucas found him.

Temptations saved him in more ways than one.

Like ice water, the memories cooled his curiosity about the new governess.

To be intrigued only led to disappointment.

And disappointment was kin to heartbreak.

And he had vowed long ago, never again.

He'd survived once.

It wasn't that he didn't think he could survive again.

Rather, he was afraid he would.

And death was welcome over surviving any more loss.

Chapter Eleven

Miranda went down to the parlor, where they would meet before dinner, praying Iris had heeded her admonition and dressed for the occasion. What she needed was a distraction, and Iris was a blessed buffer for the evening, or so she hoped. Her nerves tight, she scanned the foyer for the viscount, praying he wouldn't mention their earlier misadventure. Heaven only knew what Iris would say, let alone the questions she'd ask. Her face burned at the thought.

She was thankful for the gloves on her hands as they kept her palms from sweating with anxiety. Taking a deep breath, she straightened her back and walked into the pale blue parlor. At a quick glance, she noted she was the first to arrive. Her gaze passed the settee and armchair and scanned the wall, with a delicate bookcase framing the window. The sunset was illuminating the evening sky, and she welcomed the distraction of its beauty. She passed the small table with a polished wooden box, ornately painted with gold. Pausing, she turned toward the beautiful treasure. The box was heavier than she anticipated as she lifted it from its place on the shelf. Delicate flowers wound around the wooden frame, a blue ribbon interlacing the gold. With care, she lifted the lid. Silence.

Her brow pinched as she turned over the box, only to discover the windup knob was missing. In its place was a hole marring the bottom of the masterpiece.

"Please, if you wouldn't mind . . ."

Miranda startled, her fingers fumbling with the box before she righted her hold and tenderly set it back in its place. "My apologies. It's quite lovely," she stuttered, her face heating painfully with a blush.

The viscount nodded once. His gaze had lost all the merriment she'd seen earlier. The room felt chilly with his entrance, and she fought a shiver that traveled down her spine. "It's a keepsake." He lifted a broad shoulder, reminding her of the power they had held when carrying her. Glancing away, she fought for control.

"A family keepsake?" she asked, anxious to make small talk that would prevent him from alluding to their earlier encounter.

His gaze clouded ever so slightly, as if controlling his reactions with precision. "One might say that," he answered cryptically.

Miranda decided it wasn't a subject about which he wished to converse. Glancing about the room, her gaze landed back on the light filtering in from the sunset. "It's a beautiful evening. I must say, the sunsets here are vastly different from London." She gave a tight smile and walked to the window.

There was a short pause. "London?"

Miranda was thankful she had her back to the viscount. Her eyes widened at her possible faux pas, but she reminded herself that he was originally supposed to meet her in London, so it would follow that she was originally from that location. "Yes."

"Were you raised in Town?" he asked, his voice much closer than before, and she resisted the temptation to turn and discover just how close he had come.

"Yes," she answered, wondering how long she could continue offering monosyllabic answers.

He stood beside her, evaluating the scenery beyond the gardens.

She breathed in and out calmly, her mind spinning, wondering what to say should he ask for further details. Not wanting to lie, she wasn't sure how to respond.

"It has its charms," he said after a moment.

"Indeed it does."

The sound of footsteps was the most welcome sound in Miranda's world as she turned to see Iris walk into the parlor, Mrs. Keyes on her heels.

"Evening." Iris executed a much-improved curtsey. Belatedly, Miranda realized she hadn't offered any sort of polite greeting to her employer; rather, she almost had dropped a family treasure.

She was just thankful Iris hadn't been there to witness it.

"Good evening, Miss Iris." The viscount bowed smartly.

Well, he hadn't exactly bowed to her either, so perhaps they were even.

"Dinner is served." Mrs. Keyes gave a broad smile to the room as she gestured to the hall.

Traditionally, the gentleman of the house would escort the highest-ranking lady. But with keeping country hours, Miranda suspected a less-formal attitude and was proven right when the viscount simply gestured to the door, indicating that the ladies should precede him into the hall. Miranda walked toward the door, her body still tense, and gestured for Iris to precede her into the hall.

After all, Iris ranked higher as far as everyone else knew.

Miranda followed her, all too aware of the viscount close behind her. Was it possible to feel someone's gaze? She certainly believed it was. She could feel it now. The temptation to turn around and face him and satisfy her theory was great, but she soldiered on ahead, ignoring her curiosity. As they came into the dining room, she watched Iris pause, then turn to her. "Where do we sit now?" she asked in a loud whisper.

The viscount's chuckle vibrated through the air.

"To either side, Miss Iris," Miranda coached, indicating with her hand which seat Iris should take.

"That's right." Iris nodded, her brow furrowed with concentration. "Thank you." She waited beside the richly carved chair as a footman withdrew it for her.

Miranda followed suit, watching as Iris folded her hands in her lap. She cast a glance to the viscount, who seated himself last. His frame made the chair appear small in comparison. He cleared his throat while the footman placed a steamed beef consommé before each of them. Miranda glanced at Iris, watching to make sure she waited to lift her spoon till the viscount did it first. Iris's gaze lifted to Miranda, clearly awaiting instruction. When the viscount lifted his spoon, Miranda did the same and inclined her head toward Iris, who mirrored her actions.

"Is dinner often this formal for you ladies?" he

asked after swallowing. His caramel gaze inquired of Miranda just as much as his words.

Miranda swallowed her own mouthful and nodded before responding. "Indeed, my lord. This is the best way for Miss Iris to practice her table etiquette."

"Ah, I see," he remarked, then continued with his soup.

Miranda did as well, watching as Iris ate with perfect manners.

As the minutes stretched on, Miranda's nerves grew tighter. This was the most dreadful dinner party she'd experienced in some time.

Granted, it wasn't exactly a dinner party, but the least the viscount could do was initiate conversation.

Usually, she'd have no qualms about starting it herself, but she didn't want to overstep.

As another silent minute passed, and the soup bowls were removed, Miranda took matters into her own hands.

"Usually, conversation would begin with discussing the weather, or possibly a current play at Drury Lane. I'll start." Miranda waited a moment while the footman placed the second course before them. The scent of roasted venison and potatoes made her mouth water.

"Have you seen Kean's newest performance of Hamlet?" she asked Iris.

The viscount gave a low chuckle.

Miranda glanced to him, tempted to raise a brow of inquiry, but chose to offer a smile instead. "Ah, you have, my lord?"

His manner shifted to amusement, and he tilted his head as he reclined in his chair slightly. "I have. But it wasn't nearly as brilliant as his first, Shylock."

Miranda nodded, taking a sip of water, then replied,

"I wasn't blessed to see that performance but read the reviews in the *Times*. Quite an enthusiastic response."

"The house went mad." The viscount gave his head a little shake. "But my favorite performance was Macbeth."

Miranda's grin widened. "I am quite fond of that performance myself. I attended the evening the front stage light caught an actor's costume on fire! Thankfully, it was put out almost immediately. I don't believe the man was injured."

The viscount leaned forward, his brow furrowing. "I attended that night too. Did you hear, they are now considering renovating the lights to the new gaslights?"

Miranda shook her head, intrigued. "No! I hadn't heard that! My sister—" She paused, then continued. "My sister mentioned there had been titter about the potential risks with candles. There have been several fires."

"Sister?" The viscount's eyes betrayed his interest, and Miranda's inclination was to retreat from the conversation. Yet if she did, wouldn't he suspect something? Did it matter? Wasn't Liliah supposed to disclose their secret soon?

She resolved to soldier on, and hopefully avoid speaking any lies that would need to be unwound in the future. "Yes, I have an elder sister." She kept her expression open and turned to Iris. "See, Miss Iris, this is a brilliant example of dinner conversation."

Miranda's face heated with a blush as Iris's gaze slid from hers to the viscount, then back. "I see."

Miranda didn't know what she saw, but she was sure she wouldn't approve of it.

"Well, in India there are several different ways to

keep candles from becoming too dangerous, but there is no gaslighting, at least that I saw. However, they do have the most beautiful lamps."

"Very good." Miranda nodded. "My lord, have you ever visited India?" She turned back to the viscount, thankful to direct the conversation to a different venue.

His gaze was studying hers, as if attempting to read her thoughts to answer whatever questions his mind had conjured up from their previous conversation. The intense look faded, and he gave a dismissive gesture with his hand. "I've never been that far East. But I've read several journals of notable explorers."

Miranda turned to Iris.

Iris glanced to Miranda.

Miranda glanced to the viscount.

Apparently, she was going to have to save the flow of the conversation once more.

"The weather has been lovely recently." She introduced another topic of conversation, hoping this one took a longer turn than the last.

"A little cold, if you ask me." Iris shrugged.

"You mustn't shrug," Miranda coached gently. "It's vulgar in a proper setting such as this."

"Vulgar." The viscount chuckled. "It's been an age since I've heard that word. Outside of Almack's, that is, and I avoid that place like hell itself," he remarked. "My apologies for my blunt speaking."

Miranda nodded. "Lord willing, you'll be invited there, Miss Iris. Lady Jersey will need to be applied to for vouchers beforehand, however," she explained, suddenly wondering if those vouchers would be impossible to procure if the viscount wasn't a familiar of the famous meeting place.

"We shall get them for you, Miss Iris. Have no worry." The viscount lifted a crystal glass of wine, as if toasting her.

"Lovely." Miranda breathed an inward sigh of relief. She thought she could potentially procure an invitation through Lady Rebecca, her sister's dear friend, but it was a bit of a stretch. It was nice to know Iris wouldn't need to find a voucher in a roundabout way.

"What exactly is an Almack?" Iris asked, taking a sip of the red wine served with dinner.

If Miranda hadn't just swallowed her bit of venison, she would have surely choked on it.

Clearly, they had work yet to do.

Iris directed the question to the viscount, who turned to Miranda with a wry expression. "I do believe Miss Miranda is best suited to answer that question, Miss Iris. My answer will not be taken favorably, that I can assure you." He grinned unrepentantly.

Miranda took a deep breath, resisted the urge to let her irritation show, and turned to Iris. "It's a lovely—"

The viscount coughed; rather, he coughed in order to cover a laugh.

Miranda ignored him.

Iris did not.

"It's a lovely place in St. James's where those who have vouchers are invited to attend a weekly Wednesday ball during the Season. Lady Jersey is a patroness, and you must apply directly to her or another patroness in order to gain entrance. It is said Seasons are made or destroyed by a single word of approval or derision from the patronesses," Miranda instructed in a serious tone.

"I see." Iris bit her lip in a concerned manner.

"Don't be alarmed. You'll do famously. It would be

a great boon if you should debut your first week in London at such a notable establishment." She turned to the viscount, hoping her subtle hint hit its mark.

The viscount grinned casually. "I'll make arrangements soon. I assure you, there is nothing of which you need to concern yourself, Miss Iris." He took another sip.

Miranda turned back to Iris, about to continue their discourse, when the viscount began speaking again.

"Of course, Miss Miranda left out the rather unremarkable aspects of this highly esteemed establishment." He gave a daring glance to Miranda, then turned his attention fully to Iris. "But I must adjust your perspective. The lemonade is sour, the orgeat is terrible on a good day, and the room is overly hot, with little air circulation. The men are often dandies, and the ladies all parade about like prize hounds waiting to be snatched up. It's rather dull, and if you only remember one thing, eat before you attend. Or else you'll surely faint from hunger." He leaned back, crossing his arms, clearly proud of his additional information.

Miranda wished she could offer some sort of redeeming words, but never having been to Almack's herself, she was rather helpless.

Iris turned her bright eyes to her governess.

Miranda swallowed.

"Oh my. That's certainly disproportionate for the amount of weight the place has in society, is it not?" Iris asked.

Miranda took a breath through her nose, searching her mind for a proper response.

"Miss Iris, I've learned that society rarely makes sense. And that is probably the best lesson I can give you this evening."

"Hear, hear!" The viscount lifted his glass.

Miranda lifted hers; after all, it was the polite thing to do.

Iris mimicked their movements.

If there was one thing Miranda understood, it was that life rarely made sense.

Especially if one was the daughter of a duke.

Chapter Twelve

The dinner soon ended, and Heathcliff sent up a silent prayer of thanks to the Almighty for delivering him.

For more than one reason.

His extinguished curiosity was now burning brighter than before.

A governess who was familiar with Kean's work?

A governess who was able to simplify the truth of society's nonsensical hierarchy?

A governess who wouldn't let him simply ignore her and eat his meal in peace?

He was in trouble, and he wasn't sure he wanted to accept that ill-fated truth.

So much of their conversation that evening had created far more questions than answers, and he rather hated unanswered questions.

Bloody nuisance.

He'd retreated from dinner to take his port in seclusion in his study. The warm, sweet-tinged flavor was thick on his tongue as he watched the sun start its descent over the hill. Country hours were far more conducive to a peaceful existence, he affirmed that truth once more.

Yet the beautiful sunset wasn't enough to distract him from his mind returning to the mystery that was Miss Miranda Smythe.

He swirled his brandy around his glass, the bouquet of its fragrance teasing his senses as he took another sip. It was one thing to be attracted to a woman's body, an entirely different, and far more dangerous thing, to be attracted to a woman's mind. And Miss Miranda had an intriguing mind, which was far more dangerous than her beautiful face and lovely form. A mind that was engaging, challenging, ever growing and developing, learning.

He swallowed the last of his port and set the glass on his desk, abandoning his study to take an evening stroll in the gardens. As he strode down the hall, he went out the front door into the warm, early fall evening. The scent of the sea gave the air a hint of a salty fragrance, along with the mixed blooming heather from the hills. The scent calmed his tight nerves and his shoulders relaxed.

Of course, the two glasses of brandy assisted in that relaxation.

He glanced to the front of the estate, debating on whether to take the road in front or find a path in the back of the house to wander. After a short debate, he started around the front courtyard and took the path toward the back of his property. A swallow darted overhead, followed by its friends, adding a bit of activity to the otherwise quiet evening. He started by the stables when he noted the door slightly open. He frowned, then strode over. It closed abruptly, and his body tightened with caution. It was probably nothing of note, but he was inquiring regardless.

He leaned back and opened the door wide, making sure any shots fired would go by his position.

When only silence met him, he peeked around the edge of the doorframe.

A horse nickered.

He relaxed.

Upon entering the stable, he met the curious stare of a chestnut mare and Miss Miranda.

"What an interesting way to enter a stable, my lord." She tilted her head slightly, her eyes dancing with restrained amusement.

He tugged on his shirtsleeves, then continued into the warm stable, the scent of hay and linseed oil perfuming the air. "One can never be too cautious."

"Are there often reasons to open doors, then hide from those within?" Miss Miranda inquired, a delicate brow arching in query.

He chuckled, though without real humor. Desperate men were often dangerous. More than once, a gentleman had come to the club with pistols, threatening to take back what he rightfully lost. Heathcliff had learned quickly to be cautious. "Depends on where you find yourself, Miss Miranda," he answered simply.

"I see." She turned back to the mare, stroking her nose softly. The horse leaned into the gentle touch and nickered.

"She likes you." He nodded toward the mare.

"She has good taste, then," Miss Miranda remarked, casting a sidelong glance to him.

"That's left to be decided." He shrugged one of his shoulders and approached the mare as well. "You see, she likes me too. Now what do you think of her taste?" He scratched behind the mare's ears.

He glanced at Miss Miranda, curious to see how she'd respond to his invitation to flirt. Would she back away like a proper governess or would she rise to the occasion?

He hoped she wouldn't back down from the challenge.

Even though it was the wiser of the two options.

"That's left to be decided." She inclined her head, but he read a fire in her expression that was daring, yet at the same time restraining, as she tossed his previous response back to him. She wasn't giving away her secrets.

The lady would have been a good gambler.

Her wit pleased him. "That's a fair answer. After all, we did just meet." He spoke as he traced along the jawline of the mare. "But I must say, I wasn't quite expecting your level of expertise in discourse. It was a pleasure to converse with you this evening."

"I almost feel insulted," she responded with a saucy grin. "But because I'm in your employ, I'll simply accept it as a compliment." She met his gaze, held it for a moment too long, then glanced away while a lovely pink tinted her cheeks.

So the lady wasn't a gambler after all. He wasn't sure why, but he appreciated that about her. It was better to read people, to know what they were thinking, rather than be left in the dark.

But it was also dangerous.

Because you couldn't unsee the truth.

Like the truth she had just revealed; she was attracted to him.

Which was one of the most dangerous things she could have revealed.

Dangerous for her.

Dangerous for him.

"I'll leave you to your evening, then." She smoothed her skirt and turned to leave.

Before she could move a step, he reached out and grasped her hand. She froze at the contact and turned back to him. "Yes?" she asked, her tone wary.

He released her at once, but his hand burned from the contact, sending a pulsating energy up his arm and into his chest. "I interrupted you." He took a step back, needing to remove himself from temptation.

Ha, irony was thick in his life.

"It is your horse, and your stables, my lord," she reminded him.

"Actually, Lady is . . . was my father's horse," he answered, feeling the dark cloud of his past creep up around him.

"Was." Miranda nodded once. "My condolences for your loss."

"It was long ago." He spoke too quickly for it to be believed.

She studied him then. "I take it you were close with your father?"

He hitched a shoulder, regretting his inclination to keep her from her departure. He'd already revisited the past enough for one day—one decade. "Yes," he answered.

She nodded, and when a few moments had passed without further questions, he relaxed his posture.

"It is good to at least know her name," she remarked.

It took him a moment, then he realized she meant the horse. "Yes, Lady. Not exactly original, but adequate."

"Isn't that so much of life? Adequate, but not original?" she murmured, her gaze lingering on the horse as if lost in thought.

Heathcliff reflected on her words, finding them refreshingly observant. The burning curiosity that seemed never to remain dormant for long in regard to this woman ignited once more. "How do you mean?"

She blinked up at him, as if remembering her words. "Oh, I suppose nothing of import." She shook her head delicately, a curl coming down from her loose chignon at the nape of her neck, trailing along the delicate structure of her clavicle.

The innocent curl almost distracted him from the subject matter of their conversation, yet he dragged his gaze upward. "I find it hard to believe you'd say anything of little import, Miss Miranda. Rather"—he took a slight step toward her, watching as her breath caught— "you strike me as someone who puts an inordinate amount of thought into her words. It's intriguing."

She glanced away. "You must lower your assessment of me, my lord. Or I'll surely disappoint."

His attention was once again arrested by the wayward curl, and without thought, he lifted his hand to touch its thick and silky length. Her stunned gaze shifted back to his, and he wondered—had Miss Miranda ever been kissed?

It was a dangerous, rogue thought.

One he became obsessed with the moment it entered his mind.

"Have you ever been kissed, Miss Miranda?" he asked before he could use his better judgment.

Her bright eyes widened further with shock at his forward question, but rather than retreat, as he half-expected, she simply gave a simple shake of her head.

No.

Damn if he didn't want to initiate her education on the subject.

"I find that hard to believe," he hedged, fighting an internal war he was fully expecting to lose.

Her head tilted slightly, tugging the loose curl from his fingertips with the movement. "Why is that?" she asked.

The ill-fated war was already lost as he reached down and traced his fingers down her elbow to her wrist, then loosely gripped her fingers, caressing them. "Surely you've experimented at least a little?" he asked, not fully believing her innocent nature, even though nothing had indicated otherwise.

Weren't women masters at deception?

She shook her head. "I'm not sure I understand." She spoke softly, her tone breathless as she closed her eyes, breathing through her nose as if drawing strength from the air.

She tugged her hand away, but like the rogue he was at heart, he chased after it, not willing to accept her rejection.

Rather the idea of the chase fanned the flames more.

How long had it been since a woman, any woman, hadn't thrown themselves at him? An age at least, and he quite missed the thrill of the hunt.

"I don't think—" she started, but as he gave a slight shake of his head, she paused.

"Don't think," he remarked. "Feel." He traced up her arm this time, touching her with a featherlight caress. He lingered at the curve of her elbow, then moved over the bare skin of her arm till he reached the light cap sleeve of her day dress, hiding only a small square of her shoulder. His fingers leaped over the offensive fabric hiding his view, and he slowed his ascent to the curve of her neck, watching her eyes flutter closed as she sighed.

"What do you feel?" he asked.

"Too much," she replied, then stepped back, away from his touch. "Enough to know this is not the wisest of choices, my lord." Her chest rose and fell with the depth of her breathing.

The horse nickered, as if sensing the powerful intensity in the stable.

He regarded her for a second, studying her expression. Was she feeling pressured? Yes, but it wasn't unwanted.

Which was all the encouragement he needed to continue his pursuit.

"I should go." She glanced to the door, then to him.

Grinning, he walked toward her slowly, starting with a single step. "That is a viable choice before you."

Her gaze flickered to the door once more, and he measured another step to give her more than adequate time to take that route of escape if she wished.

He suspected she was trying to talk herself into it, and he hoped sincerely that she'd fail.

But it had to be her choice.

He wasn't going to force himself upon her, even if was just a kiss.

It was a seduction of sorts, a choice to surrender rather than run away.

He closed the distance methodically, and her gaze flickered back to his and held.

Checkmate.

He brushed the wayward curl behind her shoulder and leaned down to kiss where it had first touched. The fragrance of lemon and sunshine held him spellbound for a moment as he lingered with his lips brushing against her skin. He noted her soft gasp and nipped her playfully, allowing his hands the freedom to circle around her waist and pull her a few inches closer. As he leaned back from her neck, he fleetingly noted that she seemed at a loss as to what to do with her hands, clasping them in tight fists. He released one hand from her waist and guided her arm to rest on his shoulder.

"Like a dance," he whispered, watching as her clear eyes met his. Her hands settled on his shoulders, and he could feel her fingers relax from their fisted position and tremble against the skin of his neck.

A wave of tenderness washed over him at the realization of her truly innocent nature. He leaned forward, tracing along her jawline with his nose, inhaling the sweet scent of her, feeling her arms tense around his neck as if holding on for strength. She was erotic in her inexperience, and he nibbled at her skin as he gently made his way toward her full lips. Anticipation flooded him the few lingering moments before he allowed himself the pleasure of tasting her.

Soft, yielding, untried, her lips seduced him with their intense pleasure. It was the most chaste kiss he'd ever given a woman, yet it was the most powerful in its effect on his body. Everywhere she touched him felt aflame, and his body responded with enthusiasm, sending his blood to boiling in all the lower regions, begging him to follow his instincts and lean into her feminine form and claim more than her first kiss.

He exercised a restraint he hadn't used in nearly a decade and leaned back from the kiss, wearing the flavor like a victory banner. He awaited the verdict from her first experience as her eyes fluttered open. Wonder, confusion, and arousal all flooded her gaze, and rather than take a moment to appreciate them, he rather found it impossible to resist initiating her second experience.

This time, as he met her lips, he ran his tongue along her lower lip, then pulled it playfully between his teeth ever so slightly. She pulled back, as if a little shocked, but didn't withdraw further, and instinctively, he met her lips once more. He repeated the action, pleased when she didn't retreat again, rather leaned into the kiss further, her fingers teasing the hair at the nape of his neck in the most alluring way. Tentative at first, her confidence clearly grew as she began lacing her fingers through his hair as he continued to deepen the kiss.

He flicked his tongue against her lips, tracing along the slightly open space and caressed her lips from the inside out. After a moment, she mimicked his actions, and he knew it was his turn to retreat.

Retreat, or he'd surely meet the swift end of his restraint and seduce her fully.

He gentled the kiss, then slowly, regretfully, withdrew.

"Oh my," she whispered as she met his gaze.

He chuckled softly. "I'm pleased your first lesson has met with approval."

A rose-colored blush tinted her cheeks as her gaze flickered away. "Yes . . ."

"Speechless as well," he interjected.

She shot him a wry grin. "You look far too pleased with yourself."

"I am," he answered honestly.

"Well . . ." She glanced down. "I find I'm at a loss

as to what to say now . . ." She glanced to him expectantly.

He grinned at her stark honesty. "Allow me to help, because I'm the instructor in this area, as it were."

She arched a brow.

"It's only fair. You are a teacher, are you not? Is it not your duty to assist your pupil when the need arises?" he asked, knowing he was drawing attention to their employer/employee relationship but certain he could find a way to validate the scandal of it.

For him.

Maybe for her too.

For now.

Sure enough, her skin took on a pale hue at the reminder, but he continued, not waiting for her to panic.

"I will be your tutor, Miss Miranda. It's only fair, is it not? You're assisting Miss Iris, I shall assist you."

She blinked, then narrowed her gaze slightly. "My education?" she asked wryly.

"Yes. For surely your education is severely lacking, and I find I cannot abide by it."

"Is that so?" she asked dryly, a smile bending her well-kissed lips.

"It is. It is quite thrilling subject matter, is it not?" he asked, giving her his most seductive grin.

Her color returned and heightened into another blush. "I wouldn't say thrilling," she teased.

Minx. "Ah, you've simply proved your education is incomplete. After all, I wish your experience to be . . . satisfactory," he murmured softly, reaching out and tugging on her hand till she was closer.

"And you are concerned I wasn't impressed by your tutoring?" she asked, breathless.

"One can never be too certain, Miss Miranda." He

kissed her once more, playfully nipping, tasting, and delighting in her quick learning.

He leaned back, murmuring against her lips. "I'm afraid I'll have to continue your lesson tomorrow. Practice makes perfect, you know."

"So, I've not mastered the subject matter, is that it?" She leaned away just enough to meet his gaze.

"There's always room for improvement." He tugged the curl that had started the whole thing and allowed it to rest over her shoulder once more. "Good night, Miss Miranda." He gave an unrepentant grin, turned, and left the stable.

He no longer wanted a long walk to clear his mind.

He wanted a cool bath to calm his feverish instincts.

He wasn't sure who was in more trouble, Miss Miranda . . . or himself.

Chapter Thirteen

As Miranda lay in her bed, she called herself a hundred different kinds of fool.

A fool for being alone in the stables.

A fool for not running when she had the chance.

A fool for kissing him back.

A fool for enjoying it.

A fool for anticipating it happening again.

Dear Lord, what had she become? Yet even as she knew of her folly, she wasn't repentant.

Not in the least.

She'd never known nor expected a kiss to feel that way. It was astounding, and for the rest of her life she'd relive that experience over and over. Her mind flooded with the memory as her body remembered the hundreds of pleasurable sensations his touch evoked. It was beyond impossible to ever forget, and for the first time she understood how ladies were ruined.

The temptation was quite powerful, and while she hoped she had the fortitude to walk away, she wasn't sure she would have wanted to if he had pressured her to do more.

Not that she knew what *more* exactly entailed.

The unknown haunted her, and she wanted to understand . . . to know what happened beyond the first kiss, the first touch. If the pleasure brought by her first experience in simply kissing were any indication, whatever *more* entailed, it may surely overwhelm her.

How delicious!

What a dichotomy, to know the folly of her behavior yet to be utterly ravenous for more of it. If only her sister could see her now. Would she know? Would she be able to look at Miranda and instinctively know something had changed? She rose from her bed and walked to the mirror, studying herself. She didn't look different, but she felt different.

A little more feminine.

A little wiser.

A little more powerful.

Had Liliah experienced this same rush of awareness? Desperately, Miranda longed for her sister, to sit and chat, ask questions she knew Liliah would be kind enough to answer.

Loneliness flooded her.

Then trepidation.

She had hoped the viscount would understand her need for duplicity. Only she wasn't sure, she'd just met him.

And kissed him.

My, that hadn't taken long. He'd been in residence for merely a day and her world had tilted. She walked back to her bed and snuggled into the sheets.

Mrs. Keyes had informed her that she was to take up residence in the nicer room, the one where the viscount had taken her after the pond fiasco. She wasn't about to argue with the new arrangement; it was far more to her liking. The bed was much softer, the coverlet a bit thicker, and the fireplace much larger. As if proving her point, the wood in the hearth crackled loudly. It wasn't as opulent as her room in London, but it was a far cry better than the room adjoining the nursery.

She wasn't sure why the viscount had insisted she move to a guest room, and she wasn't going to ask either. Simply enjoy.

As she drifted off to sleep, her mind lingered on the memory of the kiss, her body flooding with warmth from within as unconsciousness overwhelmed her. She awoke in the morning with the sensation that she had merely blinked, only to be greeted by the rising sun. It had been a chore to accustom herself to rising early. She'd always awoken when she pleased in London, and that was certainly unacceptable here, while employed.

But she had grown rather fond of the sunrise, and so, with only a slight reluctance, she rose from bed and padded over to the window. The rich orange color tinted the sky, and she breathed deeply of the crisp morning air as she curled her toes against the cool floor. A shiver ran down her back, and she decided it would be wise to dress before she caught a chill.

In short work, she'd donned a simple day dress and proceeded to pin her hair into a modest chignon. She wasn't as skilled at producing the perfect coif, so she maintained her simple hairstyle day after day. Ready, she silently slipped out into the hall, wary to be quiet in case the viscount's room was nearby. She rather expected it to be somewhere else in the house—she was clearly in the guest wing—but she would be cautious nonetheless. She would rather have a fortifying cup of tea before she faced him once more.

That was one aspect of the day she both anticipated and dreaded. Pushing the thoughts aside, she took the stairs down to the main floor. As she rounded the corner, she raised a hand in greeting to Mrs. Keyes, who was bustling down the hall.

"Mornin', Miss Miranda. I trust you slept well in the new room?" she asked, pausing and folding her hands before her ample form.

Miranda nodded. "Indeed, thank you, Mrs. Keyes. And how did you sleep?" she asked kindly.

"Bah, well enough." She waved a hand dismissively. "I thank ye for asking, though. I'll leave you to breakin' yer fast." She nodded and bustled away.

Miranda watched her departure and then proceeded the rest of the way down the hall, passing the suit of armor, then turned left in to the dining room. The sideboard was set with rashers of bacon, ham, coddled eggs, and toast with marmalade. She selected some bacon and a slice of toast, then found her seat at the table, wishing for *The Times* to look over while she ate. She had an hour or so before Iris would be ready to start her instruction, and it was at these moments that she missed several of the comforts of home.

But most of all her sister.

Perhaps today would be the day Liliah and Lord Heightfield would arrive.

She poured herself a steaming cup of tea and enjoyed her breakfast in silence, the clock chiming the hour midway through.

She was almost finished with her second cup of tea when she heard footsteps in the hall. The teacup she was holding froze halfway to her lips as she listened intently. A few moments later, Iris walked into the room, her eyes slightly bleary from being newly awake.

"Good morning," Miranda greeted her softly.

Iris took a deep breath, as if mustering the energy to speak. "Morning, though I wouldn't say it's good." She muttered the last part and selected a plate.

Miranda chuckled softly and took a sip of her cooling tea. "That depends on one's perspective."

"You're always happy about the morning, so I find that your opinion is one I will not take into account," Iris replied, though Miranda noted a hint of a grin.

"Someone is cheeky this morning."

"Someone is far too cheerful," Iris responded, but her grin had grown into a full smile as she took a seat across from Miranda.

Iris took a bite of toast, and Miranda lifted the teapot in silent query.

Iris nodded, and Miranda poured her a cup of tea, then refilled her own.

"Shall we review last night's conversation?" Miranda started.

Iris gave her an irritated expression as she swallowed her food. "After tea. Not that there is much to discuss. I didn't speak very much, which means that there's little to criticize." Iris smirked, then sipped her tea.

Miranda sighed impatiently. "I was leading by example. And my question wasn't referring to your involvement in the conversation; rather, I was seeking your opinion and whether you had questions regarding it."

Iris lifted a shoulder in a shrug. "I—"

"Ah, ladies don't shrug," Miranda corrected.

Iris arched a brow, then swallowed another bite. "I do not have any questions."

"Very well, provided the viscount doesn't have other arrangements, tonight for dinner conversation, I'd like you to initiate a topic upon which you can practice conversing. Something you feel comfortable with the extent of your knowledge."

Iris tilted her head. "Something I know well?"

"Yes."

"Very well," Iris replied, then gave Miranda a curious expression. "The viscount seemed quite . . ." She frowned.

Miranda froze, curious and slightly concerned about what Iris had noticed.

"It was of no consequence," she finished, taking another bit of bacon.

Miranda wasn't about to question her further, thankful Iris didn't press.

It wasn't proper breakfast conversation.

But then again, her behavior had been anything but proper concerning the viscount.

Miranda turned her attention to the day ahead. "Today, I think we shall work on your needlepoint and discuss some of the details pertaining to Almack's, the establishment I mentioned last night at dinner."

"Anything but dancing," Iris remarked. "I never thought I'd see the day I'd actually want to do needlepoint. What has become of me?"

"A lady. You are becoming a lady, Iris."

"I always was a lady—a miss of gentle breeding. My father was a gentleman, and I am a gentleman's daughter, Miss Miranda," Iris replied archly, a wide grin making her eyes sparkle.

"I'm simply helping your behavior match your birth," Miranda replied, proud of her little turn of phrase.

"Ah, well done." Iris lifted her teacup in a salute.

As Miranda chuckled, she smiled at Iris, thankful for their budding friendship, even if it was that of governess and pupil.

It went a long way in keeping her from feeling so alone.

And she expected it did the same for Iris.

She finished her tea and stood from the table. "I'll be waiting for you in the library. It has the best light."

"Anticipation floods me," Iris replied, lifting her last piece of toast.

Miranda quit the room and started down the hall toward the library, where the east-facing windows stood tall and allowed the room to be full of a cheery glow each morning.

As she walked into the room, she considered Iris's word choice.

Anticipation.

While Iris may not be authentic in her anticipation for her next lesson, Miranda couldn't help but reflect on the viscount's promise to further *her* education.

And the anticipation she felt for such an education was frighteningly real.

Chapter Fourteen

Heathcliff rolled from bed far later than he had expected. It had been a difficult night, with sleep eluding him. His attention was arrested by the woman only a few doors down.

Each time he'd try to relax into his bed, his mind would linger on Miss Miranda. Her quick wit engaged his mind, her intellect challenged him, and her innocence inflamed his body. The sun had fully risen when he made his way downstairs to break his fast. As he sipped his tea, the grandfather clock chimed ten, reminding him that he had much to accomplish before the day ended.

After breakfast, he headed to his study, passing the library. Feminine laughter halted his steps and he paused to listen.

The voices were muffled enough that he'd have to step closer to hear their words.

His damned pride didn't allow him such an effort,

and he settled on listening to the laughter once more before striding forward to his study down the hall. Had it only been a day since he'd arrived home? How had so much happened? As he sat behind his wide desk, his thoughts lingered down the hall, wondering what Miss Miranda was teaching Iris. What had caused their laugher?

He forced his thoughts to submit to his will, and he began to lift several papers from the stack to read.

Several hours later, he was rubbing his temple as he read over the notes from his steward. A knock sounded on his study door, and he blinked at the sound, his mind snapping to attention. "Yes?"

Sothers entered, his gray head bowing in respect. "My lord, there are guests here to see you. Lord and Lady Heightfield."

Heathcliff rose from his desk. "Show them in at once."

Sothers gave a twitch of his lips, surely anticipating the acceptance of Heathcliff's old friend. "Yes, milord." He quit the room, and Heathcliff came around his desk and leaned against the front of it, partially sitting as he waited for his friends' arrival.

Moments later, Lucas Mayfield, the Earl of Heightfield, strode in, his lovely wife, Lady Liliah Heightfield, holding his arm engagingly. He smiled at her familiar face, something striking him, like a fragment of a memory, but he dismissed it and pushed off from his desk to greet them. "Heightfield, and Lady Heightfield!" He reached out and grasped Lady Liliah's hand, kissing it softly, lingering there just to irritate his friend.

"Enough of that," Lucas retorted hotly, tugging his wife's hand from Heathcliff's slightly exaggerated welcome.

As he anticipated, Lady Liliah giggled softly, and Lucas glared. "I see not much has changed. I quite expected her to soften you up a bit, but I see you're still a pain in the arse." Heathcliff chuckled.

"Only when the occasion, or person, calls for it," Lucas replied, reaching out and grasping Heathcliff's hand in welcome. He grinned widely. "It's good to see you, my friend."

"Eh, I suppose I'm glad to see you as well. Though I must say, this is something of a surprise. Aren't you still newly married? Why come here and torment me with your calf-eyed self?" He arched a brow, teasing his friend.

"It pleases me to torture you."

"Truer words have never been spoken." Heathcliff chuckled. "Brandy?" He gestured to the sideboard. It might be early, but then again, if he were in London and it were after one of their parties, it could be considered overly late—especially if you hadn't gone to bed the night before at all.

Heathcliff's smile froze as he noted the glances exchanged between Lord and Lady Heightfield.

"Out with it." He backed up and leaned against his desk once more, crossing his arms.

Lady Liliah turned to her husband, her expression questioning.

"Damn it all, you're making me jumpy. I know that face, Lucas. What the hell has happened?" He frowned.

"Perhaps we should converse in private?" Lucas directed the question not to Heathcliff but his wife.

Heathcliff waited impatiently for the verdict.

"That may be best," Lady Liliah answered deliberately, then turned to Heathcliff. "I'll give you two some time alone, then join you later. I'm sure your housekeeper can help me find your ward. Iris, correct?"

Heathcliff frowned. Something didn't ring true about her words. Not the words themselves, but the tone.

He turned to Lucas. "How bad is it?"

Lucas grinned unrepentantly. "That, my friend, depends on you." He shrugged. "But I am enjoying watching you squirm. Lord knows what scenarios you're cooking up in your depraved mind. I assure you, it's nothing like your imagination is concocting."

Heathcliff nodded, then rang for Mrs. Keyes. When she arrived, he instructed her to take Lady Liliah to the other ladies, who were in the library.

Mrs. Keyes nodded, glanced at Lady Liliah, then blinked. "O-of course, my lady. . . .tMight you be related to our Miss Miranda?" She shook her head. "Forgive me. It just shocked me, the likeness. Follow me, my lady."

Heathcliff didn't see them quit the room.

He didn't hear Lucas's chuckle.

He simply put the puzzle pieces together.

Lady Liliah—Miss Miranda. His mind worked at lightning speed, making sense of all the questions that had been unanswered. It was so obvious, yet he hadn't seen it till now. The sister who was supposedly in America, who was not actually abroad but much closer. Under his roof, in his employ, for heaven's sake.

A duke's daughter.

Parading as a governess.

Why in hell—then his eyes snapped up to meet his friend's.

"*You!*" he roared.

Lucas tilted his head slightly, then shrugged. "Your response is not equal to the knowledge. Interesting."

Heathcliff narrowed his eyes at his friend as Lucas helped himself to the sideboard and poured a liberal helping of brandy into two snifters, then offered one to Heathcliff.

He wanted to ignore the offering, but he also needed to calm the hell down.

Lucas was right.

His response wasn't equal to the knowledge.

And whenever that happened in the club, it only meant one thing.

Guilt.

And Heathcliff was guilty as sin.

"Care to explain yourself?" Lucas asked, taking a slow sip of brandy, as if the world hadn't just shifted.

"No." Heathcliff downed his drink and set the glass on the desk, re-crossing his arms like a petulant child. He uncrossed them and glared.

"Fascinating." Lucas remarked, and took another slow sip, as if doing his damnedest to annoy the hell out his friend.

It was working.

Heathcliff stalked over to the sideboard and poured himself another helping of brandy, then took a long sip.

"So, how much have you compromised the girl?" Lucas asked, just as Heathcliff was swallowing.

He choked on the brandy, sending the burning liquid up his nose and down his throat at the same time, leaving a fiery trail everywhere it touched.

He coughed, set the glass down, and tried to master his reactions, failing with each cough.

"Interesting," Lucas remarked, again.

Heathcliff glared at his friend as his eyes watered, "Don't say that damn word again," he choked out, then coughed a few more times for good measure.

"Fascinating," Lucas replied, grinning wildly.

"I hate you," Heathcliff remarked, but without heat as he stood up and glared at his friend. "Why didn't you tell me?"

Lucas hitched a shoulder and took a small sip. "It was safer, for you and for her. Those bloody investigators were like dogs with a bone."

"Not good enough. I need a better reason. Those investigators were a joke."

Lucas continued. "Yes, but it was still safer for *her*. And, my friend, she was the one who needed protecting, not you," he added.

Damn and blast, he was right, but that didn't negate the fact that Lucas had used him.

"Why not tell me later then, when she was safely away?" he asked.

"Would it have mattered?" Lucas asked, swirling the remaining brandy in his glass.

Heathcliff opened his mouth, then closed it. "Yes."

"Why?"

Because then I wouldn't have kissed her, wouldn't have been so curious about her history. I would have stayed away . . . "Because," he answered inarticulately.

Lucas raised his brows, as if waiting for the rest of the explanation. It was bloody irritating having a friend who knew you so well.

When Heathcliff didn't respond, Lucas helped himself to a chair and made himself comfortable. "You do realize that my wife is content to spend the entire day here, with her sister whom she's been worried to distraction about, and I have nothing better to do than sit here and wait?" he threatened coolly.

"Damn you," Heathcliff replied.

"So, my question remains."

"Which one?" Heathcliff replied with heavy sarcasm as he took his seat behind his desk.

"The first. How much have you compromised her?" he asked, as if discussing the weather.

Heathcliff closed his eyes. "It was only a kiss."

Lucas whistled under his breath. "And how long have you been in residence?"

Heathcliff opened his eyes and leaned forward. "Twenty-four hours."

Lucas choked on the sip of brandy he'd just taken, and Heathcliff took sadistic pleasure in watching his friend's much smaller, yet still satisfying, coughing fit.

When he recovered, he speared Heathcliff with a pointed look. "You didn't waste time."

"I'm not often accused of wasting time in any situation," Heathcliff replied, leaning back.

"I suppose the question I should ask next, as her brother-in-law, is what type of kiss? And what are your intentions toward the girl?" Lucas leaned back, giving Heathcliff a hard, inquisitive glare.

"You'll make a terrifying father one day, but I'm afraid your threats are ineffectual on me." Heathcliff sighed. "It was enough of a kiss to cause me a hell of a difficult night's sleep, and my intentions toward women in general have remained unchanged."

Lucas nodded.

Then another thought ricocheted through Heathcliff's mind.

She knew.

Bloody hell, Miss Miranda knew!

Was that even her real name? He expected not, which elevated his level of anger at the situation.

"Bloody hell." He spat. "She knew!"

Women were deceitful, the lot of them. Innocent ones as well!

Lucas chuckled. "She did, but in her defense, I did request she not tell you anything."

"Then I shall take my anger out on you." Heathcliff glared.

"You know a fight would end in a draw, with us both bloody and weary. You're stronger, but I'm faster," Lucas reminded him.

Damn it all, the bastard was right.

"What a mess." Heathcliff rubbed his hand down his face and leaned back in his chair.

"Women often create problems as much as they solve them," Lucas offered sagely.

"Oh, shut up." Heathcliff wasn't in the mood for his friend's attempt at wisdom. Only a few months earlier, Lucas would have wholeheartedly agreed with him.

Now he was of the converted sort.

And utterly useless.

"Are you going to tell Liliah?"

Lucas paused. "Tell her?"

"Anything," Heathcliff answered.

"Perhaps. It depends on what she asks."

"Traitor," Heathcliff remarked.

Lucas chuckled. "It will be interesting to find out

what my wife discovers regarding what . . ." He paused. "Is it Miss Miranda?"

"Blast, yes. What's the chit's real name anyway?"

"Samantha. But under the circumstances—"

"I know, Miss Samantha it is." Heathcliff waved a tired hand, then thought over the name. Samantha. It fit her.

"Of course, as her brother-in-law, I could demand that you come up to scratch," Lucas remarked.

Heathcliff's eyes narrowed. "You wouldn't."

Lucas chuckled. "No, I wouldn't. It wouldn't be fair to her, and in turn, my wife would have my hide. No, Liliah is convinced her sister needs a love match because she enjoys one of her own." Lucas preened.

Heathcliff wanted to gag.

"How lucky for her," he remarked dryly.

"And since you are not that love match, I'm afraid I can't force the issue." Lucas dusted off his hands.

"How magnanimous of you," Heathcliff continued in dry sarcasm.

"However, I must insist that you cease taking liberties with her, you understand."

Heathcliff nodded. "Consider it done." He refused to acknowledge the hint of regret that passed through him.

"I have your word?" Lucas leaned forward, spearing him with his sharp blue gaze.

Heathcliff gave a shrug. "Of course."

Now that he knew the conniving nature of the girl, it would be easy to remain on guard.

No more touches.

No more kisses.

Nothing beyond cool detachment.

He could do that.

Couldn't he?

He had to.

Yet, even as Lucas leaned back, trying with little effort to hide a grin, Heathcliff had an errant thought.

What if the lie he was telling wasn't to Lucas . . . but to himself?

Chapter Fifteen

Iris's eyes grew wide as the door to the library opened. Miranda studied her pupil for a moment, then turned the direction of Iris's gaze, then gasped.

"Liliah!"

She all but tossed her needlepoint aside and rushed to meet her sister.

"Sa—Miranda!"

Mrs. Keyes took a quick step back, her gray head shifting between the two girls as Miranda rushed forward to embrace her sister. Tears pricked her eyes as she held on to her elder sister, feeling the loneliness melt from her like snow in the sunshine.

"Oh, how I've missed you," Liliah murmured, holding her tightly, then releasing her just enough to lean back and examine her.

Miranda's face ached with the span of her grin of delight as she studied her sister. Her golden hair was neatly pinned into a beautiful twist and her eyes danced with joy, a deep-seated joy that came from her once-restless heart finding its home.

Miranda had the suspicion her brother-in-law had much to do with that peaceful state in Liliah's life. Affection for her little-known brother-in-law flooded her at the sight of her sister's joy. "You look lovely as always, and utterly joyful," Miranda replied, reaching down to squeeze her hand.

"And you!" Liliah tilted her head slightly. "There's something different, something confident in you. Freedom looks well on you, love." Moisture gathered in Liliah's eyes as she spoke the words.

Miranda nodded, understanding their deep meaning. Freedom. It was worth the risk.

Because even though she had fought loneliness, she was free to live her life without the oppressive nature of their father, and his tyrannical rule over her life.

Liliah had fled first but, thankfully, had never once considered leaving Miranda behind.

"Come, sit." Miranda gestured to the library's sitting area and watched as Mrs. Keyes stepped forward.

"If I may, would you care to take tea?" she asked with the utmost civility.

Miranda nodded. "Yes, Mrs. Keyes, thank you."

To her credit, Mrs. Keyes didn't ask the questions clearly written on her face, and quickly quit the room, presumably to fetch tea.

"Allow me to introduce my pupil, Miss Iris." Miranda gestured to her, noticing her silence.

Liliah moved forward with grace and nodded kindly to Iris.

Iris remained frozen.

"Iris?" Miranda asked.

Iris blinked, then stood. "My apologies. It's a pleasure to meet you." She curtseyed, albeit slightly awkwardly.

They would work on that later, Miranda decided.

"Miss Iris, please meet my sister, Lady Liliah Heightfield." Miranda bit her lip after the introduction, suddenly concerned that she had given too much detail. It would be helpful to speak with her sister, and her brother-in-law, to decide how much could be potentially dangerous. Not that her father would suspect her to be hiding in Scotland, but one could never be too careful.

Especially when dealing with the Duke of Chatterworth.

"It's a pleasure to meet you, Miss Iris. I've been looking forward to making your acquaintance," Liliah said as she took a seat across from her.

Iris nodded, then turned wide eyes to Miranda. "Perhaps you would like some time alone?"

"Yes, but promise me you'll continue your needlepoint and then do something to improve your mind? Likely we will practice conversation at dinner as well, and I'd like for you to enter into the conversation more than last night."

Iris nodded, the sparkle returning to her countenance. "If I can get a word in edgewise," she teased.

Miranda tilted her head in query.

"Yes, Miss Miranda." Iris stood, curtseyed, and then left the room.

"She seems like a lovely girl; a bit on the precocious side, but that's only to her credit." Liliah grinned.

"She reminds me of you in many ways."

"She'll be a sensation for sure, then." Liliah giggled. "Now, tell me everything. Start with the first day you arrived." Liliah leaned forward, anticipation radiating from her.

Miranda was more than willing to indulge her sister's curiosity.

She was just telling of the first time she was introduced to the viscount when Mrs. Keyes arrived with the tea. Liliah assured Mrs. Keyes that they would pour for themselves, and the housekeeper left, her footsteps slightly reluctant, as if she wished she could stay to solve the fascinating mystery of the two ladies.

When the door closed, Miranda continued her tale. She debated speaking of the story of her fall into the pond but wanted her sister's opinion on the matter.

Once she finished with that, Miranda purposefully poured herself a cup of tea and waited for Liliah's response.

"That is certainly out of character." Liliah poured herself a cup of tea as well, blowing across the top.

"How so?" Miranda asked.

"You say he was abrupt in his departure once he set you down in the room?" Liliah asked.

"Yes."

"Hmmm. Continue. I'm saving my opinions till I've heard everything," Liliah said.

Miranda suppressed a groan, then gave a description of last night's dinner conversation.

"Ah, so that is why Iris said it would be difficult to get a word in. It seems you and the viscount have much in common," Liliah said with a significant look.

"Some. I would not venture to say much," Miranda corrected, but as she considered the rest of her story, her cheeks flamed. Did she dare tell her sister?

"Oh! There's something you're not telling me," she quietly exclaimed and set down her teacup. "Surely there is something delicious or you wouldn't blush so!"

"I'm not blushing." Miranda calmly took a sip of tea.

"Liar," Liliah replied. "Regardless, I will not cease in pestering you till you give me what I seek. What happened?" She leaned forward with a wide grin.

Miranda sighed. "It is nothing as forbidden as you are anticipating."

Lilah bit her lip. "The fact that you said such a thing tells me that you know something you did not know when you left London . . ."

"You are utterly irritating," Miranda replied.

"Lucas says it's part of my charm."

"I find that hard to believe."

"Love is blind," Liliah said with a wave of her hand.

"Love is ignorant." Miranda giggled, immensely enjoying the camaraderie she shared with her sister.

"I'm still waiting," Liliah singsonged.

Miranda's face heated as she opened her mouth to speak, then closed it.

"The anticipation is horrific," Liliah lamented.

"Such theatrics," Miranda said in an effort to delay.

"You kissed," Liliah guessed, then bit her lip as she awaited the verdict from her sister.

Miranda's face heated to a painful degree, then closed her eyes as her sister applauded with victory at guessing correctly.

"My, this is wonderful, and not necessarily surprising. Why, I told Lucas—"

"You told me what, darling?"

Liliah startled as the door closed quietly.

"I didn't even hear you enter," Liliah scolded playfully.

Miranda turned and watched her brother-in-law stride

into the room, his eyes solely on his wife, affection apparent on his face.

"You were quite enthralled in the conversation, love." He came beside his wife and took a seat, kissing her softly on the cheek. Miranda watched as a lovely rose-colored blush tinted her sister's cheeks.

For a moment, they just gazed at each other. It would have been almost theatrical in its drama if it weren't so lovely. Miranda was thankful for the obvious love between the two, but also felt a sense of loss. She couldn't quite place it, but it was there nonetheless.

Lucas was first to look away, and he turned to Miranda. "It's a pleasure to see you again, Miss Miranda." He spoke smoothly, as if her borrowed name were her true identity.

"It's a pleasure to see you as well, Lord Heightfield," she said warmly.

"Lucas, if you please. I've never been fond of being called by my title. Reminds me too much of London society."

Miranda nodded. "Lucas, then." It was slightly awkward to call him by his Christian name, but if he requested it, who was she to deny him?

"I trust you had a productive conversation with the viscount?" Liliah asked, her eyes sparkling with knowledge.

Miranda held her breath as Lucas studied her. Would he notice her overly exuberant expression? Probably. The true question was whether he'd inquire about it.

"Indeed. It was quite . . . enlightening," he added meaningfully.

Miranda released her held breath, then grew curious at the tone of his voice.

"As was mine." Liliah arched a brow. "The question now is what to do with them?"

Miranda would have choked on her tea had she taken a sip. Blessedly, as it was, she was practically frozen with dread at their conversation.

"Hmm. That remains to be seen." He arched a brow and turned to Miranda. "I trust you are comfortable with your position here?"

Liliah served him a cup of tea while Miranda nodded. "The viscount has been very kind, and Iris is . . . challenging," she finished with a smile.

"Challenging; that's an interesting way to put it." Lucas arched a brow and accepted the teacup from his wife.

"She's educated, but not in the more feminine arts. It's been a learning experience for both of us."

"I see. And are you happy here?"

Miranda smiled warmly at her brother-in-law, thankful that he'd care to ask. "Yes. The viscount moved me into a very lovely room, and I do adore Mrs. Keyes and the other staff."

"That's very good to hear."

"And Iris and I get along quite well, as long as we don't practice dancing too much. I'm afraid it is a bit of a sore subject, which in turn gives me sore toes," she added with a grin.

Lucas chuckled, turning a warm gaze to his wife, then back to Miranda. "That is something that certainly must be remedied. However, if she insists on dancing on all the gentlemen's toes in London, she surely will at least be remembered."

"I don't think Iris has the personality to be forgotten, my lord. She has quite a colorful personality. She will either take the Season by storm, or she will offend many with her bold nature," Miranda replied. "I rather think she will make a splash."

The door opened, and before Miranda even turned, she knew who had entered.

Her skin prickled with energy, and her body warmed. Keeping her eyes lowered, she studied her teacup, hoping her controlled demeanor wouldn't give anything away.

"Ah, speak of the devil," Lucas remarked with a teasing tone.

"And he shall appear," the viscount finished, his tone slightly strained.

Miranda glanced up then. He met her gaze, then flickered his away, studying his friend. "I see you've made yourself right at home." He took a seat close to Miranda, on a wingback chair.

"I thought it was only fair to return the favor," Lucas replied.

"Eh, fair enough." The viscount chuckled.

"You have a lovely estate, Viscount Kilpatrick." Liliah spoke with civility. "I see from the windows that you have a courtyard behind the house."

The viscount nodded. "It's home. But I must say, my favorite location is the pond over the hill."

Miranda's gaze shot to him, but he didn't seem as if the words held any undercurrent.

They surely did for her.

Lifting her almost empty teacup, she took the last cool sip of tea, needing something to do.

"What about you, Miss Miranda? Have you enjoyed the estate?" He directed the question to her.

She glanced up, her mind quickly spinning to come up with an articulate answer.

She could be cautious.

She could say something benign.

But in those few seconds, as she thought, everything within her revolted against doing the proper, the right thing.

She could have said a hundred things, but instead, she met his gaze with a bold one of her own and replied, "I quite prefer the stables."

The freedom the truth gave was powerful.

As was the shock in his gaze.

That warmed into appreciation, but then cooled into a frosty indifference as he turned away. "If you're visiting the stables, I'd take a footman with you."

Miranda gave a single nod, then turned toward her sister.

There was something in her sister's gaze that fortified her confused heart.

She almost didn't recognize it, but it fed her soul.

It was hope.

And if Liliah saw hope, she could see it too.

Chapter Sixteen

Heathcliff paced the length of his bedchamber, waiting until the last moment to head downstairs for dinner.

He knew the folly of it, yet he hadn't been able to restrain the words that had tumbled forth. Filtering the space between his mind and his mouth had always been difficult, and that was certainly the case this afternoon.

What had he been thinking?

Not ten minutes before, he had sworn off the chit, reminding himself of her duplicity. Even if it weren't entirely her fault, he still held it partially against her character. But when he'd seen her, his resentment faded like a highland mist. She practically glowed as she sat with Lucas and her sister.

He was taken aback as he considered just how much bravery it took to take such a leap of faith.

Faith that ended up being placed in him.

Which he'd shot to hell when he kissed her, and wasn't even gentlemanly enough to regret it.

Rather, when he was asked the question about his estate, his mind immediately leaped to the pond, where she'd ignited his intrigue.

Then the blasted woman had to mention the stables.

He'd nearly choked.

It had taken all his self-control to turn away and somehow save his resolve.

As weak as it may be at the moment.

He hadn't looked back at her till he was assured of his impassive expression. Lucas and Liliah had left shortly after, promising to return in a few days.

Which meant that for dinner tonight, it would just be Miss Miranda, Miss Iris, and himself.

Last night's dinner conversation had started the whole fiasco. He wasn't holding out hope for this evening's to be any better. Half of him wanted to request a plate sent to his study, but his damned pride wouldn't allow such a cowardly act.

No.

He would dine with the ladies.

He would ignore the sparkling intellect of Miss Miranda.

He would eat his meal and be done with the whole thing.

Surely she would understand, now that the truth had come to light?

Reaching into his pocket, he withdrew his watch and frowned at the time.

He couldn't delay any longer, as much as he wished he could.

The door opened silently, and he strode down the hall with purpose, taking the stairs downward and entering the parlor, where they were to congregate before dinner.

"Good evening," he said as he entered the room. The ladies nodded their greeting, and he swore he could have heard crickets fill the awkward silence.

Miss Iris cleared her throat.

The proverbial crickets started up once more, and he cast his gaze about the room in an effort to break the damned silence with something intelligent. Of their own accord, his eyes darted to Miss Miranda. His gaze narrowed at the slight twitch of her lips. Then he remembered last night. She had initiated the sparkling dinner conversation, yet here, when her talents would be most welcome, she remained silent.

And if his suspicions were correct, she was doing it on purpose.

The minx.

He almost allowed a smile to slip through his control, but he cast his gaze away from her sparkling eyes and turned instead to Miss Iris. "I trust you had a good day?" he asked.

"Oh, yes," she replied, then shot a glance at her governess.

Heathcliff refused to glance to her as well. He was saved from the temptation when Mrs. Keyes walked into the room, announcing that dinner was ready.

He sighed in relief before he could expose his true emotions. He hazarded a glance at Miss Miranda, noting that her lips twitched once more.

It was a good thing he wasn't gambling; he'd have lost before he'd even been given a fair shot.

Not that gambling was ever fair.

He should know; he helped run the books at Temptations.

Of course, it wasn't exactly unfair either. It was all about the odds.

And right now, he didn't feel they were in his favor.

It was a disconcerting feeling, one he wasn't familiar with and not comfortable experiencing.

He increased his pace toward the dining room, seeking a bit of escape.

"My lord, would you mind?" Miss Iris asked, a slightly irritated tone to her words.

He slowed, turning toward her. "My apologies."

She nodded, then glanced behind her to Miss Miranda, then to him, raising a brow.

Dinner couldn't begin and end soon enough.

After he led Miss Iris to her seat at the table, and then Miss Miranda, he took his own and motioned for the footmen to start serving.

When the clear chicken broth was served, he had the impish thought of pushing the limits of Miss Miranda's current silence.

What could it hurt? The thought relieved some of the tension in his body, the idea that it was simply a game of dare thrilled him.

Damn it, even in her silence she was challenging.

Intriguing.

But surely a game of silence couldn't be dangerous?

He played his imaginary hand, and purposefully ignored Miss Miranda and, as a result, Miss Iris.

The soup was finished and the second course served, the silence continuing. The footman must have sensed the tension and even set spoons in the dishes quietly, as if afraid to break the silence.

When the second course was finished and the dessert was served, he allowed himself a glance at Miss Miranda. She lifted a fork full of lemon tart to her mouth and took a delicate bite. Her pink lips were dabbed with a bit of whipped cream, and her tongue darted out to lick them clean.

Heathcliff swallowed.

Looking wasn't his wisest action. Then again, he wasn't exactly sure what he had done this evening had been of the wiser variety.

She met his gaze, pausing, then shifting her expression to one of daring. He expected her brow to arch in a silent question, but she simply waited, holding his gaze.

He leaned forward slightly, studying her.

A silent game of waiting for the other to fail and blink.

It would not be him.

"Miss Miranda?" Iris's voice pierced through the fog of challenge.

Heathcliff didn't try to stop his grin as he watched Miss Miranda. To her credit, she didn't so much as flinch when Iris spoke her name, but, after a moment's pause, she very intentionally turned to face her charge.

"Yes, Iris?" she asked, as if they weren't burning down the dining room with their intensity.

Heathcliff didn't cast Iris a glance, but watched Miss Miranda with that same intensity, hoping the force of his gaze would fluster her. It was an immature choice, but he found it quite satisfying. If she noted his regard, she didn't appear to be affected by it.

Or perhaps she was overly skilled at self-control.

Iris continued. "I, that is," Iris's tone was hesitant, but as she continued, it carried a resolute confidence, "I loved the food in India. Have you ever tried Indian foods, Miss Miranda?"

Heathcliff tilted his head, awaiting Miss Miranda's

answer. It was a curious question, and quite random, but he found it pricked his curiosity as well, so he waited.

Miss Miranda's head tilted ever so slightly, giving him a lovely view of the clavicle that had utterly distracted him last night. The memories of their kiss flooded his mind, and his body responded in kind. Slightly uncomfortable at being so aroused at the dinner table, he relaxed his position and leaned back in his chair, thankful for the tablecloth and table adding further discretion.

"I haven't had the pleasure of trying a great many diverse dishes as you have, Iris. I'd love to hear more about them." And, leaning forward slightly, she gave a warm smile. "Brilliant question."

Heathcliff pieced the conversation together, realizing Iris had been following earlier instruction on conversation and was attempting to apply her skill to the task. He awaited Iris's response, thankful for the distraction from his more engaging thoughts.

"The curry is quite potent and can be very spicy. I do adore spicy food, but my mother always was cautious. If she ate too much, it would cause her to lose sleep over a bit of a fire in her belly," Iris explained.

"We normally don't discuss bodily maladies at the supper table, just for reference, but continue," Miss Miranda instructed kindly. She hadn't turned her gaze to him once, but kept her attention on Iris.

Iris nodded, accepting the gentle reprimand, and continued: "In India there are a great many dishes that implement the use of lentils. Because they don't eat their cows, you understand. They use lentils in many ways that we'd use as a source of meat. It's fascinating, and I found that while I'm as happy with a beef roast as any other Englishwoman, I didn't miss it as much in India. They are quite talented in the kitchens," Iris finished, and Heathcliff turned his gaze to Miranda, wondering how she'd respond.

"I don't believe I've ever eaten a lentil. What about you, my lord?" She turned to him, and he felt Iris's gaze as well.

He blinked, thought over the question, and frowned. "You know, I don't think I have." He'd been offered a few dishes that contained them, but he hadn't ever actually partaken.

He met Miss Miranda's gaze, then froze.

She was grinning, far too eagerly to be associated with his response.

Damn it all.

He belatedly realized he had played right into her hand.

After keeping his silence all evening, in one quick turn, she'd cracked his silence and disarmed him entirely.

It was dangerous, it was delightful, and he felt as if he should bow to such a worthy opponent.

But instead, he merely gave a tight smile, remembered his resolution to keep himself from her, and stood from the dinner table.

The ladies followed his example and stood as well. He didn't meet either of the ladies' gazes, but gave a smart bow and quit the room as if the devil were on his heels. Because if he stayed, he would surely fail, and likely fall for her charms once more.

And failure had never been so tempting.

Chapter Seventeen

Miranda watched the viscount flee from the room. There wasn't any other way to describe it. Iris met her gaze with a confused one of her own, then hitched a shoulder and followed the path of the viscount, though at a much more moderate pace.

When they had both made it into the hall, Iris seemed to glance about, then turned to Miranda. "Did that seem odd to you as well?" Her gaze flickered farther down the hall, then back to Miranda.

"Yes. It was indeed."

"Do you . . ." Iris paused. "Do you think my talking about not eating the cows offended him? I rather thought Scotsmen preferred sheep."

Miranda gave Iris a swift smile. "No, I think he's just unsettled." It was her best guess, and if she were assuming further, she was quite certain he was more than a little put out with earlier discoveries. He'd been quite standoffish and aloof since her sister and brother-in-law had paid their visit. It was an assumption, but she felt confident she was right. If she were to speculate further, he was regretting his earlier scandalous behavior with her.

Which was a pity.

She hadn't regretted it for a moment.

"What makes you so certain?" Iris asked.

Miranda had to think back for her answer. It was rather specific. She decided it would be prudent to have a frank conversation with Iris. After this afternoon, when Iris had seen Liliah and Miranda together, she was owed some sort of explanation. Or, at the very least, it would be polite to offer one.

"Come, Iris. Let us take a walk. The evening air will do us both good. It had been a busy day, and surely you have some questions."

Iris nodded. "Indeed, but I wasn't wanting to pry."

Miranda gave her a wry expression.

"I'm learning! May I at least have credit for not asking immediately? I'm quite proud of myself that I thought before speaking, and then I waited further." She gave a little tilt to her chin with pride.

Miranda gave a soft chuckle. "I suppose you're correct. Forgive me for not offering accolades where they are most certainly due." Miranda bowed her head. "That was very good of you, Iris. And I'm proud of the progress you are making."

"Thank you," Iris replied cheekily.

They descended the front stairs of Kilmarin and walked out onto the gravel circular drive. Miranda chose a path that would wind around the house and lead to the back maze, giving them more than ample room to walk and talk while they did so.

As they passed a small bush blooming with white flowers, Miranda turned to Iris. "You're probably wondering about our guests today."

Iris met her gaze. "I did have a certain amount of curiosity."

Miranda grinned. "How delicately put."

"I was quite proud of that." Iris grinned mischievously.

"That was my sister and brother-in-law, Lord and Lady Heightfield."

Iris gave her a slow nod, her expression full of questions and slight confusion.

"You're wondering why, if my sister has the title of lady, I am relegated to being a governess." Miranda supplied the words.

Iris nodded, remaining silent.

Miranda paused, considering how to answer the question while still keeping as much of her secret as possible. She trusted Iris; it was not that she felt her word of silence on the matter would be questionable. It was rather that she questioned the wisdom of disclosure. After a moment of debate, she followed her instincts. "Do you remember when I spoke of never knowing my father?"

"Yes."

"That was true, yet at the same time misleading. It implied that my father was no longer among us but, in fact, he is very much alive. What I meant by such a statement is that while my father is still alive, I do not know him. And he, as much as he'd like to think otherwise, does not know me. He's a proud man, and that isn't always a fault. To a certain extent, we all are proud, but in him it is the sole element of his character. Every aspect of his life is to feed his vanity, and the result is a man who is hard, cold, and commanding in everything. My sister and I fled London because we were going to be matched very inappropriately. I'll not give the details, but it was my sister's bravery that spurred my own, and in a roundabout way, it led me here. But because of my . . ." She paused, thinking of the right word. "Fear of my father, and his determination to keep me under his rule, it was imperative that I remain silent on the matter, assume a different identity and position."

Iris blinked at her, then tilted her head.

Miranda expected a great many questions, and she was prepared to answer them to the best of her ability.

"It makes sense." Iris gave a firm nod, then continued on her way, as if Miranda's story was a common one.

Miranda blinked in confusion, pausing her steps. She then hurried to catch up with Iris. "How?" was the only articulate response she could come up with.

Iris shrugged. "You love dancing too much not to be a nobleman's daughter. However, I assume that your sister also married into her husband's title."

Miranda started to laugh, and the laughter turned into a louder, less delicate sound as she almost doubled over with the mirth of it. "Truly?" she asked between fits of giggles. "*That* is how you explain yourself? And yes, my brother-in-law is the Eighth Earl of Heightfield."

"Of course!" Iris replied, laughing herself.

"Dancing?" Miranda asked.

"Indeed. There are a great many worse things, I assure you." Iris gave a mock glare.

Miranda calmed her mirth just enough to give a soft sigh. "Indeed, there are."

"Does this mean you're still going to be my governess?" Iris asked unexpectedly.

Miranda frowned. "Why would it change anything?"

"Because your family is here, certainly you'll live with them?" Iris replied, and Miranda saw the clear logic, but immediately revolted against it.

She wasn't sure why. "No, I'll remain in residence in Kilmarin. I am not only employed here, but I like it here. I like you, Iris. And I will not leave you," Miranda replied firmly.

Iris paused, her gaze turning slightly moist. "Thank you." She turned back to her path, and Miranda gave her a moment to collect herself.

They passed by the manor and continued on toward the maze before Iris spoke again. "It's just that, with my parents gone, I feel quite alone. The idea that you would leave as well, as short as our acquaintance has been, gave me a great deal of uneasiness. Ever since this afternoon, I had my suspicions, and that is probably why I hesitated to ask about your relations who visited. I didn't want my fears to be realized and see you leave."

Miranda's heart pinched at the confession. She and Iris had so much in common, loneliness being paramount of those similarities. "I shall not leave you, and I'm quite certain the viscount wouldn't allow it either," she affirmed with a jaunty grin.

Iris gave her a sidelong glance. "Of that I'm entirely certain, and I must confess that its truth gave me a small measure of confidence that you might not quit Kilmarin. He's quite taken with you."

Miranda colored, turning away to hide her reaction. "I'm certain you are reading too much into his actions."

Iris didn't offer a reply, just a slight shrug of her shoulders as they wandered through the maze.

Miranda felt the acute need to change the conversation. "Did you have a nice, restful afternoon?"

"Without dancing?" Iris remarked cheerfully.

"Without dancing," Miranda said with a smile.

"Yes, it was lovely, and I took a short walk over the hill. Did you know there's a lovely pond in that direction?"

Miranda's face heated with a painful blush that came from a powerful memory. She cleared her throat delicately and turned her head to angle her face away from Iris's view. "Indeed. It is lovely."

Iris agreed, and as they wound their way out of the maze, Iris paused. "Thank you for taking the time to discuss the day with me. I treasure your friendship, and I must say I wasn't expecting a governess I actually would like, let alone admire. I'm truly grateful for you." Iris impulsively reached out and wrapped her arms around Miranda in a tight embrace. When she released her, she gave a cheeky grin and bid her adieu.

Miranda watched as Iris left the gardens and headed back toward the front of the estate. She debated following, then decided to take a few more moments to herself and wind back through the maze. She found it was a place of solace for her, where there was a solution to every problem. Two right turns, one left, follow the hedge till the end of the path; it was predictable, consistent, and she valued it.

It was likely because in her life she felt the opposite, and the maze offered her a security that felt absent in other aspects. She finished the path and turned to the house. It was growing further into the evening, and she knew it wouldn't be wise to linger out of doors as darkness swallowed the light.

As she ambled back to the house, she smiled, then gave a delightful little spin on her toes, which were only slightly sore from Iris's abuse earlier in the week. She grinned at the realization, and gave her head a shake.

She debated taking the servants' entrance but finally chose to walk through the front door, making the stairs to her room much closer than the previous option.

She ascended the stairs, the crickets serenading her, and Sothers opened the door widely, offering her a welcoming grin. "Good evening," Miranda said.

"Evening, miss," Sothers replied, keeping to his man-of-few-words persona.

She was almost to the stairs when the viscount started down the hall toward her, presumably quitting his study in search of his rooms. There was an awkward moment when he saw her, paused, then continued toward her.

Her courage was great that evening, and so, with a bit of a smile, she addressed him. "If I didn't know better, I would say I frighten you, my lord."

A rueful grin tipped his lips, almost against his will, it seemed, and he shook his head. "Is that so? What makes you come to such a conclusion?"

"For one," she took a lazy step toward him, "you all but ran from the dining room."

"I had pressing business," came his reply.

"And just now, you looked as if you wished to turn around and pretend you hadn't seen me," she continued.

He twisted his lips, then shrugged. "I thought I had forgotten something in my study."

"Tell me, are all Scotsmen such proficient liars?" she asked without heat, only a slightly flirtatious tone that surprised her, along with her frank question. Iris seemed to be influencing her. She was clearly speaking before thinking. Boldly, she waited, curious to see how her words would be taken.

The viscount tipped down his chin, hiding his expression, giving her a moment's panic, but when he glanced up once again, his expression was full of humor. "Are all ladies who masquerade as governesses so impertinent?"

"Yes. Because I'm the only one I know, so I'm an authority on the subject," she added with a grin.

"Well played." He chuckled in response. "Then I defer to your greater expertise on the subject."

"However, I am not an expert on the subject of the character of Scotsmen, and you, sir, have not answered my question."

"Relentless, are you?"

"I've been called worse," she replied, now standing only a few feet from him. She paused there, waiting.

"As have I," he replied, rocking on his heels, appearing slightly uncomfortable. "You are far more observant than is prudent."

"I've been told that before."

"I'm sure you have been." He paused, then glanced around, his brows pulling into a frown. "Come with me." He gestured to the red parlor just down the hall, turned, and started for it.

There was nothing to do but follow, and her curiosity wouldn't let her do any less. As he entered the room, he regarded her seriously.

The door was wide open, so there was no fear of scandal—pity, that—but she awaited his leisure, much as at dinner. She was patient most of the time, and in this case, it would serve her well.

"I understand why you did not confide in me, but surely now you understand that this . . . knowledge changes things."

"What things?" she asked, risking a slight step forward. She half-expected him to step back, but he did not.

"Things of a more . . . intimate nature," he finished, his gaze flickering from her gaze, to her lips, and then back.

"I see." She folded her hands before her.

"I'm pleased you understand." He nodded, but his expression didn't appear pleased in the least.

"I'm not pleased at all," she said. "I'm quite disappointed. And I'm afraid you're not doing your gender much credit, nor Scotsmen in general."

"How so?" he inquired, his gaze roaming her features, as if touching her when his hands could not.

"You promised me proper instruction, and now, less than a day later, you have gone back on your word."

He chuckled. "And you were anticipating such education? I doubt it."

"You know nothing of my mind and what I anticipate," she replied. It felt so liberating to assert herself, and her thoughts and feelings. Had she ever done so before? She wasn't sure, but it was heady, the freedom, however foolish. She was almost challenging the man to ruin her.

And, like the wanton she was, she didn't regret it.

"It would seem I do not," he muttered, taking a deep breath. "I'd like to, but I cannot offer you any more than a few stolen moments of pleasure, and I will not disrespect my friendship with your brother-in-law by treating you thus."

"That is truly a pity," she replied, and with her courage beginning to fade, she took a step back, gave an entirely proper curtsey, and turned to leave the room. She had almost reached the door when a warm hand gripped her shoulder.

She didn't turn, but did halt her progress. She'd been far braver than he this evening; it was his turn to take a risk, however small.

His breathing seemed loud in the otherwise silent room, and she fancied she could hear her heartbeat as well. "Wait," he whispered, the word spoken close, just a breath away, and her body trembled in response, in heady anticipation.

"You would be better off forgetting everything I said yesterday," he murmured, his actions in direct contrast with his words as his hand caressed her shoulder to her hand, where he delicately took her fingers with his.

"Why is that?" she asked, closing her eyes as she gave herself over to the sensation.

"Because I am not a gentleman," he answered succinctly, his hand tugging hers, encouraging her to turn and face him.

She opened her eyes and did his bidding, immediately losing herself in the warmth of his gaze. "How so?" The words were a mere whisper on her lips.

His gaze shot to her lips, and he leaned forward just an inch, his hand releasing hers and trailing ever so lightly up her arm before resting on the crook between her neck and shoulder, the warmth radiating from him, erotically delicious.

"I'm far more heartless than I seem. A flirtatious smile, a wicked grin can do much to cover a black heart. I am no saint, Miss Miranda. And more than anything, I'd love to encourage your bravery on the subject at hand, but for my own pleasure, my own purpose would I do it. In that, I'm an utterly selfish creature, and you'd be better off to remember that, and stay far away," he murmured softly, every word caressing with his rich tone. It was impossible to take him at his word when the tone and inflection were a direct contrast to everything he was stating.

"For being as wicked as you claim, you have quite a sense of morality in warning me against your charms," she replied, surprised at her own ability to form words when being so utterly distracted by his.

He gave a slight shake of his head, then traced his fingers up her neck and slid a finger across her lower lip.

Her lips parted without a thought, and before she could comprehend what was about to happen, he leaned down and kissed her. It wasn't a kiss that was gentle and leading; it was a kiss of passion, of warning.

But she was quite certain it held the opposite effect of its application. As his lips ravaged hers, nipping, teasing, and devouring, she wasn't the least bit warned, nor did she sense the danger in it. Her body rejoiced, her lips responded in kind. He pressed into her, her body catching flame as he did so, and she stepped back to hold firm against the pressure he gave. She felt his lips bend into a grin in between kisses, and when she stepped back again, she had the suspicion it was planned. But she was too lost to his attentions to care, and before she knew it, the click of a door penetrated her thoughts as the cool wall pressed up against her back. Leaning against it, she was flooded with a thousand sensations as his body deliciously aligned with hers. Her arms wound around his shoulders, pulling him in tighter, and when he groaned in pleasure, she had the greatest sensation of delight overcome her.

It was one thing to accept pleasure, but to give it? That was powerful. She tugged on his hair as her fingers threaded through it, and he responded with an urgent press into her soft form. Just when she was quite certain her own morality had flown away, he broke from the kiss and stepped back.

"You tempt me in ways I cannot withstand." He swore the words, as if they were an oath, completely in contrast with the heady sensation overwhelming her.

She caught her breath and regarded him with some confusion. "And that is not something you like?"

"It is something I cannot entertain," he replied, raking his hand through his hair. "There will be no more of . . . this." His darkened gaze flickered to her, then to her lips, then back to her wide eyes.

"You mentioned that."

"This time I'm resolute," he remarked with more feeling.

"Because you don't wish to go behind your friend's back when you gave your word."

He nodded. "And I will not do a lady such as yourself justice. I will not come up to scratch, no matter how tempting you may be, Miss Miranda. Marriage and I are old enemies, and I'd not wish that fate on anyone, especially you." With that, he made a small bow, opened the door, and left.

Miranda took a steadying breath.

And wondered if perhaps his resolution would falter.

She hoped so, more than she dared admit.

Because while he was making resolutions to keep away from her, she was making resolutions to have him.

It was that way for several days. Life continued in a somewhat normal routine, but in the evenings, when Iris was in her rooms, Miranda would allow herself to be found, if, *if* the viscount wished. And, apparently, wish he did. Because for four nights, he would find her, and they would converse. At first, she was certain he had no designs on her and was going to be stalwart in his resolution to keep from her.

But just before he'd say good night, he would kiss her.

She had no expectation that tonight would be any different, except when he walked into the library, his countenance was stormy indeed. He appeared cross, but not with her. It was curious, and she inquired. But all her inquiries were met with monosyllabic answers. She resumed her reading, and she had no sooner turned the page when he addressed her.

"I will fail if I continue to allow myself the pleasure of your affection, Miss Miranda. And when I say fail, please understand it will be entirely, and you will be left without anything to show for it. I'm a brute for taking advantage of your willing nature for far too long, and so I must, I will keep myself from harming you with my weakness." He gave a nod.

"But one final thing," he said after a moment.

Her heart picked up speed, and she couldn't find her voice.

He strode toward her and kissed her sweetly, innocently, and without any of the delicious heat she'd learned to crave.

"No more," he whispered against her wet lips, and left.

How could her heart be broken without ever truly falling in love?

Maybe knowing it was entirely possible to love someone, to have his love in return, and have that hope disappointed was enough to create heartbreak. It certainly felt as much, and with both his kiss and his solemn promise for it to be the last lingering on her lips, the tears slid down her face as she silently cried.

Maybe love wasn't everything she had hoped it to be.

Maybe it was far more damaging.

Chapter Eighteen

Heathcliff felt a shiver of foreboding filter through him as he greeted his friend. Lady Liliah gave him a sweet smile, and then slid her gaze to her husband when he gestured to a seat before Heathcliff's desk.

"I suppose this isn't strictly a social call because you're not seeking the company of your sister?" Heathcliff asked dryly, ambling toward his desk, not in any hurry to discuss the issue that certainly was about to be brought forth.

Lucas took a seat, leaning back in a most relaxed manner.

Damn, how the tables had turned.

Usually, it would be Heathcliff reclining, unhurried and unaffected by whatever scheme or mishap had ruffled Lucas's feathers. Heathcliff didn't appreciate the reversal of roles, and he adjusted his oddly tight cravat as he took a seat. Did he appear as guilty as he felt?

Folding his hands on his desk, he awaited their leisure.

"My wife and I have come to an important conclusion," Lucas started, giving a causal flick of his wrist.

"It appears quite grave," Heathcliff couldn't help but remark.

Lucas chuckled. "I suppose that would depend on how one feels about the subject matter," he replied cryptically.

"What I think my husband is trying to say, " Lady Liliah gave Lucas an amused glare, "is that we learned something that brought us to a conclusion, one that requires your assistance."

"I'm utterly at your disposal, Lady Heightfield." Heathcliff grinned, enjoying the irritated glare of his friend.

"Watch it," Lucas bit out, but he was grinning.

It was Heathcliff's turn to wave a dismissive hand. He was feeling more comfortable. If they merely needed his assistance, perhaps all his guilt, all his foreboding was for naught.

"We received word from London. I have Ramsey watching the Duke of Chatterwood. Ramsey indicated the duke has been alluding to his daughter, Miranda's, return from America," Lucas spoke meaningfully.

Heathcliff frowned. "Why would he say such a thing? He hasn't a clue where she is."

"That, my friend, is the same question we began with. And while I don't know the answer, I do know one thing." He leaned forward in his chair, his demeanor and tone serious.

The foreboding and tension returned to Heathcliff tenfold.

"It simply reinforces the truth that Miss Miranda is going to be at risk until she is safely married."

Heathcliff stared at him, his mind churning with implications and realizations that confused him further. But he saw the merit in the idea, saw the truth of such a statement.

"This is where we need your assistance," Lady Liliah chimed in.

Heathcliff felt the air leave his lungs. Surely they didn't mean for *him* to marry her? Would they ask such a thing?

He glanced at Lucas.

Yes, yes, he would.

"Don't have a heart spasm, old man. We don't mean for you to marry her." Lucas rolled his eyes.

Perhaps Lucas would *not* ask that of him.

A sharp disappointment flooded through him, followed by a slightly offended twinge to his pride.

Did Lucas find him wanting in some way?

As soon as the thought skittered across his mind, Heathcliff almost laughed at the truth of such an errant idea.

Of course he was wanting in some way, in practically every way! It was foolish to even consider.

Yet consider it he had.

Much to his surprise, he took great lengths to hide it at the moment. "Then what did you have in mind?" he asked once his thoughts cleared.

Lady Liliah spoke up. "We were hoping you knew some gentlemen, some who were perhaps local and of good breeding. Kind, and in need of a gentle wife? I so wish for my sister to have the opportunity to fall in love, and there simply will be no way for that to happen in London under my father's tyrannical eye. So, it must be here."

Heathcliff frowned at her. "You wish her to have a Season in Edinburgh?"

Lucas answered him. "Of sorts, but it will be difficult to have a proper come-out because we'd need to keep her identity hidden. London is far, but not so far that word wouldn't travel," he finished.

"So you want a titled, well-bred gentleman who isn't offended when he learns the woman he's thinking of marrying has a completely different identity?" he asked with heavy sarcasm.

"We would have to concoct a different story than one she has currently."

"Of course, of course." He shook his head. They'd lost their bloody minds. This would never work, and even if it did have a chance in hell, who in their right mind would expose her to the risk of being found out?

"You don't agree," Lucas stated.

"I think it's possibly the most idiotic scheme you've concocted in some time."

"Don't hold back your true feelings," Lucas replied dryly.

"If I'm understanding correctly, you wish to marry her off to a local, titled Scotsman who has no connection with London, and in a manner that has duplicity at its core? Surely that is the way to assure a love match!" He shook his head. "Lady Liliah, I rather expected more from you."

Lady Liliah frowned. "I expected more imagination from you, Viscount Kilpatrick." She arched a brow daringly. "Is it so difficult to orchestrate a few meetings? I'd think you'd be thrilled to have at least one unmarried lady out of your household."

Heathcliff shrugged. It was surprisingly casual, given

the tumult of emotions that spun within him. "She is providing a necessary service to Miss Iris. It is not a hardship to have her here." He didn't add that he would rather rot than have her leave his residence. Even if it were just a few stolen moments each day, it was his entire source of joy to see her, to simply know she was near.

At this, Lucas chuckled, then sobered, earning a glare from Heathcliff.

"What about a masquerade? Surely you—" Lady Liliah flickered her gaze between the gentlemen meaningfully—"know how to put on a proper masquerade? It would be a perfect event to both conceal my sister's identity and also get her out in the social world." Lady Liliah folded her hands primly on her lap, a self-satisfied grin firmly in place.

Lucas gave a short round of applause for his wife's idea.

Heathcliff rolled his eyes. "More and more secrecy? Again, not the best way to establish a tendre for a swain, or to gain one."

"And you have so much expertise in this area?" Lucas asked.

Heathcliff cleared his throat, then met his friend's gaze with a stalwart one of his own. "I know how betrayal destroys, and I don't see your scheming to marry off Miss Miranda using deception doing anything but hurting her," he bit out.

Lucas studied him, and Heathcliff had the impression he was attempting to make a decision about something.

What, he had no idea, but it was disconcerting at best.

"How would you go about it, then?" Lady Liliah asked with a slightly impatient edge to her tone.

Heathcliff took the question as a reason to look away from his all-too-aware friend and addressed Lady Liliah's question. "The masquerade idea is a good start, but not enough."

"Of course it's not enough," Lady Liliah interrupted with exasperation.

Heathcliff sighed impatiently, then continued. "A house party would be—"

"Oh yes! How did I not think of such a thing?" Lady Liliah leaped from her seat and clapped her hands. "It is a perfect way to control who is here, and how they can interact with her! You'll be the host, and we can stay here, acting as proper chaperones—"

"May I make a suggestion?" Lucas asked with an indulgent grin aimed at his wife.

She nodded.

Lucas turned to Heathcliff. "This is a brilliant plan, because then you can also use it as a trial for Miss Iris. All the better if she meets someone of note and you are able to forego the entire London Season." He gave a winning smile.

Damn the man. Heathcliff had come up with several reasons why the house party would never work, why it was doomed, even though he had been the one with the idea initially. But Lucas had neatly destroyed all his arguments.

Because if he refused now, they would suspect.

Not that there was anything of note to suspect; rather, anything that meant something . . .

Surely a few kisses didn't mean *something*.

Nor did the fleetingly tender touches stolen as they passed in the hall.

Miss Miranda wouldn't be truly interested in him, just as he wasn't seriously interested in anything more than the stolen pleasures.

But that didn't mean he wanted someone else to enjoy those same things.

The thought made his temper simmer just below the surface. But what choice had he? None. He was damned if he did and damned if he did not.

"Perfect." Lucas nodded, taking Heathcliff's silence as acceptance.

"Oh, I can hardly wait! Now, we must work on the guest list. Have you a piece of paper I may use? And a pen?" Lady Liliah came around to his side of the desk, her eyes scanning the table for the requested objects.

Heathcliff still hadn't spoken a word, still holding out for some miraculously perfect reason to tell them to go to hell with their bloody idea.

No miracle poured forth, so he withdrew a fresh sheet of paper and a pen and ink, handing them to Lady Liliah.

She grinned triumphantly.

He resisted the urge to glare.

"Now then, who shall we invite? Surely you know some local gentlemen?" Liliah leaned down over a free area of the desk, her pen poised in eager anticipation.

Heathcliff glanced at Lucas, and he tapped his finger on the desk, irritated.

"Perhaps we could ask Mrs. Keyes? She is here year-round and certainly knows everyone in the vicinity," Lucas spoke helpfully.

Heathcliff swore mentally. Damn the man.

"Perfect. I'll go and request her assistance!" Lady Liliah left the paper and pen and ink unattended and quit the room in a rush of delight.

When the door closed, Lucas leaned forward in his chair, his expression unreadable, which only meant Heathcliff was going to utterly hate whatever he was about to say.

"You . . . could always come up to scratch, if the idea of her marrying another is so abhorrent to you." He wore his gambling face, the one that gave nothing away. Not a tick in his expression, not an inflection in his tone.

Heathcliff shook his head. "The devil could also serve us tea, but just because it's possible doesn't mean it's going to happen ever. You need to stop trying to intertwine me in your family theatrics. I'm already involved more than I wish to be, simply having her in residence. Take that and leave me be." He was proud that his tone gave nothing away. Years of working at Temptations allowed him the perfect gambling face as well.

Lucas nodded, considered him for a moment, then stood. "Just don't fold too late," he murmured, and left.

Heathcliff sighed as he leaned back in his chair.

Fold? That wasn't in his vocabulary.

Yet, as he glanced down, the blank paper and pen mocked him.

Reminding him that right now, he was the only option, though that was about to change.

And competition was never something he appreciated.

In fact, he had the feeling it was only going to compound the matter . . . and that was far more frightening than a house party.

People he could manage.

It was his own heart that had him concerned.

Chapter Nineteen

A kiss meant something, didn't it? What about two kisses? Certainly then? What about after more than two? Oh, why wasn't life as easy as mathematics? One plus one equals two.

Two kisses.

Two kisses plus three more meant five. And after each kiss, a vow that it would be the last.

Five kisses meant . . . what exactly it meant, she wasn't sure. But it should mean something, she decided. Yet, as her sister paraded with an utterly focused expression as she spouted off ideas about marrying her off to some unknown gentleman, Miranda decided kisses might not mean as much as she'd hoped.

Because if they did, wouldn't the viscount have had an opinion on her involvement with another man?

Yet, if her sister's present conversation was accurate, he hadn't whispered a word against the idea.

What was worse, no one had seen fit to ask *her* opinion either.

"Liliah?" Miranda tried, not for the first time. Her sister was of quite a singular mind when she was focused on a plan.

When her sister continued as if she hadn't spoken at all, Miranda rose from her place on the settee and walked around the low table, careful to miss the cornered edge, and approached her sister, who had her back to her as she paced.

"And I do think Mrs. Keyes has a keen eye for gentlemen, because she was quite insistent on the character of a few of the men we discussed—"

Miranda grasped her sister's shoulder gently, breathing a sigh of relief when her words cut off before being completed.

"Yes?" her sister asked, spinning, her heightened color and determined expression reminding Miranda of the matchmaking mamas of the Ton.

It was almost predatory.

She withdrew her hands and folded them before her. "What if that is not what I wish?"

Liliah blinked, her wide eyes immediately confused. Miranda could see the irony. After all, a gently bred lady had but one goal in life: to marry well.

Her asking such a question was akin to asking why one thought the sky was blue. It just was.

After a few moments, Liliah tipped her head ever so slightly. "Are you against the idea?"

Miranda sighed. "Not the idea but perhaps the execution?"

Liliah frowned, creating a few tiny lines between her eyebrows. "Do you have a better one?"

Miranda felt her lips tip into a grin. Her sister had asked without impatience; she was sincerely wondering if there was some aspect of this brilliant idea she'd missed. Not likely; she'd clearly thought out more details than Miranda had expected to be involved in courtship—and the gentleman hadn't even been met.

"No," she hedged. "But it does smack of coercion." She added softly, "I'm away from London to remove myself from one tyrannical family member, and I feel as if I'm discovering another." Miranda kept her tone soft, kind, so as not to unnecessarily hurt her sister.

"Oh." Liliah's lips formed into a perfect circle. "I see. I suppose I got rather carried away."

"A little," Miranda agreed.

Liliah took a few steps toward a side table beside the window, brushing her fingers against the wood, her expression thoughtful. "What is it you want, then? It is your future after all." She turned to regard her sister.

Miranda shrugged. "That's a difficult question. I suppose the easy answer is that I wish to be happy, settled, unafraid." She twisted her lips as she considered what she would choose if she had the world before her, any options, any path to take. "I'd want to know my husband, find him not only diverting but also fascinating. Would it be so much to ask to have something in common?"

Liliah nodded once. It was a decisive nod, as if she were taking mental notes. "No, that is not so much to ask. I think your requests are more than reasonable."

"And if I could actually find a love match, I think that would be lovely." A sigh escaped her lips.

"I wouldn't want you to have anything less."

Miranda met her gaze. "You say that, but everything you've said seems so . . . ." She frowned as she searched her mind for the word. "Calculated."

Liliah had the grace to look slightly abashed. "Well, we must encourage affection and attachment where we can."

"Yes, but what happens when those circumstances change? Will that affection and attachment remain? What is wrong with allowing it to build naturally?"

Liliah sighed. "Nothing, but I don't know how much time we have," she answered, her eager anticipation fading into a concerned expression. "I don't want to risk Father finding you, spiriting you away to London, and—"

"He didn't want me there in the first place. Why would that change now? I'm out of his realm of responsibility; isn't that what he wished? Why he was willing to marry me off to the highest bidder? To be rid of me, the responsibility of me under his protection?" Miranda asked, her indignation rising to the surface, causing her voice to become harsh.

Liliah stepped toward her. She reached out and cupped her cheek, smoothing her thumb over her skin. "Yes, but never underestimate a man in love with power. I'd rather not trust any aspect of his character, not with something as precious as your future. But I do promise to listen to you, to *try*," she emphasized the word, "not to become carried away with my own plans. I just want you settled, and I want you . . ." She gave a watery smile. "I want you as happy as I am. As loved as I am. I want it for you so desperately, I'm afraid I'm going to be overzealous."

"Overzealous? You?" Miranda teased, giggling softly. "You do it with love. As such, I'll do my best to remember it."

"When I become tyrannical?" Liliah asked, laughing.

"More or less." Miranda shrugged, grinning at her sister.

"It will probably lean on the more side, rather than the less." Liliah hitched her shoulder, then grinned unrepentantly. "Let's start anew."

Miranda nodded, and watched as Liliah ambled past the settee and took a seat in the wingback chair. "Now then, have you any resistance to meeting the three gentlemen suggested by Mrs. Keyes?"

Miranda twisted her lips, then took the few steps to the settee and sat down, thinking. "What does the viscount know about these gentlemen? I'd like to have his insight. Surely he knows them?"

Liliah nodded. "I haven't asked him yet. Perhaps we should do that now, before we go any further with our plans. Just to be certain they are of the character Mrs. Keyes suggested."

Liliah rose from her seat, then strode to the corner to ring the bell for the maid. "I'd like to include my husband in the details as well. He's quite astute with social arrangements, granted his expertise is of the darker variety, but he's insightful nonetheless." Liliah walked back to the recently vacated chair and sat back down.

"I don't mind who we involve, at least in the first stages." Miranda paused, then added just to make sure her point was clear, "Only in the beginning stages, though."

"Understood," Liliah replied.

The door opened and Mrs. Keyes herself walked into the room, her expression inquiring. "How may I assist you? Tea, perhaps?"

Liliah was quick to answer. "Yes, and would you please inform my husband as well as the viscount that we request their company?"

Mrs. Keyes replied with a grin, "Right away, Lady Heightfield." With a polite nod, she quit the room, presumably in search of the tea service and the gentlemen.

Miranda took a deep breath, steeling herself in anticipation of seeing the viscount again. It was a strange juxtaposition. When they were alone, or alone enough, she had little anxiety in carrying on a conversation with him, or stating her mind.

She had little trouble with being nervous when they kissed.

But add in her sister and Lord Heightfield, and she could feel her body humming with tension. It was odd, really. She should be far more comfortable with others around, her own family! Yet, she found that only increased the stress, and she was much more relaxed when it was simply the two of them.

She mused about this odd truth, wondering why it was so, as her sister interrupted her thoughts. "After we discuss the gentlemen in question, you know, seek the viscount's opinion on their character, I think the next most important thing is to determine when we can host the masquerade."

"Masquerade?" Miranda blinked, then narrowed her eyes slightly. She hadn't remembered her sister mentioning a masquerade.

Then again, her sister had spoken so swiftly and with such vigor, she might have missed more than just part of the one-sided conversation.

"Yes, of course. We need to provide an avenue for you to mingle without risking exposure to your identity. Originally, there was to be a house party first, but I've now decided it is best to have the masquerade ball first. It will be easier to explain as well as give you insight into the gentlemen you find interesting," Liliah replied, flicking her wrist in a dismissive way, as if to say her answer should have been understood without needing to be explained.

"I see," Miranda replied. "So, I'm to meet gentlemen without them actually knowing who I am."

Liliah leaned forward, her brow pinched. "Were you listening to me at all earlier?"

Miranda had thought she was listening, or at least listening to part of it. She was realizing now that maybe she hadn't been listening nearly enough. "Yes," she answered anyway.

"I'm not entirely convinced," Liliah replied. "But it is of little importance. We are starting over, sort of." She frowned. "The viscount may be reluctant to help," she added, a little off topic.

Miranda froze. Her breathing stilled as hope and a fierce curiosity rose within her. "Why is that?" she asked, then released her tight breath, exchanging it for another.

Liliah looked thoughtful, her eyes flickering to the side as if deep in thought. "He was rather silent on the matter. And I found that odd. He's not one to be silent about . . . well, anything," she finished.

That statement was in agreement with what Miranda had discerned about his character as well.

Interesting.

"Oh?" she remarked, hoping her sister would continue speaking about that particular subject.

"Yes. Has he singled you out in any way?" Her gaze flickered back to her sister. Another person might see the wide eyes and interpret it as innocent.

Miranda knew better. Her sister was playing ignorant; she suspected something.

"What do you mean?" Miranda asked directly, the need to know causing her to be utterly frank.

Liliah dipped her chin slightly. "I know nothing. I'm simply observing."

"What are you observing?" Miranda asked, slightly impatiently.

"That—"

The door opened, and Miranda could have marched over and slammed it closed in the face of whoever was attempting to enter during such a crucial moment.

But it would be unforgivable to slam the door closed on the man who owned it.

The viscount was first to enter, effectively silencing any further discussion on the previous matter.

Yet, as he walked in, Miranda couldn't seem to muster the irritation of moments earlier. Rather, she was equal parts relaxed and anxious. It was ironic: to be at odds within herself, yet with no other way to explain it. Seeing him made Miranda feel as if a piece of her was put back in place, when she hadn't even been aware it had gone missing. Yet her heart hammered in her chest when his rich and warm gaze settled on her, her chest constricting with the power of it.

It was thrilling and frightening all at once.

And utterly distracting. She hadn't even noticed that Lord Heightfield—rather, Lucas—had followed him into the room until he spoke. "We were summoned?" he asked in a teasing manner, one that Miranda was readily realizing he used often. For all the rumors surrounding him, he was a remarkably easygoing fellow, not at all what she'd expected.

Or maybe he was simply in love.

Love changed people; isn't that what she'd heard?

She glanced at the viscount. Could it change him?

He gave her a curt nod, then took a seat to the side, reclining slightly, clearly at ease.

Well, it was his parlor, after all, so she supposed if anyone were to feel comfortable, it would be he.

"Summoned? Is that how you wish to call it?" Liliah teased.

Lucas took a seat beside his wife, rubbing his nose against her cheek for a brief moment before answering. "Yes."

"Very well, let it be known I can summon Lord Heightfield like a queen at court."

"I have a feeling the courtesy goes both ways," Miranda added, smiling.

"She's a quick one." Lucas nodded toward her.

"Thank you," Miranda felt the need to add.

There was but a moment of silence before the door opened again, this time admitting a maid with a full tea service. As she carefully carried it to the table and set it down, Miranda waited patiently for the viscount to contribute to the conversation.

Liliah stood to pour for her husband, then, in turn, served the others. Miranda blew across her tea gently, watching the swirling steam and allowing herself to become lost in the mist of it, for a moment, as she waited for her sister to break the proverbial ice and inquire of the viscount.

Would he give any hesitancy to her meeting other gentlemen? She was eager to find out, yet she wasn't sure if she truly wanted to know. Because what if he did not care? Her heart pinched a little, so she sipped her fragrant tea to distract herself from the pain. She didn't want to think she was so easily disregarded, but what did she know of love, or courtship, or even kisses?

Nothing.

It was very irritating to be so naive.

Yet she didn't want to become jaded either. She simply wanted . . .

"We spoke with Mrs. Keyes, who mentioned three gentlemen of note. Miranda and I wish to inquire your opinion, my lord," Liliah said, turning to Viscount Kilpatrick.

Miranda's eyes cut over to him, watching for any change in his demeanor or facial expression.

He cleared his throat after taking a sip of tea. "Who are the gentlemen she mentioned?"

There was no change, no hint that he might be distressed by her seeking a suitor. Nothing that would give her hope that the five kisses meant something . . . anything.

Liliah continued. "The Honorable Matthew Sarose, Lord Marrion, and," she paused, her lips twisting as she frowned in thought, "Lord Winter's son, the Baron of something or another." She flicked her wrist.

"Chester Farthingham, Baron Gant," the viscount supplied.

"Yes. That is his name," Liliah replied with animation. "Thank you. Now, do you have any opinion about who might be best suited for my sister?"

Miranda wanted to crawl into a hole. What had she been thinking, allowing her sister to ask such personal and humiliating questions of the viscount? She hadn't been thinking, that was the problem. Yet it was so clear now, she should have seen this outcome; yet she was oblivious, all she could think was that he would not appreciate such an inquiry and, in that, it would display his affection for her.

But there was no affection displayed.

And he seemed to have no qualms about such an in-quiry.

It was utterly insulting.

Who kissed a lady, then, the next day, plotted whom she should marry?

Were all the men in her life to be so easily dismissive of her?

It felt that way.

Her father.

The viscount.

One thing was for certain: She made a resolution at that very moment.

Whoever she married would not dismiss her so easily.

He'd . . . well, he'd fight for her.

He'd think she was important, vital, and necessary.

Not something to be pawned off, as her father had thought.

Not something to be used, as the viscount clearly had done.

No.

It would be more, it would be . . . everything.

Because in that moment, she knew what she wanted more than anything.

She wanted to be not only relevant but necessary.

Someone's air, someone's song, simply . . . more.

More than she had ever been to anyone.

Chapter Twenty

Heathcliff was quite certain he was in the seventh circle of hell. Because he was discussing the local eligible bachelors with the sister of the woman he'd, for all intents and purposes, compromised. Granted, the compromising wasn't complete—pity, that—but it was enough.

Enough to remind him that he was an eligible bachelor.

Enough to tempt him to come up to scratch.

Enough to give him a reason to come up with all the worst character traits in the gentlemen Mrs. Keyes mentioned.

There was no reason he should help his competition.

Not that he was considering them competition.

That would mean he was considering himself as an option—which he wasn't. No, he may be tempted, but temptation never required action.

As much as many thought the opposite.

Damn, the gambling hell made its market on that very idea.

But he knew better. Or, at least, he thought he knew better. He was growing less confident each moment that passed.

"A lady should aim higher than an untitled gentleman, unless he is of the most impeccable character," Lady Liliah emphasized, tilting her head as she regarded him. "What exactly do you know about him?"

Heathcliff suppressed his groan of frustration and thought about the man in question. He was young, with enough land to make him respectable in that aspect. It wasn't common knowledge, but the gentleman had inquired about purchasing a title, which made Heathcliff think he was seeking social promotion. A marriage to a duke's daughter would certainly be something he'd find tempting.

Damn, there was that word again.

He cleared his throat. "I have reason to believe he is in search of a way to climb the social ladder, as it were."

"Oh." Liliah frowned slightly.

"That's not necessarily a bad thing. Aren't most men in search of the same thing? It doesn't necessarily mean his character is flawed," Lucas interjected; not helpfully, in Heathcliff's opinion.

"True. I can see that point," she conceded. "We'll keep him on the list." Lady Liliah turned to her sister, and Heathcliff did his very best not to follow her gaze. "Are you in favor of meeting him?"

Heathcliff lifted his teacup, thankful for the distraction it offered, even as he listened intently to her answer.

"Yes. Keep him on the list. I'm not going to disregard a man because he is ambitious. There are worse things," she murmured the last part.

And he wondered if perhaps the words were directed at him.

But no, he hadn't indicated anything to her other than a few stolen moments of pleasure. There had been no promises, no talk of commitment. It was simply . . . he had to think about the word that would define the description . . . he failed at fitting the sensations he felt into one simple word. It was too much, yet not ready to be defined at the same time, and confusing as hell.

"Now, then, next on the list is Lord Marrion," Liliah continued doggedly.

Certainly there was somewhere he needed to be, anywhere, really.

But if he left now, they would ask why. After all, he was the only one who knew the men in question, aside from his housekeeper, that is.

"Yes?" he asked, taking another small sip of tea. He wasn't thirsty, just desperate for something to do.

Lady Liliah gave a little impatient huff. "What do you have to say about his character?"

Heathcliff considered the man reluctantly. He was a wealthy earl who spent most of his time on his estate near Edinburgh. Heathcliff searched his memory for some flaw, something that would eliminate him from the list of eligible gentlemen, but could think of nothing.

Not a damn thing.

Blast it all.

"Viscount Kilpatrick?" Liliah asked when he didn't answer quickly enough.

He waited a moment, hoping some sordid secret would reveal itself from his memory, but there was still nothing. "I can't think of anything that would strike him from the list," he remarked, not mentioning he actually had several good qualities to recommend him. In fact, they had spent time at Eton together, and he considered the gentleman a friend.

At least he had.

He was seriously questioning his friendships at the moment; he cast a wary glance at Lucas, who was grinning just over his teacup.

If there were no ladies present, Heathcliff would have made a few choice remarks to his friend and then offered to wipe the smirk off his face with a roundhouse punch. But he had to tamp down his rather heathen inclinations and lifted his teacup again.

It was almost empty, and he asked Lady Liliah, who had poured before, to refill it.

She willingly refreshed his cup, and then continued with the same conversational topic. "That is good to know. Now, finally the baron." She gestured widely, as if presenting a grand topic, not one that was tedious at best.

"Disregard him," Heathcliff took a sip of tea.

"Very well, why?" Liliah asked.

"Yes, why?" Lucas leaned forward, clearly enjoying himself in the middle of Heathcliff's struggle.

Truth be told, he didn't have a ready answer, so he simply shrugged and used the most common and widely acceptable answer. "He's a fortune hunter."

"Truly?" Lady Liliah tipped down her chin. "I'd think he'd find better luck at such an endeavor in London."

"Indeed," Lucas chimed in, earning a glare from Heathcliff.

"He isn't one for Town, and since he doesn't have

the connections to gain him access to the parties where he may have the most luck, he chooses to remain local. While there aren't as many titled ladies, there are quite a few with respectable dowries," he finished, then took a sip of tea, using the motion to close his argument, hoping it would suffice.

"I see. That is unfortunate. I'd rather have more than two eligible gentlemen on the list." Lady Liliah bit her lip.

"Two is more than enough." Miranda spoke up. "Truly, all we need is one. Rather, all I need is one, if it is the right one, you see."

The right one; the idea filtered through him, condemning him and challenging him all at once.

He could be the right one, if he wanted to be.

But he didn't. Not really.

Or at least, not enough to brave such a risk, which could create such a possible failure.

Because what if he failed? What if he was a horrible husband? What would that do to his friendship with Lucas, with his business partnership? So much hinged on success that he wasn't willing to entertain the idea of it. Better to step back, allow things to take their natural course, and maintain the current flow of things.

It was safer.

Deep within, he knew it was the coward's way out. And he hated that he was being so gutless.

"Miranda, you suggested a week from today for the party. Viscount Kilpatrick, do you think we can make that a possibility? We do not want to overtax your staff. And I should inform you that we made a slight adjustment to the plans. First, I think we should host the masquerade so that my sister can observe the gentlemen in question, and perhaps add other names to the list, and then, after she's been introduced, we host the house party. I do believe you'll find such an arrangement makes more sense. Now, what of your staff?" Lady Liliah inquired kindly.

"They will likely cheer when you break the news. I'm afraid I'm rather dull. And I have no objections to your amended plans." At least no objections he could voice without creating a problem and a solution all at one fell swoop. Rather, he distracted himself by her question concerning the staff. He hated how true his response was, but when in Scotland, he simply blended into the scenery. It kept the talk down, so history was spoken about less often.

"Wonderful! If you'll excuse me, I'll seek out Mrs. Keyes and get the plans in motion." Lady Liliah stood. "Sam—Miranda, would you accompany me? Because this event is about you, it is vital to have your input on all the details." Lady Liliah had the posture of a doting mother, exuberant about the upcoming debut of her protégé. It was almost comical, but also rather endearing.

As the ladies quit the room, Heathcliff took another sip of his blasted tea and awaited Lucas's verbal assault.

But no words were forthcoming. He hazarded a glance at his friend.

Lucas was watching him with that expression again, the one that saw too much, that knew too much. "Don't fold too late."

He repeated his earlier comment, rose, and then quit the room as well, leaving Heathcliff alone.

Odd how he'd wished to be alone twenty minutes earlier, and now that he'd gotten his wish, he resented ever thinking it.

Alone was another way to say being lonely, and for the first time in a long time, he realized it described him aptly.

Alone.

Lonely.

And he had the dangerous inclination to maybe, just maybe, do something to change that.

Chapter Twenty-one

Miranda tucked her hair behind her ear as she adjusted her hat in the windy Scottish air. After her sister had discussed the details about the masquerade with Mrs. Keyes, she had announced that she, Miranda, and Miss Iris would be leaving for town—Edinburgh to be exact. The carriage had been readied, Iris had been summoned, and dresses had been changed to be acceptable for the outing. Lord Heightfield had announced that he would be accompanying them, and after a pointed look to the viscount, who had the poor luck of entering the foyer at that moment, a fifth member to the party was added.

So it was, less than thirty minutes later, that Miranda found herself opposite her sister and Iris, while the gentlemen rode behind the carriage, enjoying the fine sunshine.

"I'm quite relieved that Lucas and Viscount Kilpatrick wished to attend us. I'm not terribly sure where to go in Edinburgh. I've heard Princes' Street is the place to shop, but I'm not entirely sure," Liliah mentioned.

"Surely a footman would have known, or Mrs. Keyes. She seems to know everything else," Iris mused.

Miranda agreed. Mrs. Keyes did seem to be a wealth of information.

"Be that as it may, it's much better to be accompanied by gentlemen on our first outing. After this one, I'd think we would be fine on our own," Liliah remarked.

The carriage shifted slightly as they traversed from the courtyard to the open road toward Edinburgh.

"I've never been to the city," Miranda said, eager expectation filling her. It seemed like an age since she'd been shopping with her sister, a lifetime ago.

"We've only recently arrived, and I haven't had the pleasure either. I'm glad we are doing it together. It seems apt, does it not?" Liliah asked, offering her sister a small smile.

"Yes. It does," Miranda affirmed.

"And I'm thankful to be out of the estate. I was growing rather impatient with the confines," Iris replied. "I'm quite accustomed to movement from place to place. I can't remember the last time I stayed in residence for more than a week."

"Truly?" Liliah asked, turning to her.

"Yes. My parents were very serious travelers," Iris added somberly.

Miranda offered her a kind and sympathetic smile. She still missed her parents dreadfully.

"Well, we shall have to take you out and about more often. There is much to offer in Edinburgh, or at least that's what I've been told," Liliah mused. "I shall love to see the castle, and possibly Holyrood House as well. Bonnie Prince Charlie stayed there once, though I don't think the Regent has any plans to visit."

"Holyrood House?" Miranda echoed.

"I'm told it's quite stately."

"That may be interesting," Iris agreed. "Do you think we will be able to see the castle from the carriage? It's on a hill, is it not?"

Miranda turned to her sister. Geography never was her best subject. But she had adored math, which only reminded her of her earlier musings regarding addition and kisses.

Blast it all.

Her sister was answering Iris's question, and she turned toward her, eager for distraction. "Yes. I believe so. It's built from the stone of the mountain, and I wouldn't be surprised if we could see it quite soon," Liliah angled herself so she could look out the carriage window.

Miranda and Iris followed suit.

"There, see that hill? On the top, I believe that's it." Liliah pointed and Miranda squinted.

"I see," she murmured. "Quite fascinating. How old is it?"

"It was built in the twelfth century," Iris answered. "My parents loved history."

Liliah turned to Iris, giving her a kind smile. "I see my sister doesn't need to further your historical education."

Miranda gave a wry smile. "No, I rather think she could educate me in some subjects. I'm helpful in other ways."

Iris winced. "I'm afraid I'm not as accomplished in other areas."

"You'll get there," Liliah affirmed, then turned her gaze back to the window.

Thankfully, the New Town of Edinburgh wasn't more than a forty-minute carriage ride away. As they drew closer, Miranda studied the scenery. Gothic buildings rose amongst the newer additions of New Town, built to draw in the English nobility who preferred their London residences to their Scottish ones. Edinburgh Castle grew large and mammoth as a sentinel over the city, the newer and older areas.

"Oh, I know that! I read about it in the *Times*." Liliah pointed. "It's the Nelson Monument. They've been working on construction but I think we can at least see part of it. Its something about paying homage to the victory at the Battle of Trafalgar."

Miranda studied the cylinderlike structure. "It's a telescope," she murmured, remembering the article.

"Yes. It was crafted to replicate his telescope," Liliah acknowledged. As they passed the stone structure, Miranda glanced to the other carriage window, watching as they passed a domed structure and, if she craned her neck ever so slightly, some body of water that was a shade of blue amidst the constant stone shade of the buildings.

"We will also see the Prince's Street Gardens, and the Register house. It's a rather interesting building, or so I've read," Iris remarked.

Miranda nodded in response. "It's quite impressive. I must say, I was expecting something less civilized than London. I'm not sure why. This is actually quite comparable."

Liliah nodded. "Indeed. Ah that's the gardens! I'm sure it's lovely this time of year." She sighed happily. "I miss Hyde Park."

Miranda agreed. It was a lovely thing, to take an afternoon stroll through Hyde Park, see friends and acquaintances and simply amble about. Not that she couldn't take various rambles at Kilmarin, but it was different, less familiar. And that was a something she missed: the familiar.

The carriage slowed as they pulled up beside a long row of shops. Miranda read their signs: Edinburgh Haberdashery, Tobacconist, Mrs. Penniworth's Shop of Lace and Frilly Things, Mrs. Anne's, and several others. Her sister waited, and soon Lord Heightfield opened the carriage door, offering his hand to her.

After she alighted from the carriage, Iris followed suit, taking the viscount's offered hand, and then it was Miranda's turn. The viscount released Iris, then turned to her.

Extending his hand, his eyes met hers. Heat flooded her, and she could no more deny her attraction than she could deny herself breath. But it was for naught. He didn't want her; that much was clear. She glanced at his hand. It was a warm hand, one she loved to feel wrapped around hers. She swallowed and steeled herself against the sensations that would surely course through her once she touched him.

Her fingers tingled, then her arm as he tightened his grasp on her hand, supporting her weight as she stepped into the sunshine. "Thank you," she murmured, relaxing her fingers, giving him a signal to release her hand.

But he did not. He firmed his grasp.

She glanced up, meeting his gaze, expecting—something.

"There is a slight step up." He motioned with his chin to the cobblestone below.

Her heart pinched with hope denied, and she hadn't

even realized she'd allowed herself to expect anything. But hope was heartless and rarely asked for permission to exist, even where it wasn't wanted or welcome.

There was nothing to do but step up, and again say thank you. He released her hand then, quickly, and strode forward to meet the rest of their party. Miranda squeezed her now-empty hand into a fist and followed everyone down the street to the sign that said William's Paper Company. It made sense it would be their first stop; the invitations were far more of a priority than anything else, with the masquerade only a week away.

It was shocking, really, to think that in a week so much could change. She found she both wanted and feared it. Change was always a brutal taskmaster, especially when considering how it would involve her future. Miranda straightened her shoulders just a fraction. She wouldn't be fearful. She'd lived in the shadow of fear for far too long, heaven knew how long. She was moving forward in . . . She paused for a moment, in midstep, and tilted her head, searching for the right word.

Her party had already entered the store, and she was given a few moments of privacy. Remembering the word from her musings a week before, she decided it was an apt description once again.

More.

She was going to move forward and expect more.

More from life.

More from herself.

It was an oddly powerful feeling, to think she had control over her own happiness, her own future, even if only some small measure. It was far more than what she would have had if she had stayed in London.

She moved forward to the entrance of the store before her sister could notice her missing. With a gentle shove, the door swayed inward and the scent of vanilla-scented papers floated in the air, welcoming her. Liliah was easy to find, already being assisted by a clerk. Miranda studied their little party for a moment. Lord Height-field and the viscount hung back, allowing Liliah to take the lead as far as choosing the paper and colors for the invitations, but it was clear they were, if not peers of the realm, men of quality. Their clothing was the first indication, with their beautifully tailored waist-coats and shined boots, but it was more the confident air they presented. Both Lord Heightfield and the viscount carried themselves with consequence, with an expectation of deference and power, not in a way that made them seem arrogant, but as if their words held weight.

And they certainly did.

Liliah was tapping her chin as she considered two colors of paper. "Miranda? What is your preference?"

Miranda navigated gracefully past Iris, then felt her cheeks burn as she skirted past the viscount, her skirt brushing his breeches as she did. It was a moment before she could focus on the two colors. One was a light shade of purple, almost blue. The other was a pink that was as light as the last hue before the sun rose in the morning sky. While both were lovely, neither seemed to convey *masquerade*.

A masquerade should be dark, mysterious and se-cretive. Nothing about those colors seemed to speak to that fact. She glanced at her sister, then back to the paper. "While both colors are lovely, they seem more appropriate for an invitation to tea, or a perfectly proper ball, not a masquerade."

A chuckle from behind had her turning toward the

sound. Lord Heightfield was attempting to restrain another chuckle, while the viscount was covering his
mouth with a gloved hand, clearly trying to keep from
making a reaction.

"And what are you finding amusing, gentlemen?"
Liliah asked, her tone less than humor-filled.

The viscount's gaze slid to Miranda, and she swore
she could read his mind, and that he'd been thinking
along the same path as she regarding the colors. He
gave a small nod, as if affirming her suspicion, and
then turned to Liliah. "Miss Miranda has a very valid
point."

Miranda felt a swell of pride that her assumptions,
both of them, were correct.

Liliah gave a slight huff, then turned to her sister.
"I'd ask them for assistance—"

"But you'd be afraid of our meddling?" her husband
cut in.

Miranda turned to Lord Heightfield, watching as his
eyes twinkled with merriment. "After all, masquerade
parties are our forte."

Miranda shot a curious glance at her sister, frag-
ments of conversations piecing together, though not
enough for her to completely understand the picture
they presented.

"That's very much what I'm afraid of. I don't wish
to create *that* type of party." She spoke in a low tone,
meant for their ears alone.

"Nor do I," Lord Heightfield answered quickly.
"But I do believe we may have more insight than you
would expect."

Liliah twisted her lips, then glanced at the viscount.
Then, finally, her gaze landed on her sister.

"What is your opinion?"

Miranda turned back to the paper, then to her sister. "What is the worst that can happen?" She hitched a shoulder, the gesture quite blasé.

Liliah raised a brow.

"You'll be in good hands," Lord Heightfield said before his wife could offer more than a dubious expression. "Why don't you two ladies see about the clothing, and Heathcliff and I shall see to the . . . details?"

"They always say the devil is in the details," Liliah remarked wryly, arching her brow.

Lord Heightfield grinned wickedly, and Miranda felt the need to take a step back, even though his grin was focused on his wife. "How appropriate."

Miranda turned to the viscount, curious about his reaction in the middle of all this. What she wasn't expecting was to see him watching her, as if gauging her reaction.

She wasn't used to people studying her; it was an odd feeling and she wasn't sure if it made her feel flattered that he was curious about what he saw in her or suspicious. As soon as her eyes met his, whatever was in his expression was shuttered and he turned away. "You'd better move along if you wish to have a dress made. A week isn't much time." He directed the comment to Liliah.

Miranda turned to leave before she could find another chink in her armor. How was it he found each one?

Chapter Twenty-two

Heathcliff ran his fingers over the engraved invitation. A deep orchid color, it was evocative, sensual, and promising. It was the promising part that speared through him. Promising because he knew each gentleman who would receive one would immediately accept it. It was worded so carefully, with enough information to tease but not to give away anything. Men would attend to satisfy their curiosity, that and because he was the host.

He never hosted parties in Scotland.

Yet they all knew he did in London.

But those parties weren't of the proper variety. They had worded the invitation carefully, to make sure it was clear this party was indeed of the proper variety, but one could never be completely sure. He'd have to watch Miranda, make sure no one got the wrong idea. Of course, that was the perfect excuse to keep her close during the party, and he was willing to hold on to any excuse available.

He studied the gold lettering on the invitation; then his gaze lingered on the color once more. Why was it that purple reminded him of her? What was it that made such a connection between the two in his mind? Perhaps she had worn a dress of that color, or maybe he just instinctively knew it would be a lovely color against her creamy skin; regardless, the connection between the color and the woman was permanent in his mind, for better or worse.

He set down the thick paper and strode to the window. It was night, darkness covering everything like a warm blanket of privacy. But he felt restless, like a caged tiger.

And he knew why.

With each day that had passed since their excursion to Princes Street, he'd kept his distance from Miss Miranda. It was too bloody difficult to be around her and keep his hands to himself, and he had nothing to offer her, at least nothing enduring, and she needed more than just a momentary escape.

She needed a permanent rescue.

And he was anything but a knight in shining armor. He was more the villain who kidnapped the fair maiden in the first place.

And wasn't even repentant about it.

She deserved a rescue, a lasting one, which meant marriage. It was the only way her father would give up on finding and lording over her. In his mind, Heathcliff understood the logic of it all. But somewhere between his heart and his mind, the translation had become muddled, and he couldn't make head nor tail of it. So he'd stayed away, though the distance hadn't helped.

It had only compounded everything.

Lucas hadn't been any help either, always suggesting he ask Miss Miranda her opinion about some aspect of the party, or inquiring about her, as if he bloody well knew the answer.

Which he didn't.

That only reminded him that there were layers and layers of her likes, dislikes, preferences, and ideas to uncover, like a present that never fully stopped bringing forth delights.

But those delights weren't for him.

They were for someone else, someone better, worthy, someone capable of being her savior.

And the whole miserable cycle would start over again, leaving him in the hell that was his life.

And to think, he had eagerly anticipated returning to Scotland. It was laughable. Yet he couldn't bring himself to return to London, not when she was here.

His life was a damn Greek tragedy.

He paced the floor of his rooms, the sound of the fire crackling in the hearth as he padded from one end of the room to the other. His pace was a lazy amble, but his mind still churned furiously. He glanced up and saw his reflection in a mirror, the low light of the fire shadowing his face. Gone was the devil-may-care grin and the charm that had smoothed his way through life, replaced with tension, uncertainty, and something else he couldn't quite name. What had changed? Or maybe nothing had changed, just had been brought to the surface, and he didn't like what he saw.

No one liked realizing that maybe what you thought you'd overcome only had been swept beneath the carpet, waiting to rear its ugly head.

It was easier to pretend, to be charming and engaging, than to deal with the demons within, yet that was exactly what he found himself doing, night after night.

All because of her.

All because he knew he wanted her and couldn't have her.

Because some misbegotten shred of decency remained, and he couldn't cross that line. As much as he wanted to.

Because what if that line was all that was left of the good within him? What if, when he, if he, crossed that line, it would be the end of the man he once was?

It was easier to be the man he wanted others to think he was. Though he was lying as much to himself as to others. Either way, he was damned. He didn't know why he cared so much.

She would marry.

It wouldn't be him.

She'd move on.

So would he.

A few stolen kisses didn't equal love, even if his heart was capable of such a miracle, which it wasn't.

He sighed, bone weary, and sat down on his bed, hands on his knees as he closed his eyes and tried to clear his head.

It didn't work.

With a reluctant sigh, he rose from his bed and walked to a tall wooden cabinet. He pulled the brass knob, then narrowed his gaze on the contents.

Brandy.

But what he really wanted was whisky. Real Scottish whisky, the kind that would burn all the way down his throat, burn away the thoughts that plagued him.

But his whisky was in his office. He'd already taken off his waistcoat and shirt, leaving on only his breeches. He cast a weary glance at the clothing on the settee. "Hell with it." He strode to the door and walked out into the hall. The cool air felt comforting against his bare chest, and he relaxed slightly. He would often run about Kilmarin in nothing but his breeches when he was in residence alone, but with ladies about, he had taken to being more of a proper gentleman. Much against his will.

A certain freedom enveloped him as he took the stairs. Damn, he hated clothing.

The cravat most of all, bloody confining thing.

He nostalgically considered wearing his kilt, a beautiful plaid of blue woven with green and red. Best of all, you didn't have to wear anything beneath it.

He crossed the marble floor of the foyer and headed down the hallway toward his study, pausing at the door when he heard soft footsteps.

Probably a maid, but he didn't wish to be seen half naked in the hall at midnight.

During the day, he would have given a quick smile and ducked into his study. But night held its secrets. Night tempted, was always far more dangerous than day, so he carefully inched back into a dark corner and waited for the person to pass or go away.

Only a few candles flickered, illuminating very little in the dark hall while Heathcliff waited. The footsteps sounded nearer, then they halted altogether. He was about to step out when they resumed once more. A footman, one of their newer staff, walked by, checking behind himself for several moments before passing down the hall, then taking a servants' door that led outside.

Heathcliff listened, and when there was a telltale squeak of the door leading outside, he left the shadows. He started toward his study, then paused. Something felt off; he couldn't name it, but it went against his instincts, so he abandoned his pursuit of whisky and pursued the errant footman instead. He quickened his steps to make sure he didn't lag too far behind, and once he made it to the same door he'd heard used before, he opened it only enough to fit his body through, avoiding the squeak. The night air was chilly against his chest, and he belatedly wished he had donned at least his shirt, but it was too late now. He leaned against the stone of the wall and watched the moon-illuminated horizon of Kilmarin. Movement caught his eye by the stables, and he ducked down, while heading in that direction. He kept his steps soft, quiet, stealthy. The tall grass tickled his chest as he grew closer to the stables, and just before he reached the door, he stepped around the corner, out of sight. He had expected the footman to materialize on a horse, but when Heathcliff looked around the corner of the stable, a dark shadow walked up a path that led to an intersecting road.

This was curious.

It would be foolish to follow close behind. It was entirely possible the footman was meeting a lover, but Heathcliff had long ago learned to trust his instincts, and now he was resolute in his pursuit.

Something, he knew, wasn't right.

Perhaps even worse. Wasn't it his duty to find out what it was?

He waited till the footman had a good head start, but not enough that he could easily disappear in the night, and Heathcliff followed. The cricket's song was loud in the night, covering the soft sound of his footsteps. The half-moon's glow was just enough light to allow him to keep his target in sight. Just as the path met the road ahead, Heathcliff saw a shadowy figure. Then he heard a horse's impatient nicker.

Interesting.

He increased his pace, wanting to be near enough to overhear any possible exchange of words. He bent lower in the tall grass, keeping his movements swift and silent as he approached where the footman had stopped.

Heathcliff slowed, taking the most silent of steps, his ears alert for the softest whisper of a voice as he drew nearer, and nearer. Kneeling down in the grass, he waited, not daring to draw closer with such a lack of cover. The night was dark, but not dark enough for him to risk moving closer. The horse and rider did nothing that would indicate any clue to their identity or purpose, but Heathcliff closed his eyes and listened.

He filtered out the noise of the crickets.

He ignored the sound of the wind rustling the dry grass.

He centered his attention on the soft voices the wind carried.

"Are you sure?"

It was a man's voice, that much was certain, and he assumed it was the rider, not the footman. Yet he wondered if he'd recognize the footman's voice. Probably not.

"Certain," the other person answered—the footman, Heathcliff assumed. The voice sounded younger, green and unsure.

"And you have proof?"

Heathcliff was expecting such a question; it usually followed when one wanted to confirm information. Hell, he'd asked for proof countless times himself. There was no honor amongst thieves, or gamblers, for that matter.

"You said if Lady Heightfield took residence somewhere other than London to follow. She visits Kilmarin every day, and always with the governess—"

"Governess?"

Heathcliff felt bile rise in the back of his throat.

He had been expecting . . . well, he wasn't sure, but not this. Maybe a disgruntled lord who had lost his fortune at Temptations seeking revenge, but not this.

Not someone chasing *her.*

He didn't need to hear anymore; he needed to take action. Creeping forward, his hands tingled with the need to fight, to feel the shattering of bone beneath his knuckles. It had been too long since he'd had a good brawl; this would be . . . fun.

Restless no longer, he planned his attack. He'd have the element of surprise for only a few moments; it was best to first spook the horse to eliminate the rider from escaping. The footman would be the least of the threats, so he'd turn his attention to the would-be rider. He counted silently in his head, creeping around the back of the horse, pausing when the beast's ears perked up.

Leave it to animals; they always knew. The night had gone still, as if the heavens were holding their breath for whatever came next. The horse stamped his foot impatiently, causing the bridle to jingle. The sound carried across the windswept moor, and Heathcliff paused, listening to see if either man had been alerted by the horse's uneasy reaction. One breath, then two; the men continued to speak in soft, angry tones.

Heathcliff raised his hand and gave a swift smack to the horse's hindquarters. It gave a startled whinny and sidestepped, knocking into Heathcliff and sending him sprawling into the dirt, then took off. The force of the horse's hindquarters was impressive, and he begrudgingly felt respect for the startled animal as he lifted his head to watch what happened next. The horse was now several yards away, increasing his pace while one of the men gave chase, yelling epithets into the night. Heathcliff kept his body low as he scanned the night for the second man. Sure enough, only a yard away stood what he assumed to be the wayward footman, his back to Heathcliff as he watched the horse bolt.

Heathcliff eased up. Taking a few silent steps, he broke into an expectant grin just before tapping the footman on the shoulder.

The man spun around, meeting Heathcliff's drawn fist. The footman went down with one facer, and Heathcliff felt a pinch of disappointment. Surely it should have taken two? There was no sport in pulling one punch, was there? He didn't wait to determine an answer to his question and cast a glance toward the disappearing horse. A loud whistle rent the air, and Heathcliff watched as the animal slowed his pace. The would-be rider ran forward and mounted quickly, disappearing into the night.

Damn.

He hated when someone got away. It always complicated matters.

Always.

He glanced down at the unconscious footman, then kicked him for good measure.

The man groaned, and Heathcliff twisted his lips, wishing for a loch in which to dunk the scoundrel to wake him up, just so he could dispatch him once again into unconsciousness.

He was spoiling for more of a fight; it was anticlimactic, really, just one swing.

Well, he couldn't bloody well stay out all night in

the field behind Kilmarin. He frowned, then knelt down. "Get up you bastard," he growled, shaking the footman.

He moaned, but didn't make any movement.

Heathcliff swore under his breath. "Get up!" he roared this time, slapping the footman's face with the back of his hand. "Wake up."

The footman rolled to his side and spat before slowly attempting to rise.

Heathcliff stood and kicked him in the ribs. "Faster, you fool," he growled.

The man groaned, then panted on all fours before biting out a low oath.

"Hell will be a holiday for you when I'm finished with you. Up, you coward." Heathcliff stood back, his hands fisted, itching for the footman to resist in any way.

"Who the hell do you thin—"

"Your judge and jury. Let's go." Heathcliff grabbed the footman by the back of his shirt and all but carried the lean man to the house.

"When the duke—"

"I don't give a rat's arse about the Duke of Chatterwood," Heathcliff said, his blood chilling at the thought.

The man ceased his words and fought Heathcliff's tight grip, but it was of no use.

Heathcliff pushed him forward, sending him sailing into the dirt. "Try that again, I dare you," he threatened. "Get up. Move it, you leech."

The footman stumbled forward as if to run, but Heathcliff was quicker. Reaching forward, he horse-collared the man and sent him flying backward. He landed in the darkness with a loud thud, the sound of air leaving his lungs in a loud swoosh.

"I've got all night and a bad temper, so please, do continue." Heathcliff spoke in a politely detached tone before stalking toward the man still sprawled in the dirt, gasping for the wind that had been knocked out of him.

"Are you going to cooperate, or do you wish me to continue toying with your efforts at escape?"

The footman rose to his knees, coughing. "What—" He froze.

Heathcliff realized he was facing the moon, which had served to illuminate his face to the man before him.

"Bloody hell," the man whispered.

"Both can be arranged. Now up," he commanded.

The footman reluctantly rose to his feet, and Heathcliff could hear him swallow. Just to be sure he wouldn't try to escape again, he grabbed the back of his shirt, pushing the man forward, toward the servants' entrance.

When they reached the door, he kept a firm hold on the man, wary of him making a desperate mistake. Inside, there would be several candlesticks and other blunt utensils one could wield as a weapon, if necessary. He'd like to avoid that if possible. It was one thing to engage in fisticuffs outside in the open, but inside his house . . . well, he'd rather not alert Mrs. Keyes . . . yet.

"Down the hall," Heathcliff whispered, keeping his tone menacing yet quiet as they made their way to the servants' hall and toward the kitchens. There was a storage room just beyond it that had always reminded him of a dungeon. Kilmarin wasn't rustic enough to boast its own prison, but that storage room would suffice in a pinch.

Once he passed the kitchen, he counted three doors in the hall and then opened the one that led to the storage room. After unlatching the door, he shoved the man inside, then shut it. Thankfully the old room bolted from the outside. For that reason, Mrs. Keyes had never let him play in it as a lad, much to his disappointment. But he found the mechanism supremely helpful at the moment.

He made sure the latch was secure and backed up as the footman rammed his body into the door on the other side, as if trying to break through it.

"Your body will break before the door will, lad," Heathcliff said. "Your punishment has only just begun."

He grinned at the truth of his statement, then started asking questions.

And as the answers poured forth, his grin faded, then disappeared.

Because he realized he was about to get everything he wanted.

And nothing he deserved.

Chapter Twenty-three

It was quiet. Too quiet. It was the kind of silence that was a dull roar in one's ears, the kind that made thoughts seem loud. And her thoughts were deafening. She should be resting, allowing her body and mind a much-needed reprieve from the planning and plotting of her future, or rather, her sister's plotting for her future. She should be focusing on the masquerade that would take place in three days.

Three days and life would be different.

She wished she had a different word for it. Maybe bright, or blissful, or some other poetic adjective one dreams of using when considering the future. But no, all she could use was the word *different*.

Because if her sister's well-laid plans came to fruition, Miranda would have one or perhaps more potential suitors. And that could easily lead to marriage, which meant there would be no more stolen kisses with the viscount.

No more gentle touches in the hallway, no more knowing, heated glances from across the dinner table, and it broke her heart.

Not that he'd done any of those things in the past week or so. No, he'd been painfully distant, utterly circumspect, and completely aloof. She'd never understand how it was that men could switch off their emotions so easily. It was practically impossible for her, which was only proven once again by the fact that she was wide awake, surely past midnight, and thinking about him.

Missing him.

Because while they had their stolen moments, there had been something more.

He'd become her friend.

And she had the sinking thought that the friendship had meant far more to her than to him.

And maybe the kisses had as well.

It was a horrible circle she kept traveling within her heart.

She sighed heavily, then rolled over in her bed. The fire crackled, the sound loud against the stillness of the room.

How she wished she could just sleep, have a few moments without dealing with the unknown.

A muted thump came from just beyond her door, and she froze, listening. She could barely make out the sound of quiet footsteps passing by her room in the hall, and she wondered.

Maybe she wasn't the only one sleepless tonight.

Maybe Heathcliff was just as restless as she.

And she wanted to know the answer, needed to know. As she rose from her bed, she told herself sternly that she'd simply peek outside, nothing more. And if it *was* the viscount, well . . . she'd address that problem when and if she met it.

She darted to the door quickly, knowing she had to hurry if she were to catch whoever it was before they disappeared into the dark hall. The door handle was cool against her hand as she twisted it.

"Dear Lord." The words were spoken before she could temper them.

Heathcliff spun on his heel and froze, his gaze startled and somewhat wild. But his eyes were the least shocking aspect of the scene before her. His shoulders were caked with dirt and mud, a thin red line trailed from his left shoulder to his midback, but she lost sight of it when he spun to face her. His hair was disheveled, and mud was splattered across his face, looking like large freckles in the candlelight.

Belatedly, she realized he wore nothing but his breeches and boots. Blinking, she awaited some sort of explanation for his state of undress and dishevelment. Was he hurt?

"Ach, Miranda, you about scared the wits out of me." His shoulders relaxed, and he frowned. "What are you doing about?"

Miranda glanced down the hall. Seeing no one, she came out of her room and approached him. "I could ask the same of you. Whatever has happened to you? Are you injured?" she asked, her gaze searching his body for any indication either way.

"I'm well enough." He shrugged the words as if they were of little consequence.

It was almost laughable. Even in the gothic novels she'd read in secret, she'd never come across a hero—or a villain, for that matter—in such a state. Now that she was assured he wasn't injured, or at least not much, she was coming to appreciate the view.

She took another step closer, studying his chest and noting how it rose and fell with each breath. It was hypnotic, and she had to force herself to look up to meet his gaze.

"Miranda . . ." He whispered her name, but his tone wasn't endearing or charming. It was intense, with something that sounded suspiciously like fear.

Her heart sped up its cadence.

"Yes?" She halted her steps and waited for him to continue.

He glanced at the floor, then at his hands, flexing them. His brows drew together as he studied his hands, as if just now seeing the dirt marring them. Miranda glanced at them as well, noting the several splits in his knuckles that were caked with dried blood.

Had he engaged in fisticuffs? If so, with whom? And at this late hour?

"I should wait till Lucas gets his sorry arse here," he muttered, as if the words were meant for his ears alone.

"Pardon?" That got Miranda's attention. Why in heaven's name was her brother-in-law coming to Kilmarin in the dead of night?

"We have a bit of a . . . situation," he hedged, then glanced down the hall, narrowing his eyes. "Ach, to hell with it all." A low groan rumbled from his chest, and he gave her his back, striding toward a nearby door. He opened it quietly but with an impatient tug.

"Wait," Miranda called out, taking a step forward.

"Get in." He gestured with his chin to the barely illuminated room.

Miranda halted her steps, swallowed, then took a hesitant step forward.

He arched a brow impatiently as his gaze slid from hers down the hall once more.

She increased her pace and walked into the room, instinctively knowing these were his private chambers.

They smelled like him, cedar and cinnamon and something wild she couldn't name, but associated with the man who was now closing the door behind her, leaving them utterly alone.

Her heart sounded deafeningly in her ears as he passed her, brushing close enough that she could feel the heat from his bare skin. It made her want to lean in, to touch him and find out if he felt as firm, and as soft, as he appeared. She wasn't even sure how that was possible, to be firm and soft at the same time, but there was no other way to describe the smooth planes of his chest and the corded muscles traveling down his arms.

He knelt before the low-burning fire. Lifting a log, he placed it on top of the coals, sending several sparks flying into the air before they burned out, disappearing. The dry wood caught fire quickly, and he stood and faced her, his expression unreadable, even in the increasing light of the room.

She wanted to say something, but she didn't know where to begin. There were so many questions, but all she could do was breathe.

"It would seem you have a decision to make," he started, his gaze shifting from her, to the floor, then back to the fire as he continued. "Your father knows you're here. How, I haven't a clue. I'm assuming he knew wherever your sister was, you'd be nearby. Regardless . . ."

Miranda felt her breathing catch.

Her father knew where she was hiding? He'd be furious! He'd be irate and utterly determined to collect her back to London. She and Liliah had made a fool out of him in the eyes of the ton; he'd not take that lightly. He was far too prideful to allow such a slight.

"I see you understand the magnitude of the situation." Heathcliff's voice broke through her thoughts.

She sighed, then took another shaking breath. "I do."

He regarded her curiously, his dark brows hooding his eyes as his lips parted just before he spoke. "Do you . . . that is, do you wish to return to London?"

Miranda stood up straighter, her brows knitting with confusion over such a . . . well, a stupid question. "London? Just so my father can lord over me and marry me off to whoever will give him the most benefit?"

Heathcliff's gaze was masked. "How is that any different from marrying for position? For wealth? The ton is famous for its alliances." His tone was harsh.

"You are a part of that world, Viscount Kilpatrick," she bit out. "But as a man, you have the right, the privilege of securing your own future and fortune. I do not. I . . ." She took a step forward. "I am at the mercy of the men around me. My father, my brother-in-law, even *you*."

He flinched slightly.

She frowned. "What is it? What are you not telling me?" she asked, narrowing her eyes.

He shook his head. "You're just more naive than you know."

She tipped up her chin ever so slightly. "How so?"

He sighed, running his hand through his hair as he walked to a brocaded chair by the fireplace. He lowed himself into it and twisted his neck.

Miranda tamped down the urge to tap her toe impatiently, but it would have been useless; she was barefoot, and the movement wouldn't have made a sound.

She glanced down anyway, realization slowly flooding her. Her legs tingled, then her arms, her fingers feeling as if little needles were pricking her a thousand times before she gathered the courage to look up.

Heathcliff was watching her, waiting for her to react to the knowledge she was just now understanding.

"I . . . see."

And she did. She was in her night rail, in a gentleman's room, and he was in a state of undress, and if all that evidence wasn't damning enough, it was night, and she remembered her brother-in-law was expected as well.

A witness.

"Did you plan this?" she asked, feeling numb. She was compromised without actually being compromised. Leave it to her to let such an event be so utterly anticlimactic.

"No, yes, I—" He stood, his movements fitful as he paced the room for a moment before continuing to speak. "I'm open to suggestions if you don't wish to . . ." He hesitated, then looked at her.

"Wish to?" she asked, arching a brow.

At least he had the grace to appear slightly abashed. "Marry me."

The words should have brought euphoria, but they were forced; he'd chosen this, but only because he saw no other option. That much was clear.

She shoved all her emotions to the side. "I don't remember being asked," she bit out.

He frowned. "Surely you understand that this," he gestured between the two of them, "is more than damning."

"No one has seen us," she shot back, not that she wanted him to alter his plans, but she couldn't quite help pointing out the obvious. Plus, she didn't like the idea of forcing his hand, and this certainly smacked of force.

For her.

For him.

"Even if no one ever knew about this." He nodded to her. "Certainly you understand that there simply isn't enough time to find you a proper husband—"

"You're saying you wouldn't be a proper husband?"

"You bloody well know I'm wouldn't be," he snapped. "But you don't have a choice anymore. Improper or not, I'm all you've got, lass."

"Because my father knows I'm in Scotland?"

"Because the only way you're going to be safe is if you're married. Your sister said as much a week ago, and so did Lucas. We all know it, and now . . . we haven't another choice. Unless you wish to go back to London with yer father." His brogue was thick and rough, reminding her of scratchy yet warm wool blankets against her skin.

She took a deep breath through her nose. "Will I never have a choice in life? At every turn, it is stolen from me, and I wish . . ." She almost bled her heart out before him, but she paused and closed her eyes.

It was no use.

"I'm sorry, Miranda," he murmured softly.

She glanced at him. "It's not your fault," she admitted.

"No, but I'm certainly not helping." He shook his head and placed his hands on his hips, drawing her attention back to his dirt-smeared chest.

"Are you ever going to tell me what happened? I'm assuming it has something to do with this news of my father . . ." She tipped her head and sighed, weary.

"Have a seat." He gestured to his recently vacated chair by the fire.

She padded to it and sat down on the soft cushion, the heat from the fire warming her as he told his tale.

And as she listened, she could almost pretend this was where she wanted to be.

In his room, listening to the soft, deep timbre of his voice while the fire crackled.

She could almost pretend she was wanted.

That he wanted her.

Maybe even as much as she wanted him.

Chapter Twenty-four

Heathcliff heard Lucas's voice before he heard the footsteps down the hall. He'd secreted Miranda back in her room a half hour earlier so he could attempt to clean up the mess that was his body. And even though it had only been a half hour, he missed her.

Oh, he always missed her when she wasn't with him. Hadn't he just been musing about avoiding thinking about her? So that meant she was the only thing he could think of. He gave a wry chuckle. This was different, though.

Because the choice had been removed from him.

From her as well.

But in taking away the choice, he'd been given a freedom he'd needed, craved, and would have denied himself till his dying breath.

He would have her.

And he didn't have to be worthy . . . he simply had to be willing.

He could be willing.

Hell, he was beyond willing.

The whole thought had him practically taking wing and flying! He only wished the same euphoria translated into Miranda's heart. As he remembered her words, they pieced him anew. *Will I never have a choice in life? At every turn, it is stolen from me, and I wish . . .*

How he wanted her to be able to choose him!

But he knew, he knew deep within, that he would never have allowed himself to give her the choice of him for a husband.

She deserved more.

Which brought him right back to the fact that he wasn't worthy.

Damn, it was a beautiful thought to be willing, though.

"How in the hell . . ." Lucas stormed into Heathcliff's room, the door making a wide arc as he strode through. He frowned slightly when his gaze fell on Heathcliff, as if disappointed the door hadn't smacked his friend in the head.

It would have been a mighty blow had it. It was, after all, an oak door, and Lucas had wielded it like a weapon.

Heathcliff decided it was quite possibly his lucky day. He was all but betrothed to the woman he had gone mad over, and he'd been lost in his musings, so he'd neglected to approach the door when he'd heard Lucas's approach.

Yes. Indeed it was a lucky day.

He'd have to remember that and see what other charms life decided to throw his way today.

"Wipe that bloody smile from your ugly face," Lucas ground out, but some of the heat had dissipated from his expression. He closed the door none too gently and strode into the room, wiping his hand down his face. "It's not even dawn and I'm in your bloody room, all because I received a cryptic message that my sister-in-law is in danger and your intention to remedy it." He took a few steps forward. "Do you have any idea what conclusions I've drawn?"

Heathcliff blinked, frowning with confusion. "Pardon?" What in heaven's name was Lucas spouting off about? Heathcliff had rather thought he'd been utterly clear in his short message. How could there be any conclusion drawn other than the fact?

"Is she with child?" Lucas asked, his expression tight.

Air rushed out of Heathcliff's lungs as he replayed Lucas's question, wondering how in the hell everything had gotten so out of hand so quickly. "Dear God, no. Why would she be?" Heathcliff asked once his air returned, and with far more shock in his tone than care.

"Forgive me if my best friend has been mooning and utterly a caged tiger because of the girl, and then I get a message implying her in danger. Am I to assume the danger is *not* you?"

Heathcliff stood and then, rather wisely, put some distance and a chair between himself and his irate friend. "There has been a misunderstanding, I believe." He spoke calmly, clearly, watching his friend as if he were a snake about to spring forth and bite him.

"Explain." It was one word, but it was enough.

Heathcliff gave a shortened version of the evening's events, starting from his discovery of the errant footman—still imprisoned in the storeroom and heavily guarded by Heathcliff's most trusted men—and then skimmed over a few of the details, such as his state of undress, as he relayed the agreement he'd reached with

Miss Miranda. Adding, finally, that the magistrate had been notified and would be picking up the prisoner sometime that morning.

When he finished, Lucas's anger had shifted into an alert expression that caused Heathcliff no longer to fear bodily harm.

Or at least a facer.

"You could have bloody well given me more information in your message, Heathcliff. You have to admit, the note you sent wasn't to your benefit at all." Lucas shook his head and then all but fell into a chair, his hand coming to rest on his forehead, as if fighting a headache.

Heathcliff came around from the back of the chair he'd used to create distance, an obstacle between himself and his friend, and took a seat across from him. "You didn't tell your wife, did you?" Heathcliff asked, groaning.

"I was woken up in the dead of night by my valet, my wife right beside me. Do you think she would have ignored such a commotion, not made herself insistent on knowing the cause?" Lucas asked with little patience.

"So I gather she's on her way here, then?" Heathcliff asked, resigned.

"I'm surprised she didn't force me to wait for her. Although I may have implied that I would wait for her, and then . . . didn't."

Heathcliff winced. "You may pay for that later."

Lucas returned the grimace. "I'll tell her it was your fault."

"She'll still take it out on you," Heathcliff assured him.

Lucas signed. "I know."

They sat for a few moments in silence. Heathcliff's mind continued to spin over the events of the evening, and the events that would need to take place that day.

Which reminded him . . . "The masquerade; we need to have the party, but with a different intention."

Lucas turned to him, nodding for him to continue. "It should be a presentation of Miss Miranda—"

"Just call her Samantha. It's not as if she's in hiding any longer if what you say is true."

"Are you implying that I'm not being honest?" Heathcliff asked in an impatient tone.

"No, I believe you. Never mind what I said; I'm simply already weary and the whole bloody mess is just starting. Continue."

Heathcliff nodded, deciding to let the remark go by. Heaven only knew Lucas had done the same for him countless times. He paused to think where he'd left off before Lucas interrupted him.

"You were talking about a presentation," Lucas supplied helpfully.

"Ah, yes. It should be a presentation of my wife. That way we can begin the circulation of the news."

Lucas nodded. "That's probably for the best. But you do know we'll have to make a trip to London regardless, just to make everything official."

Heathcliff nodded. "We would have to return shortly anyway. Ramsey has been left quite alone with the whole bloody mess of the club, and he's probably in need of a little assistance."

"Ha, that's laughable," Lucas remarked, chuckling dryly. "He's in his element. The man loves to control things. It feeds his soul. Without us there, he can keep the ribbons tight to his chest and drive the whole lot however he wishes."

Heathcliff gave a shrug. "You're right."

"You always did think highly of your role in the club," Lucas remarked, his grin wide and teasing.

Heathcliff arched a brow. "I'm the only one willing to get his hands dirty."

"I take umbrage at that statement, sir." Lucas feigned offense.

"You'll stay far from any scandal now. You're married, proper and surely about to be accepted into the bosom of society."

Lucas eyed him, watching expectantly, as if Heathcliff were missing something obvious and humorous.

Heathcliff frowned.

"Calling the kettle a bit black, are we? Who is about to be married, and proper—"

"Ah, hell." Heathcliff groaned.

"Having second thoughts?" Lucas asked.

"No. Just the bit about society, not Mir—Samantha. Damn, I'm going to have to get used to that. How did you keep the bloody secret so well?"

"I'd suggest getting accustomed to it quickly. I don't think she's overly fond of that name, and in the throes of passion, if you were to speak another—"

"Dear Lord. You're an ass." Heathcliff glared at his friend.

"Just a little marriage advice."

"Because you're the expert, being married for all of . . . what is it, a month? Two?"

"Long enough." Lucas shrugged. "And to answer your earlier question, I was not around, so it was easy not to slip up with her real name. Also, technically, it's Lady Samantha."

A knock sounded at the door, and Heathcliff rose from his chair and answered it. "Yes?"

Mrs. Keyes was waiting outside, a worried expression on her face. "My lord, it would . . . that is . . . I've been informed of the events of the evening and I was . . ."

"Spit it out, Mrs. Keyes." Heathcliff gave her a boyish grin, hoping to set her at ease.

"Don't look so satisfied with it all," she scolded him. "It's terrible news, and to think, I was treating the daughter of a duke like an in-between! She's a proper lady, for pity's sake! I had her in the servants' quarters!" Mrs. Keyes paled at the words. "How unforgivable."

"I do think Lady Samantha," he silently applauded himself for using the right name, "will be quite forgiving. She needed the ruse for protection."

"From her father, I heard. Dear me, I can't even imagine. She must have been scared out of her wits!" Mrs. Keyes clucked her tongue even as she wrung her hands, clearly agitated.

"She had a few champions," he reminded Mrs. Keyes.

"Yes, yes, she did. I'm going to offer her a proper apology, but I wanted to see if you'd be wishing for tea or to break your fast? I realize it's early, but the whole house is up already with the ruckus." Her gray brows drew together in a bit of a disapproving frown.

"Aye, it would be a good idea, I'd imagine." Heathcliff glanced to Lucas, then back to Mrs. Keyes. "And tell Cook that we've guests for the morning meal. Lord and Lady Heightfield will probably be in residence most of the day, I'd imagine."

Mrs. Keyes nodded. "Of course, my lord. I'll tell Cook straightaway. And when I speak to Miss . . . Lady Samantha, is it?" She tilted her head questioningly.

At Heathcliff's nod, she continued. "I'll let her know as well. I'm assuming she's already aware of last night's events?"

"Technically, it was this morning's . . ." Heathcliff drawled, earning a disapproving glare from Mrs. Keyes. "But yes, she's aware, and I'm certain still awake. Probably hoping someone will rescue her from propriety and tell her the house is awake so she may quit her rooms."

Mrs. Keyes gave a glance down the hall. "Poor dear. I'll go directly." She gave a stiff curtsey and then darted down the hall in the direction of Miss . . . well, it was Lady Samantha's room, wasn't it?

Heathcliff closed the door and gave his head a wry shake. It was easier if he just referred to her by Christian name, rather than her title. Soon enough, she would be his wife, and formalities would be unnecessary.

He anticipated that with acute ferocity.

"That's a disturbing expression on your face," Lucas broke into his thoughts.

Heathcliff glanced at his friend, reading the guarded expression on his face. "Is it now?" He grinned wolfishly.

"It was . . ." Lucas drawled out. "Now I recognize it." He gave his head a little shake. "Go easy on the girl, will you?" Lucas said warningly. "Sexual tension can be quite powerful, and while you weren't exactly the monk I was—"

Heathcliff snorted.

"I'm ignoring that," Lucas replied flippantly. "It will be best for you, and for her, if you take things slowly."

Heathcliff's grin sobered. "I understand." And he truly

did. He wasn't some animal in rut, but he also knew he was already experiencing delicious anticipation for when he'd have the delight of living out several of his nighttime fantasies.

"You're wearing that expression again. It makes me bloody uncomfortable." Lucas sighed.

"You were an utter cake when you were in denial over your wife, so forgive me if I'm actually delighting in the idea of being married. Words I never thought I'd utter." He shook his head astoundingly.

"I know how it feels." Lucas gave a knowing grin. "But it pleases me that you've come full circle. If you love her half as much as you are distracted by her, you'll have a good marriage indeed."

Heathcliff nodded distractedly. It was a solid point, and he hadn't quite considered that aspect of love. Was he in love with her? He wasn't sure; he honestly didn't know what love felt like. He'd imagined himself in love long ago, but it clearly had not been love. Would he know the feeling when or if it happened? He wasn't sure.

"We should assemble in the parlor downstairs. My wife will be arriving shortly, if she isn't already here." Lucas stood, twisting his neck. "I'm sure she will have much to say to me."

"Scold you, you mean," Heathcliff added helpfully.

Lucas arched a brow. "Your time will come soon enough." He headed toward the door and placed his hand on the handle, pausing. "Just in case you were wondering, I'm glad it's you."

Heathcliff adjusted his shirtsleeves and tugged on them. "Oh?"

"Yes." Lucas gave a curt nod. "After all, she's wanted

it to be you all along. And I think the feeling is more than mutual, is it not? That's far more than most couples start out with."

Heathcliff's heart soared at the implication that Lady Samantha had wanted him, had wanted to choose him all along. It was a desperate type of hope, the kind that he wasn't sure was utterly true; it was simply too good, too lofty. Heathcliff didn't trust himself to respond and not make a cake of himself, so he just nodded.

"Don't screw it up," Lucas finished, then left.

Chapter Twenty-five

Samantha Durary. She whispered her name out loud and sighed with the rightness that washed over her. It was strange, really; it was only a name, yet it had felt like a weight around her had just been lifted. She hadn't realized how much of her identity was wrapped up in her name, in how others saw her. When it was taken away—rather, exchanged for a different one—she had felt bereft, lost, and insecure in who she was. It didn't make sense because she hadn't changed, just what others called her. But it had seemed like more.

And now, now she was free. Her name felt like the softest, most comfortable day dress, the kind that fits perfectly and is exactly the perfect shade of blue that highlighted her skin. Calling herself Miss Miranda had felt like wearing itchy wool, in the wrong shade of pink and poorly fitting to boot. There was no other way to describe it. From now on, she would simply be Samantha, well, Lady Samantha if one had to be utterly correct.

Mrs. Keyes had been a dear, apologizing profusely when she'd knocked on her door a few minutes earlier. Samantha had accepted her unnecessary apology quickly, assuring her it was nothing of consequence, but the poor housekeeper was scandalized by her mistreatment of a gently bred lady.

Samantha had tried to keep her smile in check because she was the one soothing Mrs. Keyes's ruffled feathers, not the other way around.

And when Mrs. Keyes had left to alert Cook about seeing to the morning meal, Samantha had closed her door, allowing her thoughts to flit back to earlier.

She was betrothed.

She didn't feel differently, at least about the betrothal part. Yet something monumental had altered in her life. She was to be married, and knowing Heathcliff, it was probably going to be soon.

Which was perfectly acceptable.

It was perfectly perfect. She couldn't think of a more apt word. *Perfect.* Now, if only she could be convinced it was more than just necessity and a healthy dose of attraction that was leading them down the aisle. Was it wrong to want more? Yet she didn't exactly have a choice.

But it would be nice for it to exist regardless.

A knock sounded on her door and she opened it, not having moved away from it when Mrs. Keyes had gone.

"Oh!"

Her sister gave a little jump, then pulled her into a tight hug. "Were you directly behind the door? Never mind, I'm so happy to see you! What in heaven's name is going on?" Liliah asked, releasing her and frowning with concern. "Lucas is in the parlor with the viscount, I'm to take you there, but I only just arrived myself, and neither of those beasts have told me a farthing's worth of news."

Samantha gave her head a little shake. "That doesn't surprise me. Let's go, and I'll give you the shortened version on our way."

Samantha watched as Liliah's mouth popped open as she started to relay the story to her sister. When they approached the parlor, she finished with the fact that she and the viscount were betrothed.

"Well, that was certainly an eventful night." Liliah blinked, then walked into the parlor.

"Ah, Wife." Lucas stood and opened his arms.

"Ah, Husband, who will be sleeping alone." Liliah glared, then made a wide arc around the room and took a seat far away from her husband.

Heathcliff's snicker pulled Samantha's attention away from her sister. His amusement was a warm sound, and it echoed in his expression, drawing her in, causing her belly to do odd flips of attraction as she soaked up the sound.

Heathcliff's gaze met hers, and he gestured to the seat beside him, inviting her.

How often had she wished for him to give her any real indication of his affection? It was so much the opposite from what she had expected. He would kiss her, caress her, speak kindly to her—but only in those stolen moments. All the other times, when he could be tender or attentive, he would alienate himself. Yet, finally, blessedly, it seemed that the man he was in those private, stolen moments, was the same man all those other times. She wondered if maybe he had been that man all along, but had some misguided sense of propriety . . . though she never thought him as one who followed any social protocol.

Men, she decided, made no sense.

"I'd stop laughing." Lucas cast the words toward his friend, and Heathcliff sobered the tiniest bit.

Samantha glanced at her sister, who was shooting daggers with her angry eyes toward her husband. "Liliah?" she asked, curious. The earl must have done something nearly unforgivable to earn such a response from his usually quite amorous wife.

"I do believe my husband should explain what happened, and I'm also quite certain part of that explanation will have a very humble apology," Liliah remarked, arching a brow.

Heathcliff coughed, trying to cover up a chuckle.

Samantha slowly sat beside him, her heart pounding with a nervous pleasure. As she placed her hands demurely in her lap, she cast a sidelong look at Heathcliff, her betrothed. His warm gaze met hers, and he reached out and placed a warm hand over hers. The heat seeped through her, warming her hands, then her arms, and then spreading through her chest, causing her heart to increase its pace before slowing into a comforting rhythm.

For a moment, she felt quite treasured.

It was a lovely feeling.

When he didn't remove his hand, she slowly relaxed, and then turned her gaze to her brother-in-law, who was clearing his throat.

"I was under the impression time was of the essence."

"Never did I hear anything about time from your valet, only that there was a missive—"

"In the bloody dead of night." He paused. "Forgive me."

"For what?" Liliah asked, tilting her chin.

"The vulgar choice of words, but also for not waiting for you to accompany me." He spoke with a contrite tone.

Samantha couldn't quite decide if he was being utterly honest. He sounded repentant, and he certainly looked it, but it was a little too quickly requested, the apology.

"Why, Sister . . ." Liliah turned to Samantha. "Do I feel as if this is a situation where the quote, 'It is better to ask forgiveness than permission' is quite apt?"

Samantha lifted her gloved hand and hid a grin. "I hardly think your husband needs your permission for anything, Liliah."

Liliah sighed. "I suppose you're correct."

"But I do understand what you mean. And I do think it's appropriate," Samantha finished.

Liliah turned a triumphant smile to her husband.

Lucas sighed, then turned his attention to Heathcliff. "I hope you know what you are getting in to. She is a copy of her sister in many ways."

"Of that I'm quite aware," Heathcliff made by way of response.

"I take that as a compliment," Samantha chimed in, grinning widely. Growing up, how often had she imagined that she and her sister would marry men who not only tolerated each other, but were friends? She imagined the parties they could have, and Michaelmas, and all the holidays they could enjoy as a beloved extended family, something she never had experienced growing up but had seen in other families in the ton.

It wasn't common, it was extraordinary, and she'd dreamed about such a blessing in her own life.

It looked as if the fates had heard her silent prayers and given her what she'd almost not dared to ask for.

"That's a lovely smile. A bit wistful, however," Heathcliff murmured softly, for her ears only.

She turned to him, offering a small smile. "Just musing. Happy thoughts."

He gave a slight nod. "It's been quite an eventful morning."

She met his gaze, wondering how much of her heart she should reveal.

Nothing ventured, nothing gained.

"But a good morning, in many ways," she allowed. Let him take that however he wished.

He studied her, his eyes deep and rich. "On that we are in agreement."

Samantha felt a smile start in her heart, then travel to her lips as they spread into a grin.

"Now, if we can simply get those two to make up." He arched a brow and glanced in her sister's direction.

"I'm not worried." Samantha followed his gaze, noting the small smile on her sister's face. All would be forgiven soon.

Movement by the door had Samatha glancing away from her sister. Mrs. Keyes walked into the room, followed by Miss Iris. Poor Iris! Samantha watched as her gaze moved around the room and then landed on her, as if asking for reassurance that everything was all right. Heaven only knew what she thought of all the commotion of the morning. Why, Samantha had heard so many sets of footsteps in the hall earlier, it was a wonder Iris was just emerging now. The house had seemed alive with all the activity. Even though it was clear the servants were trying to be discreet, it was still uncommon, and disconcerting.

Samantha nodded warmly, then stood. She was still Iris's governess, was she not? She hadn't resigned her position, nor had she any intention of leaving Iris to fend for herself, not that Heathcliff would allow that either, but still. Samantha had a responsibility, and she took her responsibilities very seriously.

"Come, Iris. It has been a full and early morning. I expect we all are in need of some tea and breakfast before we can do anything further about it."

"Well said," Miss Keyes asserted. "Speaking of which, Cook has set out everything necessary to break your fast." Mrs. Keyes bowed her gray head respectfully, then gestured toward the hall.

Samantha noted how Lucas stood, then tugged on his coat. His gaze went to Liliah, and he offered his elbow and arched a brow questioningly.

Liliah's lips pursed, but she placed her hand on his arm, then straightened her spine and followed him to the door.

Samantha bit back a grin, then cast her gaze toward Heathcliff.

His eyes were amused, and he arched a brow as he turned to her, offering his arm.

Samantha gave an accepting smile and waited for him to approach, knowing Iris was certainly putting two and two together at that gesture.

He offered his arm, his shoulders impossibly broad and his frame making her, not for the first time, seem delicate and small as she reached out and placed her hand on his sleeve. Such a sense of rightness, of home, washed over her. She glanced up, watching as Iris's eyes darted from the viscount, to her, to their arms, then back to Samantha. Her expression was a perfect question mark, eyebrows slightly raised, her lips in an O, just the right amount of confusion in her gaze.

"I'll explain later," Samantha said softly.

Heathcliff paused, and she looked up to see him raise a knowing brow.

Samantha bumped him just a little with her elbow, earning a wide grin.

"Is that the way of it, then?" he asked, leading them toward the hall.

Samantha replied archly, "Would you expect any less?"

"No. Nor would I wish it," he murmured, making her feel warm and soft inside. Who knew that words could hold such power?

The sideboard was loaded with a feast for breaking their fast. The cook at Kilmarin had always set a generous table, but it was as if this morning was an attempt to test the integrity of the table's ability to hold weight. Rashers of bacon were piled high on several white plates, and thick, fat sausage links had been fried to a golden plumpness, rising in pyramids on other platters. The coddled eggs were steaming hot, as were several slices of ham, a nice brown crust over the outside from being pan fried.

Samantha hadn't realized how hungry she was, and she was quite certain the others were as well as their breakfast party descended upon the spread like locusts. This was one time she wasn't about to offer insight or correction on a meal. Part of wisdom was knowing when and where it should be used.

And amongst the hungry and emotionally charged was not the time or place.

The gentlemen allowed the ladies to travel through the line first, and Samantha bit back a grin when Liliah selected one piece of toast, then another, and then muttered something under her breath and applied a thick layer of strawberry jam to each.

Samantha followed her sister's example and anticipated the delights of breakfast as she filled her plate and then took a seat at the table.

The men's plates were loaded down with the weight of the food they'd selected. Samantha expected Heathcliff was probably hungry in the same way a bear is after hibernation. He'd had quite the evening, and fisticuffs no less.

Their breakfast party was silent, with no one offering any anecdotes to launch conversations, simply a few groans of appreciation and the rustling of napkins being used.

Mrs. Keyes soon served tea, and Samantha inhaled the rich steam with great appreciation.

Mrs. Keyes glanced over to the sideboard, and Samantha noted the way her eyes widened with astonishment, but she didn't offer any remark.

After several minutes, Samantha glanced at Iris, who was watching as she politely ate her food, exceeding all the others in her manners.

It was quite monumental, Samantha decided. It was always rewarding when a teacher saw her lessons bear fruit in her pupil.

Samantha licked the corner of her mouth, tasting a sweet, tart hint of jam.

Iris was certainly surpassing *her* at the moment in manners.

It was amusing, and Samantha let out a little chuckle.

Heathcliff's gaze darted up, and he arched a brow, then glanced around the table. His grin widened. "We do appear to be a pack of wolves, do we not?"

Iris giggled behind her napkin. "A bit."

Samantha shared a knowing smile with Heathcliff, then turned to her sister.

"Pardon?"

At her sister's obliviousness, Samantha giggled louder. It felt so delightful to release the tension and simply laugh.

Heathcliff joined her in amusement, and soon Lucas joined in.

This had to be a promising sign for the future, didn't it?

Tomorrow would come with problems of its own.

But today, now, in this moment, they could laugh, they could let their worries go, they could simply be.

That would be enough. She'd make sure of it.

Chapter Twenty-six

Heathcliff didn't wish to have a grand wedding. Hell, he hadn't even been planning on marrying ever again. Yet, as he listened to the women discussing his upcoming nuptials, he wondered if perhaps Samantha had other wishes, bigger dreams, and maybe he was falling terribly short.

Didn't most women dream about their wedding? And women of the ton dreamed about fashionable weddings at St. George's, with all the frills and decadence London had to offer. They would include a wedding breakfast that was a generous sampling of the deep pockets of the parents, along with a heavily attended wedding, where everyone of note appeared. Not to mention banns being read weeks before, along with an announcement in *The Times*, leading to the gossip surrounding whether it was a good or poor alliance. In short, it was all about the attention.

And here in Scotland, Samantha would get none of that.

Hell, in Scotland, you could get married over any blacksmith's anvil.

It was why scandalous marriages were all known to take place in Gretna Green. No marriage license, no approval, just a willing man and woman and some smithy wanting to make a few extra pounds. While it wasn't socially acceptable, it was still a binding marriage.

And, he supposed, that was the important bit, but he still felt a slight uneasiness.

Samantha was a lady, a proper and gently bred lady— and he felt as if he was behaving like a villain in a gothic novel.

Damn, he hated that feeling.

Not that it wasn't true. It was closer to the truth than he was willing to admit. But that didn't mean he had to like it.

"You're oddly silent," Lucas said softly to him while the ladies continued discussing their plans.

Heathcliff turned to him. "It seems quite anticlimactic."

"That's for you to remedy later." Lucas arched a wicked brow.

"You're such an arrogant pain in the arse," Heathcliff bit out.

"Yes. I've learned from the best. Now, what's got you acting like a caged tiger? You're marrying the woman you're quite besotted with; don't tell me you're angry about marrying. You're the one who bloody suggested it. Honestly, I'm almost proud you succeeded in pulling your head from your arse in time."

Heathcliff gave him a frustrated look. "Oddly, I'm not resentful about entering into marriage. It doesn't make a pint of sense, but I'm not going to worry over much. I'm just feeling like an ass because she is getting a rather ramshackle wedding."

Lucas blinked, then tilted his head slightly. He breathed in, paused, then glanced away. "Is that so? You're worried she's unhappy with the lack of pomp?"

Heathcliff gave a curt nod.

Lucas looked back to him. "Does she bloody well look upset?"

Heathcliff turned to watch Samantha's expression. She was speaking with Mrs. Keyes, her movements wide and enthusiastic, a sharp contrast to the way she was normally, so self-aware and controlled. She appeared . . . happy, excited even. It didn't make sense.

"You're confused," Lucas stated.

Heathcliff turned to him, his mind offering several remarks of the more vulgar nature.

"Welcome to the club, my friend."

"That doesn't sound encouraging."

"My wife confounds me on a regular basis. You remember, do you not? When we were first . . ." He paused.

Heathcliff grinned. Because what Lady Liliah and Lucas's beginning of the relationship entailed wasn't exactly proper behavior, nor was it something that should be mentioned out loud.

"I was going to say courting—"

Heathcliff snickered.

Lucas glared. "Getting to know each other."

"Is that what we're calling it now?" Heathcliff asked with an air of superiority.

"Go to hell," Lucas bit out, but without heat. "What I'm trying to stay to your dim-witted self is that I never was able to understand what was going on in that astonishing mind of hers. It vexed me, tortured me, drove me mad, and utterly captivated me at the same time. It is very much the same way, being married to her. But I'd not change a thing. And you'll soon discover that Samantha will both drive you mad and drive you to your knees because who she is will both humble you, vex you, and astonish you. And I look forward to watching."

Heathcliff glanced at Samantha, replaying Lucas's words and tasting the truth in them. "'Misery loves company' and all?" Heathcliff remarked after a moment.

"Something like that," Lucas finished.

"Then you're saying I shouldn't worry?"

Lucas chuckled. "I'm saying that worry means you care, and that, my friend, will take you, and her, far."

Heathcliff nodded, taking a deep breath.

"What do you think?" Liliah turned to him, her light brows raised in question.

"Of?" he asked, utterly at a loss as to what they'd been discussing.

"Of the party. If you're to have such a small affair for the wedding—" She spoke with a little air of frustration.

Lucas cut in. "May I add that we had quite a small affair for a wedding too, my dear. You offered no complaint." He grinned wildly; it was an expression of victory.

Liliah pursed her lips, then her mien seemed forced as her eyes glowed with an amused expression that finally caused her smile to break free. "Very well. You have a point. But what I'm saying is that if the masquerade is to be the event we wish it to be, the event that brings word all over Scotland and back to London—" she said meaningfully, "we are going to need your help. Which means giving us your opinion."

"I do believe they just asked us for insight," Lucas said in an astonished tone.

Heathcliff turned to him, nodding. "Miracles do happen."

"You're impossible," Liliah ground out. "But unfortunately, we need you. As much as I'm loathe to admit it, you're much better at throwing a . . . noteworthy event."

"We do have experience."

"Years of it," Heathcliff added.

"I know," Liliah said through clenched teeth, her patience running thin if her expression were any indication.

"So, the invitations are sent, the décor is set, the food is established, but what we need is the something that makes a party the event of the Season. Do you know what I mean? The little something extra, maybe even scandalous."

"And being the proper lady, you don't know what that is?" Lucas added, his smile wide.

"No," she bit out the word.

Lucas leaned forward, his countenance secretive and devilish. Heathcliff knew what he was thinking; it was the same thing they'd often discussed when creating events.

"Secrets."

Heathcliff grinned, fully expecting the confused expressions he found on the ladies' faces.

Lucas continued. "You spread the word that there is some secret, some deep and startling undisclosed piece of news, and you tell the servants, who tell other servants. You let the rumor mill do the work for you. Because if there's something that no one can resist, it's scandal. If you have gossip and knowledge, you have power. And we have the perfect bait."

Liliah and Samantha blinked, an owl-like movement. Even Mrs. Keyes appeared lost.

"Why, Lady Samantha, you've escaped His Grace, the Duke of Chatterwood. You ran off to Scotland, hiding away as a governess only to marry your employer. The only thing people love more than good gossip? A good romance. And we, ladies, have both."

Heathcliff chuckled as understanding dawned on Liliah's face. Samantha's expression was thoughtful, reflective. "I had never thought of it that way."

"How so?" Heathcliff asked.

"Escaping. I rather think I did, didn't I?" A small smile grew into a larger, more confident one.

"You did." Liliah reached out and placed her hand on her sister's.

Heathcliff's gaze darted between the two sisters, both so alike yet unique in so many ways. Liliah was all energy, with light hair and sparkling green eyes. But Samantha 's eyes were soulful, aware and provoking. They disconcerted him with how much they saw, as if she were able to see past pretense and emotional barriers. Where her sister was light featured, Samantha had darker coloring, yet their smiles—they were almost identical.

"I suggest we start the gossip today, allowing the word to have time to spread. The masquerade is in two days?" Lucas paused, then nodded to himself, as if confirming something internally. "Ideally, I'd like more time to get a buzz going, but it will have to do, I suppose."

"Which means your wedding should happen tomorrow, as we discussed." Liliah turned to her sister, as if confirming that she agreed with the assessment.

Heathcliff watched as she gave a slow nod. Was she questioning her decision? His heart froze inside him, reminding him of just how much he wanted this forbidden fruit.

He needed to have a moment with her, to simply—hell, he wanted assurance that she wouldn't leave him at the altar. It would be poetic justice of a sort. He'd been avoiding her so unforgivably, yet now that what he wanted was just within reach, he had an irrational fear that it would be somehow snatched away, or truer still, that she'd run in the opposite direction from him once she realized just what she had agreed to.

He needed to steal her away; that was all there was to it. Certainly betrothed couples were allowed a measure of privacy? It had been long since his disastrous marriage, and he'd blocked so much of it from his memory that he didn't trust his recollections on protocol. He'd never thought he'd need to revisit that aspect of social convention. Samantha arched her back slightly, giving a delicate stretch as she continued speaking with her sister and Mrs. Keyes. The movement gave Heathcliff a delightful view of her form, and, not for the first time, his mind wandered to the way her body would appear without the dress, in the candlelight of his room—her hair splayed on his pillow, her lips wet from his kiss.

He took a long breath and glanced way. This wasn't the time or place to allow his fevered fantasies to spin out of control. Thank the Good Lord he'd have time to play each one out . . . and soon.

But soon was most certainly not right now in the parlor.

Pity that.

But he could at least taste her lips should they have a moment alone, and that, he decided, was the most important goal of the day.

Not planning the wedding.

Not spreading gossip.

But kissing Samantha.

It wasn't the most noble of endeavors, but it was most assuredly paramount.

And his patience was wearing thin.

Even though he reminded himself that they would have the rest of their lives together, there was something hot and needy in him. Something impatient and urgent. Maybe it was that irrational fear that she would realize the full magnitude of her decision to marry him and run in the opposite direction, but regardless, it made him damned impulsive.

So, without preamble, he stood from his place on the sofa and tugged his coat into place. His movements caused the conversation to grind to a halt, and he felt the gaze of every person upon him.

"Lady Samantha, a word?" He arched a brow and stepped toward her. Her chin tilted ever so slightly, her eyes flashing with curiosity, and then a twinge of amusement as she rose, her hands instinctively smoothing down the front of her blue skirts.

"Have I a choice?" she asked with a bit of an impish tone. He glanced to her, noting the heightened color of her cheeks, the almost bashful smile teasing her full lips.

"Do you wish for one?" he asked, the words having two meanings, at least for him. He watched her, considering the way she angled her head just slightly to give her a better look at his expression. She paused but a moment, and in that moment, his heart stuttered with that same fear that was becoming so familiar now.

"No," she answered. It was such a simple word. But it carried far and wide to soothing his shameful insecurities. Perhaps it was because his first wife had fooled him so perfectly, he didn't trust his instincts. Hell, that was an understatement. *He* hadn't trusted his instincts concerning women for a long while. It was difficult to put any confidence in his ability to understand Samantha, but he wanted to.

How desperately he wanted to, and to be able to trust those instincts.

To be able to trust *her.*

It was almost too much to ask, too lofty to imagine.

But when had love ever been rational?

And if he were honest with himself, this was, at least, the beginning of love.

Which terrified him.

Because when you loved someone, they could hurt you far more than any other.

He wasn't sure he'd survive such a blow from Samantha's hand.

Rather, he wasn't sure he'd want to survive.

As she placed her hand in his, he led them to the door. Silence followed them, as he was quite certain every eye followed their departure from the room.

After all, they were just discussing their upcoming wedding, and the bride and groom had quit the conversation and the room.

But he wasn't sorry for such an interruption. There were far more important things to accomplish today.

And the most important accomplishment would start with a kiss.

Chapter Twenty-seven

Samantha bit the inside of her lip as she followed her fiancé into the hall. A few candles flickered in the now daylight, surely a leftover aid from their eventful night. It was clear Heathcliff had something quite singular on his mind, or at least she suspected as much, but his silence had let her know he wasn't quite ready to disclose his reason.

So, she followed him down the hall toward the foyer. Sothers noted their approach, nodded his head, and opened the door without as much as a word. Heathcliff gave a curt nod in thanks and escorted her into the morning sunshine.

It was a lovely Scottish summer day. The sun was arching over the eastern sky, and somewhere a rooster crowed belatedly in welcome of the sunrise. Hazarding a glance at Heathcliff, she noted he was frowning slightly, as if concentrating on some invisible dilemma.

"Penny for your thoughts?" she said by way of conversation.

He glanced at her. "They aren't worth that much," he teased.

"Let me be the judge of that," she replied.

He gave a low, deep chuckle and led them around the gravel of the semicircular drive of Kilmarin. Samantha tried to convince herself to be at ease; certainly there was no reason to be concerned. Yet her fears, irrational beasts that they were, hinted at several problems, and she found herself growing more impatient to discover Heathcliff's intention in whisking her away from the parlor.

Before she could ask anything, Heathcliff released her hand and walked over to a stone fence that divided the drive from the road that led to the main gate. He leaned his forearms on the fence, resting his weight on it. Folding his hands, he breathed deeply and turned to her. His expression open, unguarded, not at all what she was expecting.

"It's odd to have such a lovely day after such a hellish night," he said, his tone reflective.

Samantha let out a sigh that alleviated some of her tension and walked up beside him. She stretched out her arms and allowed her fingers to bump along the stone of the fence. "I've found that such things usually are that way. They always say dawn comes after the night, and I think that's quite accurate."

"Indeed."

She opened her mouth, closed it, then turned to him. He met her gaze, his brows furrowing for a moment before his eyes lightened with understanding. "You're wondering why I stole you away."

She shrugged, able to be slightly less desperate now that he'd introduced the topic. "The question has crossed my mind."

He gave a twitch of a grin. "Something you said earlier this morning has been simmering in the back of my mind," he started, his expression sobering.

"Oh? I said a great many things this morning."

"That is also quite true. But you mentioned that at every turn, your freedom to make a choice had been thwarted. That, I think, is a very apt statement. And I find I'm quite guilty of putting you in that very same position, even just this morning."

He grimaced, as if the words he said weren't actually the ones he had planned to say. She regarded him. He was such a contradiction. She'd seen him overconfident and charming and revered by others. She'd also discovered an insecurity that lurked deep within, the kind that few would ever notice unless they looked deep, unless they cared.

She cared.

And it humbled and astonished her to discover he could have such a chink in his otherwise impenetrable armor.

"Yes, I did say that this morning," she affirmed. "But I wasn't saying it in response to the betrothal. Well, I was, but not in the way you're likely to assume," she amended.

He turned to her, his expression unreadable. "How so?"

She bit her lip, thinking. Instinctively, she knew it was of the utmost importance that she explain herself well, or else she could tap that Achilles's heel of his and shatter what they'd begun to build.

But to do so meant she would have to take off her own emotional armor, and that was, in a word, terrifying.

Because what if he didn't return the strength of her

regard? What if he was flattered, but nothing more? She didn't think his attachment was so fickle that he'd disregard hers, but she wasn't sure either. It was a quandary.

One that she had very little chance of avoiding. So, with a resolve that was more determination than courage, she continued.

"I, that is . . ." she started quite inarticulately. "Because my father most assuredly has the intention of coming to collect me from Scotland, soothing his damaged pride, you have little choice. Your friendship with Lord Heightfield is very strong, and I am his family." She breathed out a tense sigh, casting her gaze to the gray stones of the fence and directing her words to them, rather than Heathcliff. "And it is difficult, because I can understand and even appreciate how you would remedy the situation I find myself in by marrying me. But that marriage isn't necessarily based on your attachment to me. And I rather . . . that is, I wished your choosing to marry me was based on something more than a lack of other ways to save me." She sighed, then continued. "It always feels as if someone has to save me. Never once have I been given the chance to save myself. Just once, I wish I could be the hero of my own life, but each time I find that eludes me. It's quite frustrating. And that is why I said what I did this morning. I hate that there is a possibility that, because I can't save myself, you're having to play the hero, regardless of your inclination to do so for any other reason than your friendship with Lord Heightfield." She huffed the last sentence, her emotions running away with her words. It was a moment before she could collect herself and look up to meet his gaze.

His breath was measured, his gaze searching hers.

"So, you don't resent my taking away your choice; you simply wish I would have chosen you for another reason?" he asked.

Samantha nodded once, her heart pounding hard as she awaited his response to such a revelatory truth.

He glanced down at the fence, shaking his head and giving off what sounded dangerously like a scoffing sound.

Samantha wasn't sure how to interpret such a response, so she waited.

He glanced up at her, pushed off from his position against the stone wall, and reached out to take her hand. His touch was warm, comforting, and immediately soothed her. She expected him to say something, but his lips didn't part. Rather, he lifted his other hand and smoothed his thumb across her lower lip, caressing it. His hand traveled down her jaw to her neck, then back up as he cupped her cheek, his thumb drawing a lazy circle she felt vibrate through her entire body. Her lips parted to ask a question, but he stole the words from her much as he stole her breath as his lips captured hers. His hand at her cheek trailed down to her neck, and he gently pulled her in closer while his wicked tongue caressed her lower lip, making her lose all train of thought. His other arm encircled her waist, pulling her into his body tightly as his lips continued to make love to her mouth, teasing, tempting, devouring. She cared not that anyone could look from the Kilmarin windows and see their display of affection.

She cared not that people passing on the main road could look past the gate and see their romantic embrace.

All that existed in her world was the warmth of his

arms, the feverish intensity of his kiss, and the insistent need inside her that demanded more.

He tasted her fully, swiping his tongue just past the barrier of her lips, dancing with her tongue before retreating, only to perform the erotic dance once more. She leaned into his frame, her fingers tracing up his arms till they intertwined behind his neck, pulling him closer.

She didn't think he could ever be close enough.

Her fingers wandered up the back of his neck and were lost in the glory of his slightly curly hair, so irresistibly soft. His kiss intensified, and she wantonly pressed her lips into him, instinctively acting, though she hadn't a clue what it meant.

He let out a low groan and released her lips, pressing his forehead against hers while his breathing came in short gasps. "And this is why I took you out to the front of the estate."

It took a moment for the words to settle into her mind and make sense, but when they did, she simply asked, "Why?"

He kissed her, lingering at her lips before drawing away slowly. The moisture from his kiss made her lips cool as it evaporated on the morning breeze.

"Because if I had you inside, without a soul to interrupt us, you'd be in my bed already, and while I have many sins to answer for, I don't wish for that to be one of them. I'll bed you right and proper, but after you bear my name, lass." He spoke the words like a promise, like a vow, like an oath.

Samantha wondered why it was so bloody vital; she was quite of the mind that his bedroom wasn't too terribly far away. And they were to be married, quite soon as well. What could be the harm?

"You're an impatient one, aren't you?" Heathcliff asked with a slightly teasing tone. She leaned back and regarded him.

"Perhaps."

"And you're wondering why I'm being so honorable when, before I knew who you were, I was a little freer with my affection," he stated.

Samantha tilted her head and leaned back slightly. "The thought had crossed my mind." She arched a brow.

"Because the expectation was different."

Samantha frowned. That was not what she was expecting him to say, nor did it bode well after her earlier statement. If the expectation for a governess was less, than didn't that mean he *was* marrying her out of obligation, because she *wasn't* a governess?

"I can see you misunderstand me."

"This reading of minds is helpful, but later on I don't know if I'll find it as beneficial," she commented, adding a bit of a tease to her tone.

"You're quite easy to read; like a book, I'd say. But not always, only when you are impatient. When you're willing to take your time with something, you're practically unreadable. Quite frustrating, that. Especially when I pride myself on reading people quite well."

Samantha grinned. "I'm pleased to know I can still keep at least some of my thoughts a secret."

Heathcliff nodded. "Now, what I was saying was not that the expectation was different because you are a lady, and not to be dallied with, but . . ." He paused, thinking. His brow furrowed slightly, then he continued. "But you were far more attainable as a governess, perhaps you even needed me, or at least my protection or what it could afford. But as the daughter of a duke, you do not need me at all."

Samantha shook her head. "It would seem I need you very much," she replied meaningfully.

"Yes, but not in the same way. I wasn't worthy of you. I'm still not. But what I am is willing. And, blessedly, that is enough."

Samantha reached up and caressed his face, feeling the scruff of his beard through her glove. "When has that not been enough?"

"More often than you know," he answered.

She trailed her finger down his cheek and then traced the outline of his jaw. "I would wish for more than just a willing spirit, Heathcliff," she murmured, speaking his name for the first time out loud. Many times she had spoken it in her mind, but to hear it out loud was utterly delicious.

His eyes ignited as his gaze darted to her lips. "Say it again."

She frowned.

"My name; say it. I've always wanted to hear it on your lips." He kissed her quickly, then retreated, waiting.

"Heathcliff," she murmured softly, the word a litany on her lips.

He kissed her again, deeper, searchingly. When he pulled back enough to speak, he breathed her name.

Samantha.

How long had she waited to hear her name, her true name on his lips? It had been a delight to hear it earlier that morning, and its power hadn't weakened at all. A smile tipped her lips, and she reveled in the sound, the way his masculine voice caressed it.

There was something so deep, so searchingly beautiful about hearing your name on the lips of your beloved.

It might not be love yet . . . at least not for him. But as long as he said her name like a prayer, it would be enough until his heart caught up with his words.

Chapter Twenty-eight

Heathcliff strode into Kilmarin, whistling a tune and earning an amused grin from Sothers. After sliding a peevish glare at his longtime employee, Heathcliff ambled down the hall in search of his friend, who, he hoped, hadn't made himself *too* comfortable in his house. Just to be sure, when he reached the library, the place he had left Lucas along with his wife and the housekeeper, he knocked on the closed door and stepped back. He could only assume Mrs. Keyes had long vacated the room and, judging by the closed door, Lucas was doing exactly what Heathcliff suspected.

There was a curse from the inside of the room in a familiar voice, and Heathcliff bit back a grin. The devil take it, he was all but certain Lucas had taken liberties with his wife in the library. Damn the man. Not that he blamed him; hell, when Heathcliff had the pleasure of secreting Samantha in the library, he'd take the same liberties.

Though, hopefully not in the same location, he

thought belatedly, and made a mental note to have the servants scrub the library's horizontal surfaces quite thoroughly.

The door opened, and Lucas ran his hand through his rather tousled hair, giving his friend an irritated glare.

"Am I interrupting something?" Heathcliff asked, arching a brow with a knowing grin.

"Not any longer," Lucas bit out. "Come in." He opened the door wider, and Heathcliff gave a skeptical glance inside.

Lady Liliah was smoothing her skirt as she stood to welcome him.

Satisfied that all was in order, he turned to Lucas as he crossed the threshold of the library. "How kind of you to invite me into my own library."

"Lord knows it's about bloody time I turn the tables on you. How many times have I found you in my office, sipping my French brandy?"

"A few." Heathcliff shrugged, thinking that brandy sounded quite wonderful just then.

"More than a few, I'd wager," Lucas muttered.

"I wasn't exactly behaving badly in your study, however." He shot Lucas a pointed stare.

A delicate gasp came from Lady Liliah, and he flashed her an apologetic grin. For what he was apologizing, he wasn't sure. After all, they were the ones who had been behaving in a rather scandalous manner. However, he found himself in such a jolly mood that he was inclined to be more than gracious to the object of his affection's sister.

"Did you have some other reason for your presence other than to irritate and interrupt me?" Lucas asked with an unapologetic grin.

Heathcliff turned back to him. "Do I need another reason?"

Lucas paused. "No, but it would be nice. You were the one who disappeared a short while ago . . . Care to explain that?" he asked with a wicked grin.

"I do believe I'll go find my sister." Lady Liliah stood, then strode past her husband. Lucas reached out and grasped her arm gently, halting her progress. When she turned to him, an inquiring expression on her face, he lowered his head and kissed her sweetly on the forehead. Heathcliff noted the quick flush of color on Lady Liliah's cheeks before she gave her husband a warm smile, then, as he released her, she quit the room. She gave one longing look behind her, then disappeared into the hall, closing the door firmly behind her.

Lucas stared at the door for a moment, as if willing it to reopen and have his wife reenter. When that didn't occur, he turned to his friend. "You were saying?"

Heathcliff paused, reflecting on what exactly he *had* been saying.

Lucas must have noted his confusion. "Why you abandoned us."

"Ah." Heathcliff nodded, then walked to the window, which overlooked the back gardens. "It was a private matter."

"Of that I'm absolutely certain. But because there seems to be no privacy to be had this morning . . ." Lucas said meaningfully.

Heathcliff chuckled.

"You will forgive me if I press you for further details."

"If I must," Heathcliff answered. "I was affirming some of the details of my engagement to Lady Samantha," he answered vaguely.

Lucas didn't have a ready reply, but he moved to stand beside his friend. "Oh? And was your conversation fruitful?"

Heathcliff couldn't restrain the grin that broke out over his face at the reflection of the earlier conversation. "It was indeed."

When Lucas didn't offer any comment, Heathcliff turned to him, giving a questioning arch to his brow.

"It's bloody wonderful to see you in such a state. I swear, you're about to start spouting sonnets. I believe the sentiment you offered me, when I was in a similar state of mind, was of the more *Oh, how the mighty have fallen* variety," Lucas remarked significantly.

Heathcliff gave a frustrated groan. "How that has come back to roost."

"Indeed. And it is glorious. Never did I think I'd see the day when you'd fall," Lucas remarked.

"I do believe I said something of the same to you, not long ago."

"Yes, yes, you did. And I am taking no small pleasure in returning your words. It's quite vindicating," he answered with a smug smile.

"Bastard," Heathcliff said without heat.

Lucas chuckled. "I do believe I called you something of the same."

"We could do this all day."

"Yes, that happens when you have long-established friendship such as ours," Lucas offered, as if it were a helpful statement.

"And bloody annoying."

"That too," Lucas agreed. "But that aspect is lost on me at the moment. I'm having a jolly good time."

"At least one of us is."

"And I do believe Ramsey will have his say in this as well." Lucas strode away from the window and walked to the bellpull, ringing it. "I need more tea."

"Ramsey will certainly have words to say," Heathcliff agreed, his mind already spinning with what his friend would think and then say in response.

"Do you think you'll write to him and let him know?" Lucas asked, leaning against the wall in a rather relaxed pose.

Heathcliff considered Lucas's question. It was a valid one, and both aspects had promising points. "Hmm. Part of me takes a sadistic pleasure in waiting to tell him face-to-face . . ." Heathcliff paused, then continued. "But it is in the best interest of circulating the news of my marriage in letting him know. He will be able to artfully navigate the rumor mill on that end, helping our cause quite a bit."

"That's an outstanding point," Lucas agreed.

A maid walked into the room at that moment, giving a small curtsey. "How may I assist you, my lords?"

Lucas nodded to Heathcliff. He was somewhat surprised that his friend had actually deferred to him. They had always been on equal footing, but, now that he thought about it, it was his house after all. "Tea, Maye, if you please. And sandwiches as well. You may also check on the ladies to see if they would like refreshment as well."

"Of course, my lord." She bobbed another curtsey and left the room.

"Sandwiches, a capital idea," Lucas agreed. "It's nearly noon, is it not? Not quite teatime, but when you've been up at the ungodly hour I was, one can't be too particular about abiding by normal times for sustenance."

Heathcliff agreed, but couldn't help but add, "And when one hasn't slept at all, then certainly all times are a fluid thing."

Lucas nodded, then tilted his head, as if remembering an errant thought. "I've been meaning to ask, have you had any reports from Ramsey? Usually he is most thorough in his correspondence, and I haven't received any word from him. Of course, that may be his way of allowing me a honeymoon with Liliah."

Heathcliff shook his head. "No, I haven't, but when I left London, everything was quite sewn up. There shouldn't be any loose ends, and all seemed in order. I can't imagine he finds the need to notify us that all is well."

"Quite true," Lucas agreed.

"But if you're concerned, there is paper and ink over there on the desk. Feel free to send him an inquiry." Heathcliff shrugged.

Lucas's gaze darted to the desk and then back to Heathcliff. "Perhaps later. I do believe the most important order of business is telling him about your upcoming nuptials. It's bloody lucky you're in Scotland. Saves you all the trouble of blackmailing some sod at Doctors' Commons for a special license," Lucas said with a touch of resentment, maybe a little wistfulness in his tone.

"Ah, that's right. Who did you threaten who would dare risk the wrath of a duke, no less?"

"Trenton Hassel." Lucas flicked some lint from his sleeve.

Heathcliff nodded. "What did you offer to keep secret?"

"I forgave a substantial bet he'd foolishly placed. It was due the next week, but we both knew he had no way of paying it. Turns out, when money is involved, people fear debtors' prison more than the wrath of a duke."

"Brilliant."

"I rather thought so, and quite effective as well. It was a quick way to procure the special license."

"But the vicar?"

"It took a few pounds, but again, money can do much."

"Truly, I would have expected it to be harder," Heathcliff remarked.

"One would think." Lucas shrugged.

The food arrived, and Lucas took a seat beside the small table in the center of the library. The maid carefully uncovered several dishes, revealing a tray of cold meat sandwiches, a plate of biscuits, and not one but two pots of tea with the steam swirling around them in a most inviting manner.

"Would you care for me to fix you a plate?" the maid asked.

Lucas waved her off. "No, I'm quite self-sufficient."

When she turned to Heathcliff, he declined as well, preferring to serve himself. No longer needed, she bobbed a curtsey and left.

"Damn, I'm hungry," Lucas muttered, then took a large bite of a sandwich.

"Clearly." Heathcliff chuckled but understood the sentiment. His stomach had been rumbling as well. Breakfast seemed so long ago.

Heathcliff poured himself a cup of tea, then lifted the pot slightly higher, in a question aimed at his friend. He arched a brow as he waited for Lucas's answer.

"Yes, please. Thank you." Lucas held out his cup, and after Heathcliff poured Lucas's cup full, he set down the pot and selected a sandwich. The ham was cold and salty, the perfect match for the soft and slightly sweet bread. He savored the bite, then turned to his friend. "What did you speak of once we left?"

Lucas swallowed the last bit of his sandwich and held up a finger, indicating for his friend to wait. After a moment, he answered. "It was rather difficult to continue to plan a wedding with the bride and groom not present, so we moved on to the masquerade. I gave Mrs. Keyes strict instructions on notifying the servants. She wasn't too keen on the idea I set forth."

"Why?" Heathcliff asked, curious to know why his very accommodating housekeeper was suddenly reluctant.

"It may have been because I asked her to reveal it in a manner that looked as if she'd slipped up and mentioned something she should have kept a secret."

"Ah, that makes perfect sense. She's rather prideful on her tight-lipped household. She's been around me for far too long to let gossip flourish here. With so many of the rumors from London following me here, she's made it quite a career in stomping out whatever does, at least within Kilmarin. I quite appreciate it."

"Indeed. Such assistance is invaluable, but I was able to convince her that revealing the news in such a way would benefit you and Samantha. After that, she was quite willing to help."

"She's a godsend."

"She's a saint to have put up with you for so long," Lucas teased.

"I could say the same for your servants," Heathcliff remarked in return.

"True, true," Lucas agreed, then sipped his tea. "Regardless, that is the summary of events after your departure."

"Thank you. You're most helpful." Heathcliff gave a wry grin.

"You're still an arse."

"Don't see that changing much." Heathcliff shrugged.

"Pity, that," Lucas replied. "I take it, based on the profitability of your earlier conversation with Samantha, you are more than amenable to the haste of your nuptials."

"That's quite a way to put it." Heathcliff arched a brow. "So proper," he teased.

"One of us has to pretend to be the gentleman."

"Better you than I," Heathcliff answered. "But yes. After I finish my tea, I'll take my horse and go to speak to the local vicar. It shouldn't be too difficult to schedule the wedding tomorrow morning."

"I think I'll join you. I'm quite liable to fall asleep if I remain here in your quite comfortable library, and I'd much rather be active."

"If you wish," Heathcliff replied. "I'll have Mrs. Keyes notify the ladies. I'm sure they are making preparations of their own."

"A wedding in a day's notice? They are probably fluttering about like hummingbirds. It would be best for us to remain out of their way." Lucas gave a sharp nod.

"Agreed. Then it's settled." Heathcliff stood and went to ring the bell. Shortly, the maid appeared and was bid to fetch Mrs. Keyes. In no less than a quarter hour, the gentlemen were off to Edinburgh.

As the sunshine warmed Heathcliff's wool coat, he cast a glance back to Kilmarin, wondering just which room held Samantha. He smiled, because, in looking back, it was a way of looking in to his future. And for the first time in quite a long while, loneliness didn't follow him.

Hope, however, did.

Chapter Twenty-nine

The day had been feverish in its activity. The entirety of the afternoon had been spent planning, replanning, and then modifying said plans. Samantha finally understood why weddings took months to take place; the event itself was quite the undertaking and not to be done in a few hours' time.

But accomplishing the impossible seemed to be the order of the day, and they approached the dinner hour with not a small measure of success in planning the morning wedding.

As they gathered in the parlor while they awaited dinner, Heathcliff and Lucas brought the news that a vicar had been procured to officiate the service. Samantha couldn't help but admire Heathcliff's wind-teased hair. Her fingers burned with the memory of its texture, and her lips grew warm with desire for his kiss once more. And while, earlier, she had wondered why weddings took months to take place, she now, conversely, wondered how women waited so long to taste the passion of their husbands' embrace.

She thanked God that tonight was the last night she'd have to exercise patience and restraint. She'd tried to approach the topic of marital relations with her sister earlier, when they were alone. Her sister hadn't offered any insight. Rather, she'd given Samantha a secretive smile and told her that her heart would know what her body needed to do. As far as advice was concerned, Samantha found her sister's sorely lacking; she'd quite expected far more information. So, though she'd given her best effort, she still wasn't certain what would transpire in the marriage bed. However, she didn't fear it. Rather, she anticipated it wantonly. She blushed as her scandalous thoughts filtered through her mind and was quite thankful no one could suspect them.

Or so she thought. Heathcliff met her gaze, as if he knew what she was thinking, and gave a wicked grin that heated her very bones. Who knew that a look, a mere glance, could feel as intimate as a kiss? But it did, and she felt the power of his regard down to her toes.

Someone cleared their throat, and Samantha flicked her gaze away toward the noise. Lucas was grinning wildly, watching her with an amused expression. Heat flooded her cheeks once more and she looked down.

Sother came in then, to announce dinner. Heathcliff strode up beside her and offered his arm. She took it readily, and they proceeded from the parlor to the dining room.

"How was your afternoon?"

"Productive," she answered, collecting her wits. He was so very apt to scatter them with just a touch.

"Mine as well."

"So I've heard."

"I do believe I mentioned it," he remarked, smiling down at her.

As they walked into the dining room, he pulled out her chair and, when she sat down, scooted it into place. He then took the place beside her, at the head of the table.

The first course was served, and while Samantha took a sip of the beef and barley soup, she felt the slightest pressure on her foot. She paused, the soupspoon partway to her mouth, as the pressure disappeared. After taking the sip, she set her spoon back in her bowl, only to feel the pressure again, only this time it was more of a caress down the length of her slipper. Her gaze shot to Heathcliff, who was watching her with a bemused expression. The touch lingered up by her ankle and pulled the hem of her dress slightly away from it, giving the slightest draft on her lower leg.

He winked.

She gasped slightly.

"Is something the matter?" her sister asked, giving her a curious look.

"No, nothing. It was just . . . hot," Samantha answered, making a show of blowing on the soup on her spoon and then tentatively taking a sip.

A low chuckle rumbled from Heathcliff, just enough for her to hear and understand it.

Sure enough, a few moments later, his boot ever so gently brushed against her slipper, but this time she was prepared. Two could certainly play that game, and, she assumed, slippers would be far more agile at it than a boot. She withdrew her foot from his and, concentrating, edged her slipper forward till she came in contact with his boot. To keep up appearances, she took a

slow sip of the soup, and then as she put her spoon
back in her bowl, traced her slipper up the length of his
boot to the hem of his trousers, then caressed higher,
feeling the outline of his calf muscle against her toes.

The sound of metal hitting china startled her, and
she jumped in her chair, her foot withdrawing from his
person. She glanced in the direction of the noise, seeing Heathcliff muttering something quite ungentle-
manly as he wiped his shirt with a napkin. The spoon
that had dropped had been his and was sitting quite
awkwardly in his bowl. The sudden drop had sprayed
him with broth.

Samantha bit back a grin, then, when that failed,
tried to hold her laughter in check, attempting to cover
the noise with a delicate cough.

Heathcliff gave her a teasing glare, arching a brow
as if issuing a challenge. She replied in kind, enjoying
the dare.

"What am I missing?" Liliah asked, and Samantha
glanced to her sister, seated directly across from her.

"Don't ask, love," Lucas remarked helpfully, suddenly seemingly quite interested in his soup.

Liliah's eyes widened, then she gave a broad, knowing smile, and followed the example of her husband
and was quite captivated by her bowl of soup.

Samantha gave a delicate giggle and turned back to
Heathcliff. No sooner had their eyes met than she felt
the same pressure on her foot from his boot, only this
time he immediately slid up her ankle, then calf, pulling away her skirts.

She pulled away, deciding that part of the game
should be evasion.

He gave her a mock glare.

She gave a challenging grin.

His answering grin was predatory.

The footman interrupted their tête-à-tête, removing their soup bowls and giving them their second course. Samantha glanced at the roasted pheasant, steam swirling up to meet her with its heavenly fragrance. But even with the delicious food before her, her hunger was otherwise engaged in something quite different.

This time, she removed her slipper. Then, she moved her foot over, and when she came in contact with Heathcliff, she met his gaze. Brazenly, she traced her foot up his calf, her stockings doing little to hinder the intense feeling of his body against hers. She inched higher, watching as his eyes darkened, his breathing seeming to stop, and he watched her with the hungriest expression.

Her courage almost failed her as she inched higher, but she continued till her leg was fully outstretched, brushing against the outside of his thigh, feeling the heat radiating from him.

"I truly wish the pheasant would cool faster. It's blazing hot," Lucas said. It was a rather awkward statement, and Samantha tore her gaze away from Heathcliff, only to see that her brother-in-law wasn't looking at his food but at her, and with a quite pointed expression.

Properly chastised, she gave an apologetic smile, and turned to Heathcliff, who seemed utterly unrepentant.

Liliah, to her credit, kept her gaze downward, but a knowing smile was tipping her lips.

Samantha's gaze darted back to Heathcliff, and he met her regard with an amused expression of his own.

Dinner passed with less scandal than it had started, and soon the gentlemen stood, with Samantha and Liliah following suit.

"It's been quite an evening, and I think my wife and I will take our leave." Lucas approached his wife and gently placed his hand on the small of her back.

"Just an eventful evening?" Heathcliff asked, his tone wry.

"A gross understatement; my apologies." Lucas gave a nod.

Liliah moved from around the table to approach Samantha "I'll see you in the morning, bright and early. Get your rest, love." Then, in a softer tone, she added, "I'm certain you'll be needing it."

Samantha 's face heated at the implication, and bid her sister good night.

Lucas's carriage was ordered, and soon they were on their way.

Samantha watched the carriage roll away through the foyer window, then turned to the stairs. Though she had scarcely had a good night's sleep the night before, she was restless and not tired in the least. Heathcliff was waiting in the hall, and she turned to him, her lips bending into a grin as she noted the way he glanced to his study, then to the stairs, then to her. She couldn't resist teasing him. "Confused, my lord?"

He grinned. "With you, constantly."

"Unfair," she baited.

"Very fair, I believe." He approached her then, his eyes warm and his smile enticing. As he drew near, he whispered softly, "If you're not pretending to be a governess, you're seducing your employer under the dinner table. I nearly choked to death." He shook his head, scolding, though his eyes danced.

"I shall remember never to flirt with you again if it's such a danger to your health, my lord," she replied, but her voice didn't hold the teasing tone she'd had earlier. In such close proximity, she found herself breathless.

"I don't remember asking you to stop your flirtations. Nor was I complaining. I enjoyed them very much, and if they were a true danger to my health, I'd count it a worthy way to die."

"Quite the melodramatic statement," Samantha remarked, gazing into his eyes, losing herself in their depths.

"Quite a powerful flirtation."

"I thought you said it was a seduction," Samantha whispered, wishing his lips were closer, wishing they weren't in the foyer, but in a more secluded place.

"Flirtation and seduction are often found in each other's company," he answered, leaned forward as if to kiss her; then, just when she leaned in to meet him, he withdrew. "I think we've endured enough temptation for one day."

Samantha tried to think of an adequate reply, but her wits eluded her. All she could think of by way of a response was that temptation clearly had no real limit . . . at least in her perspective. She would have gladly continued to tease, taste, and tempt. Gladly.

"I'll see you in the morning." He gave her a curt nod, as if he were discussing an Act of Parliament, then bowed.

Samantha wasn't sure why his demeanor had so quickly changed, and she waited for an explanation. But rather than offer one, he turned on his heel and walked up the stairs in a very resolute manner.

That was not how she had hoped the evening would end. She waited a moment, to see if perhaps he would

change his mind, but when she heard a firm shutting of
a door, she gave up hope and walked up the stairs herself.

Maye was waiting for her in her chambers, with a
bath drawn. Samantha thanked the maid for her kindness, but her reply was that Mrs. Keyes had ordered it
as soon as dinner was finished.

Mrs. Keyes: Samantha would have to thank her. Not
only had she thought of this kindness, but she'd wisely
taken Iris to have a private supper earlier. That way, if
there needed to be further discussion on any sensitive
topics, they could speak freely at dinner. The woman
thought of every detail, and Samantha was intensely
grateful.

Soon she was slipping out of her day dress and stepping into the warm, lavish water of the bath. Lavender
floated in it, scenting the air. The water was just cooler
than hot, and her body seemed to melt into it as she im-
mersed herself in the luxurious warmth. Maye proceeded to unpin her hair, and the mass came down,
dipping into the water. Samantha adjusted her position
in the bath and leaned forward, allowing Maye to pour
a pitcher of water over her head. The warmth seeped
into her bones, and she began to feel the weariness of
too short a sleep the night before. In short work, her
hair was scrubbed with lavender soap and then rinsed.
It was peacefully quiet in her room, and she rested in
the bath for a few moments. The sound of boots striding down the hall had her opening her eyes and instinctively glancing to the door, but nothing came of
the noise, even though she swore she could hear the
footsteps pause just outside her door. She shifted in the
water, splashing a small amount onto the wood floor.

Maye quickly cleaned up the wayward water, and when Samantha glanced back toward the door, the sound was no longer near.

About a quarter hour later, she was ready for bed, sinking into the lavish comfort of the feather bed. Her eyelids were heavy and her heartbeat had slowed, but the last thought that entered her mind was the memory of her sister's words.

And she was quite certain she was correct in her assessment.

Tonight, she'd find her rest. For tomorrow, she was absolutely certain, there would be little sleep. And with that delightfully wicked thought, she smiled and drifted to sleep.

Chapter Thirty

Heathcliff bit his tongue to keep from swearing as he walked past Samantha's room on his way to the breakfast room. The memory of last night's ill-executed idea washed over him with new temptation. He'd be stalwart in his resolve to keep himself from her, from tempting himself to anticipate their marriage vows. It would be so easy; he knew it would only take two, maybe three kisses and a well-placed caress to encourage her to allow him more-than-generous liberties. He'd remained strong in his resolve till he'd walked into his room, and the memories flooded back from that morning. As far as proposals went, his wasn't the least bit romantic, but it was probably the most determined. But the outcome was exactly as he wished, and in a few short hours, she would be his. And those hours seemed quite the permeable and permissible barrier to pleasure, and one leniency led to another, till he found himself quite convinced it was a capital idea to, at the very least, kiss his soon-to-be wife good night.

So, with his less-than-honorable intentions, he'd strode down the hall, only to hear the softest splash coming from her room. She was bathing, and that knowledge allowed his imagination to spin in a myriad of delightful fantasies. He paused just outside her door, listening to the gentle stir of the water, knowing that her flesh would be slightly pink from the warm water, her cheeks rosy, her hair down and pooling at her shoulders . . . it was almost too beautiful to even picture. He heard a small gasp and wondered if maybe she suspected him, if perhaps she would call out to him. It was a far-fetched fantasy, but he waited, and before he could make a poor judgment, backed away and ran from the temptation. He shook his head, bringing his thoughts back to the present. The insistent rumble of his belly reminded him of his earlier intention of breaking his fast, and he continued on his way, casting a backward glance at Samantha 's door.

The irony of things wasn't lost on him. He took the stairs down, giving his head a slight shake. Samantha, had successfully escaped her father's control, and in so doing, had created a situation where Heathcliff was constantly trying to escape from the temptation she presented. It was oddly poetic and apt in representing his life.

For pity's sake, he was a partner in the Temptations club! Yet, as soon as Samantha had become part of his world, he'd been trying to resist the temptation she offered, when he'd made his livelihood telling men to give in to that very temptation.

Who said God didn't have a sense of humor?

He walked down the hall, his boots making a slight click against the tiled floor, and he veered left into the breakfast room. Cook had set out a smallish meal, and he was intensely grateful. Soon Lucas and Lady Liliah would arrive for the wedding breakfast, but that would be a little later in the morning, and he was quite certain he would be utterly distracted by the vision of his wife-to-be, and the anticipation of making her his, finally. He doubted he'd be inclined to partake of the feast Cook was surely preparing.

Unless Cook prepared treacle tart. He belatedly wished he had mentioned that to Mrs. Keyes. After all, it *was* his wedding breakfast; shouldn't his favorite treat be served? He lifted a plate and filled it with several pieces of toast and some jam before sitting down and reaching for the tea.

Shortly after breaking his fast, he noted the time and took the opportunity to write to Ramsey. The sooner the better, and if he posted the letter today, the news of his marriage would start to circulate in London. Samantha would be safer once the word had been established. He'd submit an announcement to *The Times* as well. Crossing every T and dotting every I, Ramsey would approve of his plan. His friend was the most thorough of the three, and quite detail orientated.

As Heathcliff quit the breakfast room to his study, he made a mental note to request that Ramsey take any liberties he felt helpful in spreading the news. An announcement in *The Times* was standard for any marriage, but perhaps there was some detail Heathcliff was missing, and Ramsey would surely remember it. It was quite helpful to have such a friend.

He withdrew a piece of paper from his desk and dipped his pen in the black ink. After dispatching a letter to Ramsey, Heathcliff's lips quirked into a grin, wishing he could have the added amusement of seeing his friend's face upon reading the news. Then, Heathcliff withdrew another sheet of paper, this one addressed to the editor of *The Times*. He didn't know the man personally, but the editor no doubt knew Heathcliff. It was always a boon when your reputation preceded you, and Heathcliff was certain the editor would be pleased to publish a bit of news before the ton was aware of it.

After calling for Sothers, and informing him to dispatch the missives, Heathcliff pulled out his watch and groaned.

He could begin to get himself ready, but it would be awfully early, and he found himself at odds as to how to proceed. He walked over to the window, his land stretching out before him in the morning sun. As they often did when he was in his study, his thoughts traveled to his father. A sad smile tipped Heathcliff's lips. His father would have liked Samantha. Hell, he would have loved her. It was tragic that he'd only known Margot, that traitorous wench. It was astounding, really, how one person could poison another so deeply. He was shocked that he'd even considered marriage after the wound dealt by his first go at matrimony. But that was a testament to Samantha, not necessarily his character. She made him . . . hope. Really, it was as simple as that: hope. It was something he'd pushed away, ignored and feared for so long, and to experience it was soothing, astounding, and powerful.

He sighed as his brows pinched. But just because he had hope didn't mean he didn't fear. Fear of failure, of not being enough, or not being able to love Samantha as she deserved. He thought of Lucas and Lady Liliah. It was clear they held a deep affection for each other. If he couldn't offer that depth of emotion to Samantha because of his brokenness, would she resent him? Could he endure that?

"Knock, knock." Lucas's familiar voice called out.

Heathcliff spun, half-startled by the interruption into his musings, and offered his friend a welcoming smile. "Too lazy to actually knock?"

"Yes. I'm still exhausted from yesterday." As if to prove his point, Lucas yawned.

"I can see." Heathcliff chuckled. "You're early."

"I thought I should be here for you, be supportive and whatnot." He dusted his nails on his jacket and then regarded his friend.

Heathcliff narrowed his eyes. "Your wife told you to say that."

Lucas nodded. "Yes, she did."

Heathcliff shook his head. "Taking orders from a skirt?"

Lucas gave him an expression that brokered no argument. "You will soon too, and there's no shame in it. I've learned my wife is often right. However, if you tell her, it will be pistols at dawn."

"You can't shoot to save your soul," Heathcliff replied.

"Rapiers it is."

Heathcliff winced. "I'll take pistols. That way I can do away with your irritating self far quicker."

"Afraid of a little blood?" Lucas teased.

"We're far too evenly matched, and our wives would have to nurse us back to health. Together, no doubt. It would be a fate worse than death."

"Hear, hear," Lucas agreed, then changed the subject as he took a seat opposite Heathcliff's desk. "Having any second thoughts?"

The question took Heathcliff by surprise, and he paused for a moment in confusion before saying, "About?"

"Samantha, you idiot."

"Oh, of course not." Heathcliff gave his friend an irritated glare. "Though she may be having second thoughts about me."

"You're far too hard on yourself. The girl clearly adores you, but why, I haven't a clue," he teased. "But to be honest, you're well matched, and she does have a deep regard for you, which is more than encouraging."

Heathcliff gave a thoughtful nod.

"And you care deeply for her, so what is there to be concerned about?"

"Not being enough." Heathcliff spoke the truth before he thought better of it. That was the rub when with a longtime friend; the walls that were usually fortified were nowhere to be seen.

"I thought we'd discussed this," Lucas said.

"That would imply I listened to you," Heathcliff responded, then took a seat on the edge of his desk.

"Blast it all. Very well, just try. And when you do fail—because you will, we all do—be a man about it and say you're sorry. And when she fails you—because she will—you forgive her. You don't hold it over her head like some medieval sword. You let it bloody go."

"A medieval sword?" Heathcliff asked. "That was the best metaphor you could think of?"

Lucas shot him a frustrated glare. "Is that the only part you heard?"

"No."

"Good answer. And it was a metaphor that was quite apt. You have that ancient suit of armor in the hall; I see it every time I come in. It was quite poetic for me to use it in a turn of phrase." Lucas shrugged, the gesture implying he was impressed with himself.

Heathcliff wasn't in the mind to disagree, actually. Bastard had a point.

"By your silence, I can tell you agree."

"Regardless, I see your point. And it is a valid one."

"Very good. Now, Liliah is upstairs helping your bride get ready. Have you spoken to Mrs. Keyes yet? What of Iris?"

Heathcliff strode over to the bellpull and rang for a maid. "I haven't asked Mrs. Keyes anything yet. I assumed she was quite busy with all the undertakings of the day. But I'll ask her to spare a moment to give us more details."

"Good," Lucas replied.

When a maid entered, Heathcliff bid her fetch the housekeeper, and soon she herself appeared.

"Good morning, my lords. How may I assist?" she asked, her face slightly flushed, as if still bustling about with preparations.

"I'm awaiting your instructions." Heathcliff gave a charming grin aimed in her direction.

She arched a brow. "I've taught you well, I have," she teased. "Your bride is up with her sister, as I'm sure you assumed. The breakfast will be ready in perfect time, and Iris is with me, assisting with the arrangements on the table. You'll also be pleased to know I instructed Cook to prepare treacle tart."

Heathcliff could have hugged her, but instead, he offered her a very grateful smile, and said, "Thank you. You're the most wonderful housekeeper in the world."

"How well I know it," she answered with a cheeky grin.

"Well, it sounds as if the only thing left to do is prepare the groom." Lucas turned to Heathcliff. "After you." He gestured to the door.

"Am I being pushed out of my own study?" Heathcliff asked.

"Yes. Now hurry up. We don't have all day." Lucas sounded just like a demanding mother, and Heathcliff shot him a peevish glare.

"This is far too much fun." Lucas grinned unrepentantly.

"I'll return the favor someday."

"I do believe *I'm* simply returning the favor. Remember, I've walked this road before you, my friend. And you were almost merciless."

"I do believe that's my cue to leave." Heathcliff gave a mock salute to his friend and then gave a kind smile to Mrs. Keyes before heading down the hall and toward the stairway.

He passed the suit of armor and grinned. Bastard. From now on, whenever he passed the bloody thing, he'd think of Lucas and his horrible metaphor.

There were certainly worse things.

And he had a feeling his friend was more accurate than he'd known.

Forgive, forget, move on.

Odd how he was just now learning how to do those three things.

Better late than never.

Chapter Thirty-one

Samantha tilted her head as she studied herself in the mirror. The dress was one of Liliah's, taken from London in the haste of all their packing in their efforts to escape. A sea green, it highlighted the color of her eyes, and the lighter colors of her tea-colored hair. It was sheer silk over muslin, with delicate lace trim along the décolleté. She and Liliah sported with the idea of wearing the dress they'd ordered for the masquerade ball, but in the end, they chose to keep that a secret. Her body tingled with the energy of anticipation, and she thought of how so much had changed since their escape from home.

She wasn't the girl who left London.

Her earlier musings sang to her, *something more*.

This, she glanced at her reflection, was most certainly, *more*.

A lot more.

And it was glorious, if not entirely conventional.

A soft knock sounded at the door, and she twisted her head and called, "Come in."

Maye was draping the dress and tugging on the hem as Liliah walked into the room. Her hand flew to her mouth, covering it in a universal gesture of emotion. Her eyes sparkled with glistening tears as her gaze traced from the top of Samantha's head to her hidden, slippered feet.

"So lovely," Liliah choked out, coming fully into the room and closing the door behind her. "All is in order. The question, however, is whether you are ready." Liliah took a deep breath, as if trying to be strong.

Samantha smiled at her sister, amused by the slight reversal of roles. Shouldn't *she* be the one overly emotional? Yet she found herself wanting to comfort her older sister. But that was the way of family; you were ever shifting and changing to assist the other. That was love, was it not?

"The viscount is going to be speechless. You're stunning, love." Liliah gave a knowing smile that Samantha saw reflected in the mirror. She studied herself once more, feeling beautiful down to her toes. Was it too much to hope for a grand reaction from her soon-to-be husband?

"Is everything in order?" Liliah asked, running a delicate hand down the skirt of Samantha's dress.

"I believe so." Maye had twisted her hair into a delicate chignon at the base of her neck. Loose curls framed her face, softening the look and giving her a fairylike appearance. She'd applied a bit of kohl to her eyes, as well as some rouge to her cheeks, tapping her finger along her lips to heighten the color there as well.

"Any second thoughts?" Liliah asked unexpectedly,

and Samantha's gaze darted from the study of her reflection to Liliah's inquiring gaze.

"No. Why do you ask?" A shiver of fear traced up her spine as she waited for her sister's reply.

"Breathe, dear. I have no reason to inquire other than to confirm that you are sure of your choice. Forgive me, I'm just being protective. I don't doubt the regard the viscount holds for you, nor your affection for him, but you haven't even had a Season—"

"Isn't the entire goal of a Season to find a husband?" Samantha arched a brow, knowing her point was valid.

Liliah twisted her lips. "It is, but there's so much more. I just . . . I don't want you to miss anything. And I want you to have a choice in life, to—"

"I think you're the one with second thoughts," Samantha replied, giving her sister a tender smile.

Liliah sighed. "I'm being overly cautious, aren't I?"

"It's surprising, in truth. Never once have I thought of you as cautious."

"There are other adjectives that are better suited for me," Liliah agreed.

"Impetuous, curious, daring—"

"I understand. But a worrier I am not. Till now, it seems. I just want you to be happy." Liliah gave a bemused smile to her sister.

"I am," Samantha answered simply. "And that is all that matters, is it not?"

"It is," Liliah agreed.

"Then shall we?" Samantha turned toward the door, then glanced back to her sister, raising an inquiring brow.

"We shall," Liliah agreed, her smile serene yet slightly wistful. "I can scarcely believe it. After being concerned for your future for so long, it's about to be established."

Samantha opened the door and stepped back, letting her sister pass. "It is." She giggled. "I was just thinking it was not exactly conventional."

"In that we are quite alike. I never did anything conventional in my life," Liliah teased, then entered the hall, with Samantha following.

"That is true."

They walked down the hall, took the stairs, and then proceeded into the foyer. Liliah hurried her pace to precede her sister and led the way to the small chapel in the eastern wing of Kilmarin. It would be a small affair, this wedding. The announcement would be made at the masquerade ball the next night.

Good Lord.

One day at a time, she reminded herself, waiting for a moment as Liliah entered the chapel. Samantha distracted herself by comparing a wedding in Scotland versus a London affair. It wasn't about the frills as much as it was about the steps that would have to be taken carefully. It was odd how easy the process seemed to be here. If she were in London, the banns would have been read three weeks in a row, and there would be the announcement in *The Times*, the reservation of the church, and so forth and so on. What a boon to be married in Scotland! Although she was certain many women enjoyed the lavish affair that was a London wedding, she found she was more than satisfied with hers. There was something intimate and utterly romantic about it.

Liliah opened the chapel door, then turned to her sister. She mouthed a question. *Ready?*

Samantha nodded, and then the music began. It was

a delicate concerto whose composer she couldn't recall at the moment. Her entire mind and senses were engaged as she put one foot in front of the other, anticipating the moment she'd cross the threshold and see her betrothed. Taking a silent breath, she walked in, meeting the gaze of the party assembled, searching each gaze till she found the one she wanted to see the most.

Heathcliff's reaction was everything she'd hoped for. His caramel eyes widened, then wickedly traveled the length of her before meeting her gaze with an intense one of his own. His expression was possessive, devoted, worshipful. She gloried in the feeling of it.

The rest of the details of the moment were insignificant in comparison to the delight of walking toward a future that radiated hope. Belatedly, she noted the small stained-glass windows above the vicar, pouring in rose-colored sunlight. The sound of a sniffle arrested her attention, and she noted the way Mrs. Keyes dabbed at her eyes, with Liliah doing the same. Iris watched with wide eyes full of wonder and, if Samantha were assuming correctly, a bit of a smug expression as well. She made a mental note to ask Iris later. Perhaps she had known all along.

Lucas gave her a wide grin followed by an approving nod, and that completed the small group of witnesses. It was quite reminiscent of her sister's wedding, and she found no small measure of delight in that fact. How apt, that they, the daughters of a duke, would have small, private weddings when the opposite would have been expected.

Her gaze flickered back to Heathcliff as she took the final steps toward the altar. The vicar cleared his throat, and as Heathcliff reached out to grasp her hand, the familiar words were spoken.

"DEARLY beloved, we are gathered together here in the sight of God, and in the face of this Congregation, to join together this man and this woman in holy Matrimony; which is an honorable estate, instituted of God in the time of man's innocence, signifying unto us the mystical union that is betwixt Christ and his Church; which holy estate Christ adorned and beautified with his presence."

Samantha was transfixed upon Heathcliff's gaze. His warm regard was more powerful than any words, any tradition. And while she respected the ceremony for its meaning, the depth of his gaze spoke of his personal dedication, his solemn vows, however unspoken, but utterly and undeniably true. The vicar continued with the liturgy from *The Book of Common Prayer*, with only slight pauses when he would glance to Heathcliff, or herself, awaiting their responses.

Heathcliff's hands were warm as they held hers, his thumb drawing lazy circles over the wrist of her gloved hand. The ceremony blew past like a summer breeze, warm and welcome, and before long, she was pledging her vows to the man before her.

Tears pricked her eyes as he did the same, the depth of the emotion in his gaze echoing his words perfectly.

They might not have had the most promising start, but she had utter hope that their journey would be much improved over the course of time. As it was, already she had more than she'd dared hope a few days earlier.

The vicar offered a prayer, and she couldn't force herself to close her eyes as was proper. Rather, she kept her gaze on Heathcliff, encouraged when he did the same. The blessing was pronounced, and before God, her sister, her brother-in-law, Mrs. Keyes, and Iris, they were pronounced husband and wife.

All that was left was the kiss, and with great anticipation, she lifted her gaze and was immediately swept up in Heathcliff's embrace as his eager lips sought hers.

It was a joyful kiss, one she had never experienced from him before. It was free, unrestrained, and full of something she wouldn't have been able to name unless it were so dear to her own heart: hope.

It was a common thread between them, one that seemed small upon first notice, but its depth was astounding, and she found it rooted itself in every corner of her heart.

As he ended the kiss—for certainly she would have gone right on kissing him, and with delight—his expression reflected the adoration his words had spoken earlier.

Their guests applauded, and Samantha walked with her husband down the aisle, to the edge of the chapel, where they were to sign the register.

The vicar cleared his throat, waiting beside the ancient wooden table, and pointed to two blank spaces in the old book.

Heathcliff signed his name.

Samantha signed hers, this time adding her new surname. It was the first time she'd seen it, the first time she'd dare whisper it into the world. It was almost too precious, too delicate to speak out loud.

And now it was real. It was done. And she was happy.

"No escaping me now," Heathcliff murmured against her neck as he placed a kiss there.

A shiver of delight tickled her back. "Don't you mean you cannot escape *me?*"

He chuckled and led her from the chapel. "That may be the more accurate representation."

"I think so. After all, you were quite resolved to resist my charms."

"You are temptation personified," he replied, grinning happily. His expression was far more open, the weight of so much pain finally behind him, it seemed.

"I would think it would be lovely to have a wife who tempts you. I'm especially thankful for a husband who provokes such a reaction in me," she flirted as they strode down the hall toward the dining room to celebrate their wedding breakfast. As they entered, the footmen applauded for their master, and as the others filed into the room, she noted the tears in the eyes of Mrs. Keyes, along with her sister.

Iris gave a knowing grin and took her seat just as Lucas retrieved a glass of champagne from the table and raised it high.

"To my brother-in-law. May you catch on faster than you have until this point," he teased.

Samantha glanced at Heathcliff, watching his wry reaction to Lucas's words. "I don't remember you catching on any faster."

"That is all in the past, and as such, we shall leave it there," Lucas remarked, earning a bemused grin from his wife.

Samantha was giggling at her sister and brother-in-law, but when Heathcliff grasped her hand tightly, pulling it to his chest, she turned.

Before God and everyone, he pulled her into his arms, kissing her firmly on the mouth.

His lips were tender, but there was an intensity beneath the kiss that left her breathless as he pulled away. "You're heartbreakingly beautiful," he murmured, then kissed her once more, fleetingly, and took her hand. When she came to her senses, she heard the amused giggles of their guests, and Samantha turned, first seeing the wide eyes of Iris.

That, she decided needed to be addressed in the near future. This wasn't exactly proper behavior. And she was still Iris's governess of sorts. They'd sort that all out later.

But while it wasn't proper, it was delightful behavior. Every groom should kiss his bride at their wedding breakfast, she decided. It was a pity it was considered scandalous.

Lucas and Liliah stood together, their expressions warm, and even Mrs. Keyes didn't appear shocked by their behavior. Apparently she didn't shock them all as much as she thought.

Heathcliff guided her to the head of the table, and then helped her to sit, and breakfast was served. A footman brought out treacle tart first, and Samantha caught a wink sent from Mrs. Keyes to Heathcliff, and he gave her a grin in response.

The breakfast passed with laughter, delight, and more than its share of teasing. It was exactly as she could have hoped, had she had enough courage to hope for so much.

As the celebration died down, a boot trailed up her leg, lifting the hem of her skirt.

She couldn't help the blush that heated her face. She remembered the previous evening, and she turned to her husband, who was watching her with that intensity that gave her butterflies and heat in her belly.

"I do believe it's more than time to for us to go. Come, Wife." Lucas stood, offering his hand to Liliah, who flickered a glance to Samantha, winked, and then stood.

In short work, they'd said their good-byes, with promises to return the next day, but not *too* early.

And finally, blessedly, Samantha found herself alone with her husband. She wanted to grasp his hand and run up the stairs, throw herself at him and love him freely, deeply, perhaps heal whatever scars remained in his heart.

But she was frozen, anticipation and her lack of knowledge holding her captive in their grasp.

Heathcliff turned to her and grinned, and her heart melted as much as her lack of courage, and with a wolfish grin, he swept her up in his arms and ran up the stairs. She giggled the whole way.

If love should be anything, it should be happy.

And though she'd never experienced it before, she knew without a doubt this was indeed love.

Chapter Thirty-two

Heathcliff kicked the door closed with a resounding thud, and debated whether to set his wife down gently down on her own two feet, or if he should carry her to the bed, toss her upon it, and devour her immediately.

He had wanted her since the moment he saw her, and now that the moment was upon him, he was both ravenous and resilient. It was ironic to be sure, but he thought it was, perhaps, a good thing.

"The bed is in that direction," Samantha remarked in a teasing tone. He turned to her then, delighting in the dancing expression in her eyes.

"Thank you, I had quite missed that fact." He arched a brow, then, to prove his point, he strode up to the bed and tossed her upon it, thankful for the sturdy build of the walnut frame as she bounced gently, offering him a mock glare.

"Is that how this goes?" she asked, all sass and light. The thought of living without her pierced through him like a lance, and he forced the chilling thought to the back of his mind. To think he had been so close to walking away; no, running from her affection. So much of his joy was because of her, because she brought light into all the dark recesses of his heart.

"Heathcliff?" She spoke his name softly, and he shook his dark thoughts from his mind. They were useless, and he was thankful. He had avoided a terrible mistake and, as such, deserved enthusiastic celebration.

And he knew just how to begin.

"Do you know, I've never done anything so proper in my life?" he started, circling the bed lazily, the anticipation filling him with heat.

"Oh? And how am I to respond to such a statement?" she replied, her gaze taking him in, darkening as he took a step toward the bed.

"Aren't lovers to disclose secrets in the bedroom? I thought I should start with the first."

"You're implying that there will be more secrets?" she asked

"Indeed. A great many, ones we shall share with a smile when others look on, confused."

Samantha's answering smile was all the response he needed. He continued. "Even your most innocent of smiles makes me want to be ever so wicked."

"And after charging me with being temptation personified! You, sir, have a strange reaction to temptation. Rather than be wicked, as you imply, it makes you quite resolute to be good. Odd, that." She arched a brow, an enticing grin on her face.

"Indeed it is."

"Interesting."

"Not nearly as interesting as having you here. Do

you have any idea how long I've imagined you here?" He gestured to the bed, taking in the soft pillows behind her, the draped purple velvet curtain around the headboard, the way the coverlet bunched around where she sat, watching him with wide eyes. "I scarcely can believe it, that you are here and not because my black heart seduced you but that all has been satisfied. To believe that it is right, and good for you to be here, in my bed, waiting . . ."

"Waiting indeed. You stand there with all the beautiful words I wished to hear for so long, yet you do not act on them." She gave her head a little shake.

"Forgive me." He bowed, earning a slight giggle from Samantha.

"I shall not. I require a token of your true repentance," she replied, shocking him by her demand. He grinned, thrilled with the way she caught him unexpectedly, thrilled to play the game she initiated. Love and sex had rarely followed one on the other in his life, and the one time they had, it had been one-sided. To be partners with each other, for it to be more; it was strange yet so perfect at once.

"What do you request as a token?" he asked.

Her eyes roamed over his body, setting it aflame with need. Her gaze settled on his neck and she smiled. "Your cravat."

"Is that the game you wish to play?" He approved.

"If you are willing to accept the challenge."

"Challenge? What challenge? It is a conquest, it is seduction in every form, and how I eagerly anticipate it . . . every moment." He tugged on his cravat and sent it to the floor in a whisper of silk.

"Now, it is for you to offer your own token. After

all, you have bold words, but your actions do not follow. For that, you should make restitution."

"Oh? And what do you want me to offer?" she asked, a playful smile tugging at her lips.

Heathcliff knew immediately what he wished, but he gave a slight pause, just for effect, before answering. "Your hair. Let it down for me."

She tipped up her chin. "You've already seen it down. When I fell in the pond it was almost completely undone." But she reached up and unpinned her tea-colored mane, let it fall over her shoulders, spilling like a luscious waterfall.

It was glorious. "Yes, but this . . . this is different." He took a seat on the bed, then reached out and laced his fingers through the thick softness of her hair, testing its weight. "Utterly beautiful."

Her lips parted, and the resolve he'd had earlier melted like hot wax before the fire, and he leaned in, kissing her.

It was like a match to the flame, and his body demanded more, knowing that every restraint could be released and he could make love to her without hesitation, without guilt, with abandon.

He reached up and tugged at the fabric of her dress, removing the cap sleeve and caressing the soft skin of her shoulder. Trailing his fingertips across her collarbone, he felt her shudder beneath his touch. He swallowed her soft moan of pleasure as he trailed his fingertips down, caressing her soft breast through the fabric of her dress, coming to a startling realization.

He leaned back, his lips spreading into a wondrous grin.

Samantha met his gaze, her cheeks pinking. "Liliah

didn't tell me much, but she did mention that . . . well, that less is more."

"How much less?" he asked, his imagination coming up with a thousand delightful and erotic answers.

"Much, much less," she answered, her color deepening with the confession.

"Good Lord," he groaned, then guided her gently down so that she was reclining on the bed and, rather than press into her, melting his body into hers, he leaned beside her, pulling her into his embrace as he gave his hands over to the exploration of her deliciously, scandalously nearly naked body. Belatedly, he thought it was a good think he'd not known about her lack of undergarments earlier; he wouldn't have survived the wedding or breakfast afterward. The knowledge alone would have burned his desire to ashes. As it was, his greedy hands trailed along the indentation of her hips, caressing the perfect curve of her buttocks, his body going painfully hard and insistent with every touch. But it was the sweetest of tortures, and like a madman, he was enjoying the punishment of endurance.

Her breathing was quick, and would hitch ever so slightly when he touched a sensitive area. He mentally made notes when she did so, remembering how she loved a kiss to the hollow of her neck, and a slight brush to her now-taut nipple. He cupped her, squeezed gently, and finally, when he couldn't resist the temptation of it all, trailed kisses down her neck and to the sensitive collarbone that had first distracted him. He kissed along the line of the bone, his hands spanning her hips, pulling her in as tightly as he could while still enjoying the access to her delicate skin.

He trailed lower, kissing every piece of flesh his lips graced, and he reached up, tugging down the surprisingly flexible fabric to expose her breast. He gave a gentle nip, then licked, grinning devilishly when she nearly bucked her hips from the bed, gasping with pleasure. Her hands gripped his hair, tugging in the most delicious way.

He needed her, every part, and with a reluctant kiss good-bye to each breast, he withdrew and stood beside the bed, basking in the lover's glow that radiated from Samantha's flushed face. She regarded him with a half-drunk expression, and he knew her body was feeling the same need, the same burning desire that was roaring within him.

He quickly disrobed, tossing his clothes to the side, along with his boots. Samantha's eyes widened as he removed every hindrance between them, watching in wide-eyed wonder.

"Good Lord," she murmured.

"I'll take that as a compliment."

"You're beautiful," she said, as if it were a shock to her.

"You're surprised." He grinned, striding toward her, then putting a knee on the bed in pursuit of his beautiful wife.

"I'm pleased," she whispered, kissing him gently, enticingly, searchingly. He released her from the kiss, leaning back just enough to speak. "I want to see you."

He met her gaze, watching as understanding dawned. She moved to stand, and he allowed her to move from his grasp, his body already missing the contact like a phantom limb.

"No," he whispered. "I want to do it." He followed her, and as she turned to give him her back, he started on the few buttons that held her dress in place. It was like unwrapping the most-anticipated birthday present.

He placed a kiss to each inch of skin exposed, and soon the dress pooled at her feet.

And she was correct in her words; there was much, much less than ladies usually wore under their dresses.

In fact, there was nothing.

The fabric had been just thick enough to hide her delicate curves, but it had been the only garment she wore, aside from her slippers.

Bloody hell, he could kneel and worship every curve of her skin, his body mapping every delight it held. He kissed her shoulder in reverence, and she shivered.

Grinning, he knew exactly how to remedy the chill.

He tenderly placed a hand on her shoulder and turned her to face him. Her gaze fixed on his chest, refusing to look up as he took in the view of her round breasts and beautiful form. He could feel the trembling in her body, so he lifted her chin with a finger and kissed her softly.

It seemed she only needed the slightest amount of encouragement, because she leaned in to the kiss, wrapping her arms around his shoulders and pulling him in close. He picked her up once more, only this time he didn't throw her on to the bed in play; he laid her down on the bed in seduction. Covering every inch of her body with his, he groaned as his most insistent part met her most coveted. He deepened the kiss, pressing into her, but not enough. With her, it would always be a sweet temptation, one he would refuse only long enough to build up the moment.

"Are you ready for me?" he whispered against her lips, then devoured them, not giving her a chance to reply. He needed her desperately; with every fiber of his being, he wanted to claim her, own her, fill her.

Her answering kiss gave the final spark to destroy

his self-control, and he slid carefully inside her, a hiss coming from his lips at the tight squeeze. It was ecstasy, almost too much pleasure to experience. She gave a soft gasp and tensed, but as she relaxed, he pressed in further, till the proof of her innocence was broken and she was marked as his.

He almost lost his control at the thought of having her fully. To comprehend that he was the only one to have her was erotic in every way. As he moved within her, he gave himself over to the pleasure, aware that her nails were biting into his back as she gasped in her own pleasure. The slight pain was welcome, heightening his own desire, and just when he didn't think he could deny himself any longer, she gave a loud gasp, calling his name.

He couldn't hold himself in check any longer and shattered within her, releasing everything he'd withheld for so long.

His fear.

His denial.

Himself, and it all came together as he met her wonder-filled gaze, and for the first time, he understood how two fully became one.

Because it was more than sex.

He'd never really understood that.

It was giving yourself over to the other person fully, irrevocably, losing that control willingly.

As much as he had branded her body, she had utterly branded his heart.

And he couldn't have been more at peace.

Chapter Thirty-three

The masquerade was a smashing success. Samantha watched as people continued to come through the foyer into the Kilmarin ballroom. Her mask fit perfectly, a gift from her husband only that morning. It was silver with several opals embedded in the arch; all fracturing the light and catching fire in the candlelight's glow.

It was clear her husband and brother-in-law knew how to give a party. From the dim, flickering candlelight lending a haunting glow to the masked footmen who silently offered champagne to each guest when they entered, it was a sumptuous affair. The string quartet played quietly in the corner, not enough to initiate the dancing yet, but enough to give a texture to the very air that hinted at movement, that hinted at seduction.

The news that the lord of Kilmarin had married passed around the room, and there was a loud buzz of conversation and no shortage of glances in Samantha's direction as she stood beside her husband. They stood together at the entrance of the ballroom, greeting their guests. Her back was to the wall, and Heathcliff reached out and grasped her waist tenderly.

She gave him a soft smile.

As another guest walked up and offered them congratulations, Heathcliff's hand lowered from her waist, to cup her bottom.

She gave him an scolding glare.

He squeezed.

She jumped slightly.

But she couldn't make any remark because another guest came up to greet them.

She was sure everything had been planned that way, especially when he repeated the action, this time pinching playfully.

He'd pay for that.

She gave him a challenging look but belatedly realized it would be lost because of the mask covering her face. Instead, she waited till their current guest walked on into the ballroom, then placed her hand on the middle of *his* back, but rather than cup his buttocks, she moved her hand lower, a smile on her lips as she suggestively rubbed the inside of his thigh far lower than he had teased her.

He groaned.

She smiled.

Another guest walked toward them, and she was satisfied to hear the gravely tone of her husband's voice, the same tone she heard when he spoke when kissing her softly but built toward something more.

As she bit her lip to keep from grinning too widely and perhaps attracting attention, she cast a glance to her husband, who was watching her with an intensity that made her body burn. His mask covered what was common with any mask, but his eyes, those caramel eyes that burned like a fire's glow, seared right through her, and all the lovely memories of the night before came back to the forefront of her mind with astounding clarity. Her body hummed with an energy he could release with his touch, and she burned for him.

And by the expression in his fierce gaze, he burned for her as well.

But the guests continued to arrive, and their intimate moment faded with the need to greet another lord and lady from Edinburgh society.

As the night wore on, the dancing began. Rather than start with country dances, Lucas had suggested there only be waltzes. It was not the common thing, nor was it necessarily proper, but it was delicious. As the first strains of the first dance began, Heathcliff grasped her hand and led her to the ballroom floor. The room hushed, the strings almost shivered with the hauntingly beautiful quality of the music, and with an intense gaze into her eyes, he began to lead.

She followed, her heart as much as her body. With each step, she was locked deeper into his gaze, her body catching just a little more of a flame, her heart pounding ever harder as she melted into the intensity of the dance. Never before had she realized just how erotic the waltz could be. The push and pull, the twirling, and dear Lord, the touching. To have his hand on her hip, her shoulder, his fingertips gently caressing her flesh with insinuation, was heady. He pulled her in tighter, his hand slipping scandalously low on her back, possessing her, marking her with his heat.

"Are you enjoying your evening, Wife?" he asked in a silken tone.

She gave an answering nod. "Indeed, but I find myself easily distracted."

He arched a brow in query.

"You," she answered simply.

After a low chuckle, he replied, "I share the same problem. All evening I've scarcely been able to keep my hands from you. And my thoughts: I'm afraid they never made it past our bedroom and linger there still."

A blush heated her face. "Would it be so terrible to leave our own party early?"

He glanced about teasingly. "It will only make the news of our marriage more delicious, and will certainly seal the truth of it being a love match," he added, regarding her, his gaze searching hers.

She was about to give a witty reply but paused, thinking over his words. "Love match? Is there something you're saying to me?" she asked, her tone breathless. After all their endearments, all their intimate moments, he had never once mentioned love.

He spun her, and she was anxious to return to his embrace. "Is it so difficult to believe?"

"I believe that is the question I should be asking you," she replied, giving an encouraging grin.

He gave a soft chuckle. "You're indeed right. But it is the truth nonetheless. As much as I fought it, denied it, and ran from it, you've held my heart for ransom for a long while."

"And I shall never return it," she replied firmly.

"I do not wish you to. But the question is, do I have yours?" he asked, and she detected a slightly insecure tone to his voice, so at odds with his usual confidence.

She squeezed his hand, met his gaze, and answered, "From the first day I met you, I was both lost and found. My greatest fear was that you held my heart and didn't wish to. But it's only ever been yours. And only will be," she said, a hitch to her voice as she confessed the deepest truth.

He spun her once more, not responding, but when she came back to his embrace, he didn't hold her in the frame of a waltz but in the embrace of a man entirely in love, and kissed her in front of God and everyone.

She didn't hear the titters of those in attendance.

She didn't hear the applause when Heathcliff finally released her from the searing kiss.

She did, however, hear the cheers when he swept her up in his arms and carried her from the ballroom.

And she most certainly heard him say, "I love you," as he reached their bedroom door and set her inside, closing it firmly.

Lucas had said there was nothing more enticing than gossip and a good romance.

And that night they most certainly gave a scandalous display of both.

Epilogue

It was a trial each day to leave his bedroom, when all he wanted to do was keep his wife abed and pass the morning delighting in all the activities the bed could facilitate. But there were things that needed to be accomplished, and . . . well, there was always the night. Anticipation wasn't a bad thing either. It only produced more enthusiasm.

Not that he needed any encouragement in that regard. Nor did his wife.

But that morning, reluctant as he was to leave their rooms, he found an interesting missive on this study desk, one that he'd been waiting for with great anticipation.

He used the wooden letter knife and slid open the wax seal of Ramsey Scott, Marquess of Sterling, and eagerly opened the letter.

His face broke into a grin as he read the account of all that had transpired in London on the knowledge of the sudden marriage of the Duke of Chatterworth's second daughter to a Scotsman, especially when she was supposedly in the Americas.

> *Heathcliff,*
> *You'll be pleased to know that your news cre-*
> *ated a sensation on the London scene, and I*
> *scarcely think the ton will cease speaking of it*
> *for at least a year. My only regret is not to have*
> *been there when the duke received the news, but*
> *I do have information from a reliable source that*
> *he was in such a fury he had first determined to*
> *call you out; pistols at dawn. I was also sorry to*
> *know that he changed his mind before any action*
> *could be taken, and since hasn't mentioned such*
> *rash action again.*

He was thankful, he grinned, his father-in-law didn't wish to initiate such a desperate measure. Shooting a duke in a duel would most certainly be more than a little trouble, and he didn't want blood on his hands, even if it was the duke's. He continued reading.

> *Your announcement in* The Times *was the*
> *first breaking of the news to both the duke and*
> *the London ton, but I had John watching the*
> *duke's residence, as well as more information on*
> *the inside that confirmed your earlier*
> *suspicions. There was indeed a man at Kilmarin,*
> *and he only returned with the news of Lady*
> *Samantha's whereabouts the day after the*
> *announcement in* The Times. *Your timing, it*
> *seems, was impeccable.*

Heathcliff relaxed his shoulders, realizing they had grown tense as he read that last part. But it was a thing of the past, mostly. They'd have to go to London soon to complete the circle of gossip and confirm all the news, but the most important aspect, Samantha's safety, was secure.

Also, I would recommend you come to London before the next Season, just to smooth things over with the ton. I say this only because you have a ward who needs the favor of society, and your charm can do great things to pave the way for her,; as much as I hate to admit it. The scandal alone has given me no shortage of ill sleep, and if we weren't already on the edge of proper society because of our joint venture, we certainly would be now. But I have hope you will be received well in London, if for no other reason than satisfying the curiosity of the ton. I would, however, write to the Duke of Chatterworth to notify him directly, making sure he has no reason to question your marriage. He will probably still try—the man is an arse—but you will have done all you can.

Heathcliff groaned as he read the last phrase. Damn the man; his friend was probably right, much as he hated to admit it. While Lucas and he were less afraid of scandal, Ramsey was the total opposite. He hated it, hated whispers, and loved nothing more than staying in his private room in Temptations alone with his numbers and ledgers. But he was invaluable, and Heathcliff recognized his strength was exactly where he and

Lucas were weak. It was a good combination for them all.

As he read the rest of the letter, he noticed a gentle click of the door as it opened. He glanced up to see Samantha walk toward him with her perfectly graceful movements and flashed her a wicked smile of appreciation.

> *Between you and Lucas, I've had my fill of scandal for the century, so if there's anything else I need to be aware of to prepare myself, please send word immediately. I hope all is well, that you find yourself in delightful married bliss, such as Lucas has, and I pray fervently that it is not catching. I send my hearty congratulations and expect to hear from you soon, but perhaps not too soon.*
> *Regards,*
> *Ramsey Scott, Marquess of Sterling*

Heathcliff folded the letter and set it aside as Samantha came around the desk and placed a hand at his back. "Morning," she whispered, then leaned down to kiss him on his slightly whiskered cheek.

"Good morning to you," he murmured back, then turned in his chair, pulling her onto his lap. He smiled as she gave a little squeak at the quick movement, but she settled in nicely, reminding him of just how perfect her round bottom was. He reached up to kiss her neck softly, chuckling against her warm skin as he felt her shiver with delight.

"A good morning indeed," he murmured again.

"You mentioned that," she replied breathlessly.

He gave a final kiss to her soft skin and then reached for the letter. "There's news from London."

She snatched the letter from his offering hand, her eyes quickly skimming its contents.

"He knows," she whispered, then turned to Heathcliff.

"He bloody well better know. I made sure of it."

"Claiming what's yours?" she asked with a teasing laugh.

"Exactly."

"Have I no say?"

He chuckled, pulled her in a little tighter as he caressed his fingers down her arm, tickling her ever so slightly at the elbow, then finding her hand and grasping it tightly. "My love, you speak as if you were the one without a choice in the matter. As much as I wish to claim total control in this situation, I cannot. You were the one who owned me from the moment I saw you, and the only one who did not have a choice was me."

"Are you complaining?" she asked, squeezing his hand and regarding him with a tender look.

"No. It's much better that way."

Samantha gave an answering smile, one that was full of wonder and delight. "I never thought of it that way." She tipped her chin.

"Oh?" he asked, growing rather distracted by the way her shoulders curved up to her neck, which led to an intense examination of her perfect lips, which only reminded him of how sweet they tasted.

"Yes." She touched his chin, pulling his gaze upward to hers. "I always assumed I was the one without control. It was how I was raised, and I laid the same sin at your feet as well. But in the end, if it's as you say, I chose you. It's fairly profound to discover that after thinking the opposite. Maybe . . ." She paused, her expression thoughtful. "You know, I always wanted to be more, to have the determination and drive of my sister, to plan my future without fear, or without force from another's power over me. And I think," a smile started at her lips, then reflected in her eyes, "I think the person who underestimated me, was me. How wonderful to realize that all along, I was already something more. I just wasn't willing to see it."

He kissed her then, savoring the truth of her revelation on her lips. When he withdrew, he murmured his reply softly, blowing the words across her waiting lips. "You always were more, more than I dared dream. And I think I shall prove it to myself once more."

"Prove what?" she asked, her smile seducing him all over again.

"That you're mine." And without delay, he kissed her into silence, and went about taking advantage of that silence by moving their escapades to the very lovely chaise longue just beyond.

It was a lovely thing to be in love.

It was an even lovelier thing to be in love with one's wife.

All because she was willing to escape from His Grace.

Sneak Peek at *The Temptation of Grace*

Edinburgh, Scotland—for now

Miss Iris Grace Morgan had always hated her name, and with the current schedule of arriving in London in a mere week, she made a decision.

She would come to London not as Iris, the woman who couldn't waltz to save her soul, nor as the lady who was utterly a failure at all things ladylike. No, she would arrive as *Grace*; the woman who personified all things that . . . well, she was not. It *couldn't* hurt her to have a name that implied what she was not, but she certainly hoped it would indeed *help*. After all, her governess, now her guardian's wife, had taken great pains to pull the lady from within and give her some much-needed polish, along with a much-needed friendship.

But as much as she had tried, Iris—Grace, that is—wasn't entirely sure she had taken on said polish. Viscount Kilpatrick had assured her she would make a splash, which was very sweet of him. But she wasn't concerned about making a splash. She was certain she would.

She just wasn't sure it would be a good splash. It would probably be of the clumsy variety, when she'd trip on her own two feet, smash into some cranky dowager, and spray lemonade across a ballroom. It could certainly happen.

It had almost happened last night after dinner, only it wasn't lemonade, it was white wine, and it wasn't her own two feet she'd tripped over. It had been the bloody chair.

Samantha, her guardian's wife and once her governess, had given her a smile and helped her clean up the mess before Mrs. Keyes, the housekeeper, clucked over them and shooed them away from it all.

Grace smiled at the memory. She loved it at Kilmarin. All the servants were kind, and they didn't expect her to be anything she was not. Sothers, the butler, was ever so thoughtful, and opened the door extra wide for her, just in case she misjudged the step, and Mrs. Keyes never complained once when she'd spill or trip over something or other.

Even Samantha. Grace frowned over how many times she stepped on her toes when trying to learn how to waltz. It was her utter Achilles's heel, that dance. She hoped fervently she simply melted into the woodwork of the London ballrooms.

Because while many young ladies wanted to be in the limelight, and find a suitable match, Grace was utterly content simply not to make a scene. But have a Season she would, and it wouldn't be long in coming. They were planning on leaving Kilmarin in just a few days' time to travel to the viscount's London home, where she could ease herself into society

Dear Lord, this was going to be a disaster.

If they could only just talk, not dance. She could do verbal arabesques with her words! She could speak intelligently on almost any subject, and her parents, God rest their souls, had given her an education that Eton couldn't claim, but they had neglected to teach her the one thing she needed most at the moment.

How to be a lady.

So it was with utter trepidation, more than a few prayers, and several late-night dancing sessions that she allowed Maye to pack her belongings for the trip to London.

It couldn't be that bad . . . could it?

She knew the answer to her own question.

Yes. Yes, it could.

The next book in the
GENTLEMEN OF TEMPTATION
miniseries:
THE TEMPTATION OF GRACE
by
Kristin Vayden
will be available in
May 2019

In the meantime, if you've missed the first book,
FALLING FOR HIS GRACE
Turn the page for a peek at the romance between
Lucas Mayfield, the eighth Earl of Heightford,
and
Lady Liliah Durary,
daughter of the Duke of Chatterwood

Available at your favorite bookseller and e-retailer!

Prologue

Lucas Mayfield, the eighth Earl of Heightfield, was a lot of things, depending on whom you asked. But chief amongst all the adjectives his peers or others might attribute to him, none was more accurate than the one with which he labeled himself.

Bored.

It wasn't a benign state either, rather a dangerous one—because boredom bred ideas, and the ones spinning about in his mind were of the scandalous, inventive, and daring variety. Ideas also necessitated risk, something with which he didn't dally lightly. Rather, he craved control—thrived on it, in every aspect of his life. Control prevented pain, prevented others from manipulating you—because you held the marionette strings. If you were in control, life couldn't toss you on your ear with blindsiding betrayal, death, or worse.

Because yes, indeed, there were always things worse than death.

Life, being one of them.

However, risk compromised that basic need for control, so it was with careful calculation that he even considered such a reckless and delightful diversion.

He would also need assistance, but that was easily afforded and solicited. Heathcliff and Ramsey were as bloody bored as he. Among the three of them, they had every connection and resource necessary to breathe life into this concoction of his imagination.

He tapped his finger against his brandy glass, the amber light of the fire in his study's hearth casting an inviting glow. Darkness was so predictable, so protective. Much easier to manipulate than light.

He took a long sip of the fine French brandy, savoring the burn. It was heavenly. The perfection leading to temptation . . . leading to . . .

He sat up straighter, the leather chair squeaking slightly from the abrupt movement. *Tempting*.

He rolled the word around in his mind, a grin widening his lips even as he shook his head at the audacity of such an idea.

It was the perfect irony.

His idea had a name—a bloody insightful one.

Different than all the other gaming hells about London—his would thrive on anonymity. No names. No faces. Masks and the uttermost exclusivity that no other hell could boast. No strings attached, where your privacy is also your security—your pleasure.

Temptation. Short, sweet, and directly to the point.

Where you could fall from grace and never want to go back.

He lifted high his brandy glass, toasting himself,

and took a long swig. It would solve so many of his own problems, the problems of his friends as well. And no doubt, if he struggled with such things, countless others did too.

Unable to resist such a brilliant plan's lure, he stood and crossed his study in several wide strides, heading to the door. It was still somewhat early in the night, surely his friends would be still lingering at White's. So with an eager expectation, he rode off into the night, the irritation of his boredom long gone.

In its place, something far more hazardous.

Determination.

Chapter One

Lady Liliah Durary urged her mare, Penny, into a rapid gallop as she flew through Hyde Park. A proper lady should have a care about the strolling couples about the park. A proper lady should not ride at such breakneck speed. A proper lady should obey her father in all things.

Liliah was *not* a proper lady.

And hell would have to freeze over before she'd ever even try.

Tears burned the corners of her eyes, blurring her vision as she urged Penny faster, not caring that she was in a miserable sidesaddle—or that her speed was indeed dangerous for her precarious position. She wanted to outrun her problems—rather, *problem*. Because aside from the one damning issue at hand, life was otherwise quite lovely.

Being the elder daughter of a duke had its distinct advantages.

Of course, it had its distinct disadvantages as well. Like your father demanding you marry your best friend.

Who so happened to be in love with your other best friend.

It was a miserable mess . . . and she was caught in the middle of it all. If only her father would see reason! Yet asking such a thing was like expecting her mare to sprout wings and fly: impossible.

She slowed Penny down to a moderate walk and sighed deeply, the light breeze teasing the strands of unruly blond hair, which came loose from her coiffure as a result of her quick pace. She blew a particularly irritating curl from her forehead, and tucked it behind her ear. Glancing about, she groaned, remembering that she hadn't taken a maid with her. Again.

Thankfully, the staff at Whitefield House was accustomed to her constant disregard of propriety. Maybe Sarah, her maid, would notice and make herself scarce, giving the impression she was with her mistress. Liliah bit her lip, turning her mare toward home—even if that was the last place she wished to be—simply for Sarah's sake. It wouldn't go well for her maid if her father discovered the way his staff allowed his unruly daughter far more freedom than he did, and should he discover it, such freedom would end abruptly—and badly.

Being attached to the staff—especially her maid Sarah—Liliah increased her pace. Besides, running from problems didn't solve them. As she swayed with the steady rhythm of Penny's trot, she considered the situation at hand once more.

It made no sense.

Yet when had one of her father's decisions required logic? Never.

Her best friend Rebecca was delightful and from a well-bred and heavily pursed family. There was no reason for the family of her other best friend Meyer, the Baron of Scoffield, to be opposed to such a match. Yet Meyer's father refused to see reason, just as Liliah's father refused. Only Meyer's father, the Earl of Greywick, had threatened to disinherit his son and grant the title to a cousin when Meyer had objected to the arrangement.

It was wretched, no matter how one looked at it. Love matches were rare amongst the ton, and here was a golden opportunity for each family—squandered.

It was true, Liliah was quite the match herself. The elder daughter of a duke, she understood she was quite the heiress and pedigree, yet was her breeding of more importance than Rebecca's? She doubted it.

Apparently, her father didn't agree.

Nor did Lord Greywick.

As she crossed the cobble street toward her home, she took a deep breath of the spring air, feeling her freedom slowly sifting through her fingers like dry sand. As Whitefield House came into view, she pulled up on the reins, halting Penny's progress toward home. The horse nickered softly, no doubt anticipating a thorough brush-down and sweet oats upon returning, yet Liliah lingered, studying the stone structure. One of the larger houses in Mayfair, Whitefield demanded attention with its large stone pillars and wide, welcoming balcony overlooking the drive. It fit her father's personality well, as if magnifying his overinflated sense of importance. Reluctantly, she urged Penny on, taking the side entrance to the stable in the back.

Upon her arrival, a stable boy rushed out to greet her, helping her dismount. Penny jostled the lad with her head, and he chuckled softly, petting her velvet nose.

"I'll take care of Penny, my lady. You needn't worry." With a quick bow, the boy led the all too pampered horse into the stable, murmuring softly as they walked.

Carefully glancing around, once she was certain that no one lingered about, she rushed to the servants' entrance just to the side of the large manor. The heavy wooden door opened silently and she slipped inside, leaning against the door once it was closed. Her eyes adjusted to the dim light, and she took the stairs to the second floor, turning left down a small hall and turning the latch on the door that would lead to the gallery, just a short distance from her chambers. The metal was cool against her gloved hand as she twisted, then peered out into the sunlight-filled room. Breathing quietly, she listened intently for footsteps or voices. Just before she dared to step out, Sarah, her maid, bustled down the hall, a pinched frown on her face as she opened the door leading to Liliah's rooms.

After waiting one more moment, Liliah stepped from the servants' hall, rushing her steps till she approached her room, then slowed as if she weren't in a hurry at all, just in case someone noticed her presence.

Quickly, she opened the door to her room and swiftly shut it silently behind her, Sarah's relieved sigh welcoming her.

"My lady! You've not but a moment to lose! Your father is searching about for you! When he noticed me, he bid me find you, but I fear he is growing impatient. He was in the library."

"Quick, help me disrobe. I need an afternoon dress." Liliah started to tug off her gloves, exchanging them for ones that did not bear the marks from the leather reins, as Sarah made quick work of the buttons on her riding habit.

In only a few short minutes, Liliah was properly attired—all evidence of her earlier unchaperoned excursion tucked away. And with a quick grin to Sarah, who offered a relieved sigh, Liliah left her chambers and strode down the hall as if without a care in the world.

When in truth, the cares were heavy upon her indeed.

Because her father rarely spoke to her, unless demanding her obedience in some matter—and she knew exactly what he had on his mind.

Drat.

She clasped her hands, trying to calm the slight tremble as she took the stairs and walked toward the library. How she hated feeling weak, out of control in her own life! With a fortifying breath, she made the final steps to the library entrance, the delicate clink of china teacups drifting through the air.

"Your Grace." Liliah curtseyed to her father, taking in the furrow in his expression, drawing his bushy salt-and-pepper eyebrows like thunderclouds over his gray eyes.

"At last. I was about to begin a search," he replied tersely, setting down his teacup and gesturing to a chair.

"Forgive me, I was quite absorbed in my—"

"Book, I know. Your little maid said as much. And I'll remind you that you mustn't spend so much time engaging your mind. Fine-tune your other qualities. Your pianoforte could benefit a great deal from some practice." He sighed, as if already tired of the conversation with his daughter.

Liliah bit her tongue, not wishing to initiate a battle

of wills just yet; she'd save the fight for a more worthy cause.

The only worthy cause of the moment.

"Now that you're here, I need to inform you that Lord Greywick and I have decided on a date—"

"But, Your Grace . . ."

His brows knit further over his eyes, and he glared, his expression frosty and furious. "Do not interrupt me."

Liliah swallowed, clenching her teeth as she nodded.

"As I was saying . . ." He paused, arching a brow, daring her to interfere again. "Lord Greywick and I are tired of waiting. We've been patient, and your progress with Greywick's heir is apathetic at best. Therefore, tonight, at the Langford rout, Meyer will be asking you for two waltzes. That should set up the perfect tone for the banns being read in two weeks' time. Hence, you shall be wed at St. George's in two months. That is beyond generous and I—"

"It is anything but generous and you well know it!" Liliah couldn't restrain herself any longer. Standing, she took position behind the chair, her fingers biting into the damask fabric as she prepared for battle.

One she knew was already lost.

"How dare you!" Her father's voice boomed.

"Father, Meyer has no interest in me! How long will you imagine something greater than friendship?"

"I care not if he gives a fig about you!" her father roared, standing as well.

"I refuse." Liliah spoke softly, like silk over steel as she clenched her teeth.

Her father took a menacing step forward. "There is no other way. And consider this: If this arrangement is not made, your friend will lose his title. Do you think that Lord and Lady Grace will allow their daughter to be married to a man with no means? No title?" He shook his head, his eyes calculating. "They will not. So cease your reluctance. There is no other option." He took a deep breath and met her gaze. "I suggest you prepare for tonight; you'll certainly be the center of attention and you should look the part. You're dismissed." With a quick wave of his fingers, he turned and went back to his tea, sitting down.

Tears burned the back of Liliah's eyes, yet she held them in till she spun on her heel and quit the room, just as the first streams of warm tears spilled down her cheeks.

Surely there had to be another way?

Perhaps there was, but time was running out.

For everyone.

The Langford rout was buzzing with activity from London society's most elite, the *bon ton*. The orchestra's sweet melody floated through the air, drowning out most of the buzzing hum of voices. The dancers swirled around, a kaleidoscope of pastel colors amidst the gentlemen's black evening kits. Ostrich and peacock feathers decorated the main banquet table, along with painted silver eggs. But the beauty of the ballroom was lost on Liliah; even the prospect of a treacle tart didn't boost her mood. She meandered through the crush of humanity, swiping a glass of champagne from a passing footman. Sipping the cool liquid, she savored the bubbles as her gaze sharpened on her target.

Lady Grace—Rebecca—danced gracefully as she took the practiced steps of the quadrille. Rebecca smiled at her partner, and Liliah watched as the poor sop all but melted with admiration. Stifling a giggle, she waited till the dance ended, and made her way toward her friend. As she drew near, Rebecca caught sight and raised a hand in a wave, her overly expressive eyes smiling as wide as her lips.

"Liliah! Did you only just arrive? I was searching for you earlier." Rebecca reached out and squeezed Liliah's hand.

"I stalled," Liliah confessed.

Rebecca's smile faded, her green eyes no longer bright. "Did it work?"

"No." Liliah glanced away, not knowing if she could handle the heartbreak that must be evident in Rebecca's gaze.

"We understood it was a small chance. We must now simply seize every opportunity." Rebecca spoke with far more control than Liliah expected. As she turned to her friend, she saw a depth of pain, yet a depth of strength in her gaze.

"There's always hope," Liliah affirmed, squeezing her friend's hand.

"Always. And that being said, I must now seize this present opportunity." Rebecca's face lit up as only one deeply in love could do, and curtseyed as Meyer approached.

The Baron of Scoffield approached, but Liliah ever knew him as simply Meyer. Their friendship had been immediate and long-standing. Ever since Liliah, Rebecca, and Meyer had snuck away during a fireworks display at Vauxhall Gardens, they had created a special bond of friendship. But over the years, that friendship had shifted into something deeper between Meyer and Rebecca, while Liliah was happy to watch their romance bloom. Meyer's gaze smoldered as he studied

Rebecca, a secretive smile in place. As Liliah turned back to Rebecca, she saw the most delicate blush tint her olive skin. Liliah blushed as well, feeling like an intruder in their private moment. "I'll just leave you two . . ." She trailed off, walking away as she heard Meyer ask Rebecca for a dance.

Liliah sipped the remaining champagne, watching her friends dance. Their eyes never left each other's; even if they switched partners for the steps, they always came together, their love apparent for anyone who cared to look.

It was beautiful, and it was for naught.

As the dance ended, the first strains of a waltz soared through the air. What should have been beautiful was poisoned, and her heart felt increasingly heavy as Meyer walked in her direction, his lips a grim line.

He didn't ask, simply held out his hand, and Liliah placed hers within his grasp, reluctantly following as they took the floor.

"By your expression, I can only assume you had as much progress with your father as I've had with mine," Meyer said, his brown eyes sober as his gaze flickered away—likely looking for Rebecca.

"Your assumption would be correct," Liliah replied.

Meyer took a deep breath, meeting her gaze. "We'll figure something out."

"But Meyer—" Liliah started.

"We will. We just need to bide our time till the opportunity presents itself." He nodded with a brave confidence in his deep eyes.

"But what if we don't?" Liliah hated to give voice to her deepest fears, watching as Meyer's brave façade slowly fractured.

"Liliah, I—I can't think of that. I'm damned if I do,

damned if I do not. I'm sure your father reminded you about my title—"

"And how Lord and Lady Grace wouldn't consider you without a title . . ."

"Exactly. I have to hold on to hope. But I, I do need to tell you . . . Liliah, if we are forced . . . nothing between us will change." He lowered his chin, meeting Liliah's gaze dead on, conveying words he couldn't speak out loud.

"Thank you," Liliah replied, feeling relieved. As much as she hated the idea of a platonic marriage, it hurt far worse to think of the betrayal that would haunt them all should Meyer take her to bed. It hurt to think she'd never know physical love, yet what choice did they all have? Should they take that step, Meyer would be thinking of Rebecca during the act, Liliah would know, and would not only be betraying her friend, but how could she not be resentful? Far better for them to simply bide their time till an arrangement could be made—she would simply step aside. Maybe take a lover of her own?

How she hated how complicated her life had become.

Liliah took a deep breath, mindlessly performing the waltz steps. A smile quirked her lips as she had a rather unhelpful—yet still amusing—thought.

"Ah, I know that smile. What is your devious mind thinking?" Meyer asked, raising a dark brow even as he grinned.

Liliah gave him a mock glare. "I'm not devious."

"You are utterly devious." Meyer chuckled. "Which makes you a very diverting friend indeed. Now share your thoughts."

Liliah rolled her eyes. "Such charm. Very well, I was thinking how it would be lovely if we could simply make the wedding a masquerade and have Rebecca switch places with me at the last moment! Then you'd marry her rather than me and it would be over and done before they could change it!" She hitched a shoulder at her silly thoughts.

Meyer chuckled. "Devious indeed! Too bad it will not work." He furrowed a brow and glanced away, as if thinking.

"What is *your* wicked mind concocting?"

"Nothing of import." His gaze shifted back to her. "Your mentioning of the masquerade reminded me of an earlier conversation with a chum."

Liliah grinned. "Is there a masquerade ball being planned?" she asked with barely restrained enthusiasm.

"Indeed, but it is one to which you will not be invited, thank heavens." He shook his head, grinning, yet his expression was one of relief.

"Why so?"

"It's not a masquerade for polite society, my dear. And I shouldn't have even mentioned it."

"A secret? Meyer, you simply must tell me!"

"Heavens no! This is not for your delicate—"

Liliah snorted softly, giving him an exasperated expression, before she slowly grinned.

"Aw hell. I know that smile. Liliah . . ." he warned.

"If you won't tell me, then I can always ask someone else—"

"You'll do nothing of the sort!"

"You know I will."

"You're a menace!" Meyer hissed, his expression narrowing as the waltz ended.

"So, you'll tell me?" Liliah asked, biting her lip with excitement.

Meyer was silent as he led them to a quiet corner of the ballroom, pausing beside a vacant alcove.

"This is a yes!" Liliah answered her question, squeezing his forearm as her hand rested upon it.

"I'm only telling you so that I can properly manage what you hear. Heaven only knows what you'd draw out of an unsuspecting swain. At least I'm immune to your charms and won't give in to your pleas."

Liliah almost reminded him that he was doing just that—but held her tongue.

"There is a . . . place." Meyer spoke in a hushed whisper, and Liliah moved in closer just to hear his words above the floating music. "It's secretive, selective, and not a place for a gently bred lady, if you gather my meaning."

Liliah nodded, hanging on every word.

"Only few are accepted as members and it's quite the thing to be invited. One of my acquaintances was far too drunk the other night and spoke too freely about this secretive club—mentioning a masquerade. That is all."

Liliah thought over his words, having several questions. "What's it called?"

Meyer paused, narrowing his eyes. "Temptations," he added reluctantly.

"And they are having a masquerade?" Liliah asked, a plan forming in her mind, spinning out of control.

"Yes. And that is all you need to know."

Meyer broke their gaze and looked over his shoulder at the swirling crowd.

"Go to her. We still have one waltz left and then I'll ask you all the questions you'll refuse to answer." She winked, playfully shoving her friend toward the dance floor.

"When you put it that way . . ." He rolled his eyes and walked off toward the crowd.

Liliah thought back over what Meyer had said, considering his words—and what they might mean. A masquerade—inappropriate for ladies.

It sounded like the perfect solution for a lady wishing to be utterly inappropriate. All she had to do was discover the location, steal away, and maybe, just maybe . . . she'd get to experience a bit of life before it was married away. Was that too much to ask? Certainly not, and as long as she knew the name, surely she could discover the location.

For the first time since this whole misbegotten disaster, she felt a shred of hope.

Utterly scandalous hope.

Connect with Us

Visit us online at
KensingtonBooks.com
to read more from your favorite authors, see books
by series, view reading group guides, and more.

Join us on social media

for sneak peeks, chances to win books and prize packs,
and to share your thoughts with other readers.

facebook.com/kensingtonpublishing
twitter.com/kensingtonbooks

Tell us what you think!

To share your thoughts, submit a review,
or sign up for our eNewsletters, please visit:
KensingtonBooks.com/TellUs.

Books by Bestselling Author
Fern Michaels

___The Jury	0-8217-7878-1	$6.99US/$9.99CAN
___Sweet Revenge	0-8217-7879-X	$6.99US/$9.99CAN
___Lethal Justice	0-8217-7880-3	$6.99US/$9.99CAN
___Free Fall	0-8217-7881-1	$6.99US/$9.99CAN
___Fool Me Once	0-8217-8071-9	$7.99US/$10.99CAN
___Vegas Rich	0-8217-8112-X	$7.99US/$10.99CAN
___Hide and Seek	1-4201-0184-6	$6.99US/$9.99CAN
___Hokus Pokus	1-4201-0185-4	$6.99US/$9.99CAN
___Fast Track	1-4201-0186-2	$6.99US/$9.99CAN
___Collateral Damage	1-4201-0187-0	$6.99US/$9.99CAN
___Final Justice	1-4201-0188-9	$6.99US/$9.99CAN
___Up Close and Personal	0-8217-7956-7	$7.99US/$9.99CAN
___Under the Radar	1-4201-0683-X	$6.99US/$9.99CAN
___Razor Sharp	1-4201-0684-8	$7.99US/$10.99CAN
___Yesterday	1-4201-1494-8	$5.99US/$6.99CAN
___Vanishing Act	1-4201-0685-6	$7.99US/$10.99CAN
___Sara's Song	1-4201-1493-X	$5.99US/$6.99CAN
___Deadly Deals	1-4201-0686-4	$7.99US/$10.99CAN
___Game Over	1-4201-0687-2	$7.99US/$10.99CAN
___Sins of Omission	1-4201-1153-1	$7.99US/$10.99CAN
___Sins of the Flesh	1-4201-1154-X	$7.99US/$10.99CAN
___Cross Roads	1-4201-1192-2	$7.99US/$10.99CAN

Available Wherever Books Are Sold!
Check out our website at **www.kensingtonbooks.com**

Books by Bestselling Author

Victoria Alexander